This powerful debut novel draws on Pat Barrow's extensive experience as an independent social worker in the family courts working with families enmeshed in high conflict separation and divorce. She has expertise with the many guises of parental conflict and the far-reaching consequences for children who have become the focus of their battles. Her skill is in hearing the voice of the child and understanding their pain and the dilemmas they face; and then promoting practical child centred solutions which encourage parents to put their children first. Now retired, Pat and her partner enjoy the countryside of the Welsh borders and spend a delightful time with their grandchildren.

To my grandchildren with love.

Pat Barrow

LOVE THAT LASTS FOREVER

AUSTIN MACAULEY PUBLISHERS™

LONDON · CAMBRIDGE · NEW YORK · SHARJAH

A CIP catalogue record for this title is available from the British Library.

ISBN 9781528974387 (Paperback)
ISBN 9781528974400 (ePub e-book)

www.austinmacauley.com

First Published (2019)
Austin Macauley Publishers Ltd
25 Canada Square
Canary Wharf
London
E14 5LQ

My heartfelt love and thanks to Anni for her encouragement, words of wisdom and endless patience typing and retyping.

Disclaimer

Whilst I have drawn on my extensive knowledge of the family court system and my experience of working with families involved, this story and its characters are wholly imaginary.

Chapter 1

The blue velvet curtain slowly closed and Bette Middler's 'Wind beneath my Wings' filled the lofty crematorium. I felt a lump in my throat and surprisingly, my eyes prickled with tears. I sniffed and glanced around at the sombre black clad individuals; where had they all come from? Who were they? I had a sudden urge for fresh air and freedom from the stifling hypocrisy of this place. Without a second glance, I hurried down the aisle, through the open door and across the stretch of grass to sink onto a bench under a weeping willow tree. As I cupped my face in my hands, my whole body shook, a million thoughts cascaded around my head, a whir of emotions too fast to make sense. The tears streamed down my cheeks, I sobbed big noisy sobs. I can't say for sure how long I sat there but suddenly, I was engulfed by an enormous wave of relief. It was true, my nightmare was really over and yes, I could be glad that my dad had gone. For the first time in twenty-one years, I was daring to really face the reality of the manipulating, controlling man he had been and to see the damage he'd inflicted upon me and my little brother, Jonty.

My mobile vibrated in my pocket; I pulled it out, I smiled, a text from Jonty. He was in Durham, probably between lectures, there with me in spirit if not in reality. It was his way of giving me his support. 'High five kiddo, speak later x'. I realised I had better get myself a taxi to Cardiff Station or I'd miss my train to Birmingham and the connection to Newcastle. I hailed the taxi waiting by the gate and in minutes, I was whisked to the station. I grabbed a chicken wrap, an apple and a coffee, guessing that in spite of nausea and a griping stomach that I might feel hungry during the long journey home. It would be midnight before we'd get back to Newcastle.

It was 5.45 before I finally settled into my seat giving a brief hello to the adjacent passenger, a bright smiling woman, perhaps in her early fifties. She seemed keen to chat but I wanted my own space. Time to think and to make sense of my whirring thoughts, the game playing, the deception and the immense pain and sadness that had dominated our childhood and had gone on to blight our adolescence and beyond for both Jonty and me. I settled back in my seat and closed my eyes feigning sleep as we gathered speed, the countryside flashing by in the gathering dusk.

Mum and Dad, they had always had a stormy sort of relationship. They were both forceful characters and although physically Dad towered over Mum, she was no shrinking violet, well not in those early, carefree days that I remember so well. Life was good – we had a big Welsh longhouse just outside Welshpool. Mum worked part time in Shrewsbury but was always there for us – she was the one we could depend on if we weren't well and she'd be the one cheering us on at school events. And Dad, well he was the joker, the fun maker – always ready for a laugh. I guess I was about nine when things began to change – well rather, Mum did. She became noticeably quieter, subdued, serious and I can see now that her confidence and belief in herself slowly ebbed away, as Dad asserted his authority and took control of us all.

I vividly remember the first time he hit her. I was ten and they had been shouting at each other, something which often seemed to happen. I don't recall what it was about but suddenly, he pinned her against the wall. Then slap, his hand struck her across her cheek. I was horrified. I screamed and Mum quickly grabbed me, hugged me close and then Dad had his arms around the two of us bringing instant relief. The incident vanished as quick as it came and I expected to erase it from my mind but it stubbornly remained indelibly printed in my memory.

For the next twelve months, life continued much the same as ever. On the surface, we were a typical, happy professional family. Jonty and I both went to a private prep school in Shrewsbury. He was two years younger than me and he pretty much thought that life was perfect, but I had a nagging doubt that things were different at our house. Something was not quite right, life had changed and it was different from how it was at my best friend's home. Her mum and dad were all touchy, feely and laughed and joked with each other. Somehow, my mum seemed anxious around Dad, as though she wasn't sure about something. They were always arguing but after the time he hit her, she backed off as if she was afraid of provoking him.

Our bedtime routine was set in stone with Mum and Dad each playing a part, there would be smiles and cuddles, fun in the bath, then Jonty and me snuggling up together as either Mum or Dad read us a story. I especially loved it when Dad used different voices, it was such fun. Then we were tucked up in our own rooms, the light would go out and I would lie there trying desperately to fall asleep but wide awake and holding my breath listening for my dad's loud voice and my mum's shrill response. Then came the endless shouting; angry, loud voices and the occasional slam of a door or bang of something on the table. I used to hold my breath, "If I count to twenty, they'll stop, well maybe thirty, forty." With my hands over my ears, I would eventually fall asleep, often as I listened to my mum's sobs.

The next day, I would anxiously scan Mum and Dad's faces for some clue as to what was happening. Dad, as usual, was especially loving and affectionate, playfully ruffling my hair and joking with Jonty and me. Mum seemed quieter and over the months, she sort of shrank, visibly became smaller, less significant. I loved her just the same, but she seemed, well, sort of miserable. Until then, we'd always enjoyed girly chats and she'd put my hair up or paint my toenails – just Mum and me times. Now it was like she couldn't be bothered. Dad was the fun one, the one who slipped us forbidden sweets if Mum was out. The one who let us stay up and watch our favourite DVD, "Shush, don't tell, it's our secret." I can see now how he manipulated us, encouraged our bond with him, oh so subtly excluding Mum. Jonty and I just didn't have a clue.

Slowly over the following months, the rows between Mum and Dad escalated. No longer just after bed time, but in the day time too. I can see now how Dad would provoke Mum and she would retaliate. Yes, he knew how to push her buttons, get her mad. Then he'd step back and somehow it was Mum and me arguing with me screaming at her. "Why do you hate my daddy, I hate you, I hate you!" The rage inside me, it just tumbled out; where did it come from? What was happening to me?

Dad would come across, take me in his arms, pull me tight to his big solid chest, he'd stroke my hair and calm me. "Now, now, my darling." And to Mum, "Why do you have to upset her, you bitch?"

Those insults, those undermining comments that Dad hurled at Mum. I heard them but at the time didn't realise how they were designed to slowly but surely chip away the respect I had for my mum. I watched my dad, my hero, my champion, the one with the calm exterior, blaming Mum. Demanding that she saw that she was hurting me that she was to blame. Of course, I just lapped it all up, followed his example. He was there for me, made a fuss of me and reassured me that I was his 'little angel'. But when he'd gone out and I was with Mum, I'd fling my arms around her and we'd hug and she would gently stroke my hair. I just didn't have the words to express my fears, my confusion. I couldn't even tell her I loved her and that I missed the life we used to have.

Chapter 2

9 September, I was twelve years old and that was the day my life changed forever. We had had a barbecue, the first since the new school term had started. It was a family do and it had been fun. Dad had worn a striped apron and a chef's cap and had been in charge. The sun was just sinking and it was a super warm evening. We'd had the hosepipe out with the sprinkler on and although we were supposed to be watering the garden, of course Jonty and I had got soaked amid squeals of indignation and laughter. Dripping wet, I had rushed over to the table and reached across for a towel and somehow as I grabbed it from Mum, Dad's beer got knocked over. He turned on her. "Clumsy bitch!" he screamed, as he grabbed me.

"Dad."

"Shush, keep out of it."

"Dad."

I knew it was me who had knocked the drink over. Mum pushed me away and screamed back at Dad and with a flash of her hand, swiped the glass off the table. It shattered as it hit the patio. Jonty was crying and I hugged him, fighting back my own tears of terror. After what seemed ages, Dad came across and caught hold of me and Jonty.

"Come on, kids, we're not staying here, we're going to my sister's, to Aunty Nicky's where we can be safe. Your mum she's lost it, she's mad, I'm not taking it anymore." He marched us indoors and flung a few things in a bag together with our school uniforms. We each had our school bags and as we bundled them into his car, I turned to take a fleeting glance at Mum, standing there on the patio, so small, so fragile, so seemingly lost. I longed to leap out, to hug her and be hugged back, but 'we're safe now, we're away from her' from Dad brought me back to reality with a jolt, of course he was right, he always was. He was my big strong hero.

For the next few weeks, life was very different. I was used to a Welsh longhouse on the outskirts of Welshpool with the hills and woods on my doorstep. Aunty Nicky's modern town house was much smaller than ours but the advantage was that it was very close to our school in Shrewsbury. She lived there with Uncle Colin but he was in the Merchant Navy and so he was away at sea for several months at a time. I guess that's why she welcomed us with open arms and seemed genuinely pleased to see us. Aunty Nicky and Uncle Colin had no children and although she thought the world of us, I could tell after a few days that she didn't really like the mess that Jonty and I made. To tell the truth, it was a bit boring there because we didn't have our own stuff, or the large garden with a rope swing and the old outhouses to make dens in, but at least there were no more rows between Mum and Dad.

Dad continued to be light hearted and loving. He would bring us sweets and puzzle and joke books and was always ready to hear about our day at school. I kept wanting to ask about Mum but somehow, I didn't know how to. He never mentioned Mum, so how could I? Jonty did though. "I want Mummy, where's Mummy?" he'd sob each night. The promise of extra time watching his favourite TV programme or more sweets invariably brought temporary peace. I know now just how Jonty and I were hurting, mourning the loss of our mum.

As neither of us had the words or the confidence to say how we felt, Dad and Aunty Nicky interpreted our silence as our ambivalence towards Mum. Far from it, I hurt so much and wanted her so badly, but over the coming weeks, a subtle change occurred. I can see now how Dad encouraged us to dwell on bad times, and oh yes, there had been plenty of them. The arguments which somehow always seemed to be Mum's fault – "Do you remember when Mum shouted at you in the street when she thought you'd run off and you were with me?" The mention of good times always brought a 'but' and then another example like, "Remember the time when she drank too much wine at that party and fell over and embarrassed us and spoilt our fun," or the caravan holiday when, "She forgot to pack Jonty's teddy and he sobbed half the night." And then, Dad's remarks, "I know you wanted to love her but she really only cared about herself, she couldn't put you first, it was always about her. You know how it's been with her. She got so miserable lately and never wanted us to have any fun together, she was always spoiling things. I know she's your mum but you're better off with me." I couldn't help but agree, my warm, cuddly Dad made me feel safe and brought a delightful glow all over me. We believed him when he said it was best if Mum got some help and then maybe we could see her sometimes. Aunty Nicky always agreed with Dad, she'd hug us and tell us how brave we were and how she and Dad would always be there for us and keep us safe.

Dreams which vanished before I could catch them would wake me in the night, sweaty and scared. I would instinctively call out for Mum. I'd remember how in the past it had always been her who had come if I was upset. Now I would bury my head in my pillow and the tears would soak the soft cotton. At those desperate times, I did so want her.

Dad would hear my sobs and come in and wrap his arms around me, hold me tight and gently soothe me with his 'there my angel, it's only a bad dream. I've got you tight, you're safe with, don't be scared any more'. Of course he was right, he was the one there for me; he kept me safe, not Mum. I fell back in to a less troubled sleep. I was so sure of Dad's love for me and oh so slowly realised that we never could be quite sure about Mum. Jonty and I didn't question Dad's suggestion that our school didn't need to know what was going on with Mum. "It's our business, we don't want other people being nosey," he'd tell us.

Mum worked part time at a bank in Shrewsbury and had always adjusted her hours so that she could drop us off outside school each morning. I guess that was why Mum and Dad chose a prep school in Shrewsbury. Dad was an accountant and had his own business in Welshpool and he had always been the one to collect us from school and come in and have a word with the teachers or attend to anything else that needed to be sorted out. The only thing that changed was that now either Dad or Aunty Nicky dropped us off every morning.

School life wasn't that easy though. We were doing a project this term on families, working out our own family tree; something which in the past I would have loved researching. Now I felt as though I was drowning in a sea of emotions. Nothing made sense, thinking of Mum and her side of the family triggered such a mishmash of feelings, mostly anger, but an unbelievable sadness too. I would concentrate really hard on Dad and his family and then I'd feel this huge sense of relief and know that he was the one that I could really trust. I struggled with the project and my form teacher Mrs Beddows was surprised that I didn't show my usual enthusiasm. Only that didn't help. On a couple of occasions, she tried to draw me into conversation but I just clammed up, remembering what Dad had said to me about no one needing to know our business. So I didn't talk to anyone, not even my best friends. In the past, Jonty and I had always been close. He'd sort of looked up to me, expecting me to look after him. It was different this time. My own emotions got in the way of me helping him so I'm ashamed to say I pushed him away, scared that if I didn't, my tears would never stop and I would drown as they overflowed.

My bedroom door remained firmly closed, a clear sign to Jonty that he wasn't welcome. Now I can surmise that as he experienced his own desperate sadness, it was impossible for him to make any sense of what had happened.

The October half term loomed up and Jonty and I were excited by Dad's promise of a trip to London and a chance to plan how we would pack as much as possible into our three days there. Before term ended, Jenny, one of my special friends, asked me to her Halloween party right at the end of the half term holiday. "I know what fantastic outfits you always come in," she said. The remark hit me hard. Muttering my thanks, I was overcome by this sickening realisation that in the past, it would have been Mum who would have created something amazing for me to proudly wear. Everyone would have been envious but now she wasn't here and Dad's creativity was sadly zilch, so of course I couldn't go. I'd be the only one without a fantastic outfit – I'd look such a fool and everyone would ask why. Why did Jenny want a stupid party anyway?

I was quiet that evening and Dad sensed that something was up. Eventually, I flung the invitation on the table shouting, "I can't go, I've nothing to wear, you're just no good!"

As usual, he offered his calm response, "We'll either hire something or buy something, there's no problem. Of course, Cinderella will go to the ball." He won me over and happily two days later, I chose a black cat outfit with huge whiskers and a long flashing tail from the party hire shop. Somehow, Dad always put things right and without me realising it, oh so slowly he seemingly eradicated my need for Mum.

Chapter 3

It was just before half term when 'the letter' arrived. Each morning, Jonty and I would dash to retrieve the post and hand it to either Aunty Nicky or Dad. I remember so well the long white envelope, the franked name where the stamp would have been 'Grays & Co Solicitors'. That didn't mean anything to me. Dad read the letter, grunted and shoved it in his pocket. He seemed very quiet, there was none of his usual banter, the fooling around and peals of laughter that we experienced most mornings. He suddenly seemed preoccupied and disinterested in Jonty and me.

In the evening when Jonty and I settled down for our bedtime story, Dad suddenly said, "Your mum wants to see you at the Contact Centre, there's one in Shrewsbury." He went on to explain that it was a safe place where children could see the parent that they didn't live with. There would be grownups around to make sure that we were okay. I stared at him in disbelief.

"I don't want to see her!" I screamed. "I hate her!" I stormed out of Jonty's bedroom sobbing and shouting, "I don't want my mum, I hate her!" Dad followed me. "Go away!" I screamed, but I soon relented and melted, sobbing, into his arms.

I couldn't resist him as he stroked my hair saying, "You're scared, it brings back all that bad stuff, of course you don't have to go, I'll tell them you're not ready, she's got to realise just how she's hurt you. It's okay, if Jonty wants to go, Aunty Nicky will take him." He tucked me up in bed, reassuring me that he would keep me safe.

Next Saturday afternoon, Jonty went off with Aunty Nicky to see Mum. I was in a really bad mood. "Traitor," I whispered to him. "How can you want to see her after what she's done to Dad?" After they had left, I felt an enormous pang of regret, why had I said that? Why had I said I didn't want to see her; when I did? Yes, of course I did. But being with Dad, how could I see Mum too? I tried to convince myself – Dad's right, she really is horrible, she caused all the rows like Dad said and all this is her fault and yes, I do hate her, I do, I do, I do. But deep down, I had this nagging, nagging doubt. No, I couldn't go there, it was easier just to hate her, to blame her and to love my dad, my special, wonderful dad.

I didn't want to talk to Jonty when he came home. Of course, he was eager to tell me how exciting it had been to see Mum and if I'm honest, I was curious. He had a big stack of Pokémon cards to swap with his mates and a Lego Star Wars model to make. "She said she'll give you something when she sees you," he told me. He looked anxiously at me sensing I guess that I would be expecting something from her.

"I don't want anything from her!" I screamed back at him. My anger was the only way I could hide the enormous sense of disappointment that washed over me.

I couldn't believe there was nothing for me from Mum, I heard Dad and Aunty Nicky talking in the kitchen a bit later on. "It's typical. Blackmailing the kid like that, not sending anything with Jonty for her. Typical. Rotten cow." Dad's anger shocked me. Once we'd left home, angry, raised voices had been a thing of the past and now Dad's hatred for Mum hit me with a jolt and made me all the more determined not to like her. Then Dad would really see how special he was and he would never stop loving me.

It confused me later that evening when Dad made a point of saying to me, "Of course if you do want to see your mum, that's okay by me, of course it is, just let me know when you fancy doing it and I'll make the arrangements for you." A big smile on his face, but somehow a smile that didn't make his eyes sparkle. What was that message supposed to mean? It wasn't true. Of course, he didn't want me to see her. Why was he pretending that he did? I know, it's just Dad trying to be nice to me, well I'll show him that I really don't want to see her. I really do hate her. Then he'll love me forever.

We settled in to a pattern. Every two weeks, Jonty would go off and spend a couple of hours with Mum at the centre. Dad would try and keep me amused whilst he was gone. I could see that he was getting increasingly frustrated by my moodiness and lack of enthusiasm for anything he suggested. On Jonty's return, I would try my hardest not to be interested but each time there was the same sinking feeling that there was nothing from Mum for me. I would vehemently deny that I wanted anything to do with her but the deep-seated longing just never really went away. Didn't she love me anymore? Did she just love Jonty?

No one really took any interest in Jonty's accounts of his meetings with Mum so he simply stopped saying anything. Invariably, the conversation would be, "Had a good time then, Jonty?"

"Yeah, okay." That would be it. Dad didn't make any attempt to encourage Jonty, or bring up the possibility of me seeing Mum, not after that first time. At the time, I just didn't realise that I needed Dad's encouragement and it seemed to make it easier just to let her slip out of my mind. I got pretty good at doing that.

I remember though that around that time, I started falling out with my friends at school. I got jealous when Jilly went off with Suzie and then when Suzie had tea with Georgina. Suzie had always been my special friend and now even she was deserting me. I started to believe that nobody really liked me and perhaps worst of all, I started not to like myself. I had always been a bit of a daredevil, wanting to try new things. But somehow, I started to doubt my own ability. I didn't really want to try anything new. I lost confidence in myself. I wanted my dad with me just when everyone else was starting to broaden their horizons without their mum or dad in tow. I still had plenty of friends but I was sort of on the fringe, no longer a leading light. I opted out of the auditions for the school's production of Joseph and the Technicolour Dreamcoat and little things like jumping off the top board at the swimming pool. I just didn't want to do it any more, my confidence, my belief in myself, they just slowly ebbed away. I know now that I quickly became a shell of my former self.

Sadly though, Dad just didn't seem to notice it. It's clear to me now that he was so wrapped up in his hatred of Mum that he couldn't see what was happening to me or to Jonty, maybe he didn't care. His overriding preoccupation seemed to be his need to punish and humiliate the woman who had dared to stand up to him. It's as clear as a bell, now, but when I was a child, I was oblivious and only saw Dad my super hero and my mum as the bad one just as he intended.

Parents' Evening loomed up and I remember making excuses to my friends why Mum wouldn't be coming. It was then that Suzie suddenly turned and said to me, "Hetty, what is going on at home? It's just that it's really weird, you never mention your mum any more. You don't ask any of us to come over. I am your best friend. Tell me, what's going on?" At first, I panicked. I just didn't want anybody to know. Dad had drummed it into us, this was our business, nothing to do with anybody else. I sort of felt ashamed, ashamed of Mum. I burst into tears. Suzie put her arms around me.

We found a quiet place to talk and I told her how Dad had saved me and Jonty; that we were living with my aunty and that Mum was really horrible and caused all the rows with Dad which frightened us and I just didn't see her any more. Suzie looked horrified. "I can't imagine not seeing my mum any more. Couldn't you see her as well as your dad?" I vehemently shook my head.

"No, it's just not safe. Dad knows how to keep us safe and protect us from her. I just don't want anything more to do with her." Suzie was wise beyond her years and I know she didn't believe me.

She just stood shaking her head. "That just can't be true, Het." But nevertheless, she reassured me that she would always be there for me, we high fived and went off to lessons.

I made the usual appointments with teachers for the Parents' Evening and went along with Dad. No one said anything particularly negative about me but there seemed to be this underlying suggestion that I just didn't have my heart in my work anymore.

"She just doesn't show any enthusiasm," Mr Hayley, our science teacher, said.

"I could always rely on Hetty asking probing questions encouraging everybody's interest," said Miss Bloomfield, the history teacher.

Then there was my form teacher. "I just wonder, is everything all right at home?" she said to Dad and me.

I glanced nervously across at Dad as he explained, "Well yes, there have been a few problems and the children and I are living with my sister for a while just to give us all a break." He made it sound all so plausible, the most natural thing in the world to no longer live with our mum. Mrs Goddard looked puzzled but then smiled and reassured me that if there was anything that was worrying me, I could always talk to her. But I needed to concentrate on my work and at times, she thought that I wasn't really keeping up the standards that I had set myself. I felt mortified, especially as I knew how important top grades were to my dad.

I could tell that Dad was annoyed. He hardly spoke as we drove back to Aunty Nicky's. There were so many questions that I wanted to ask him but I just couldn't. Instead, I heard myself reassuring him that I trusted in him implicitly and I knew that he had made the right decision to leave Mum and although she didn't deserve it, he was giving her a chance to, as he so often said, "Sort herself out." I reinforced my insistence that I didn't want to see her. That I was his 'good girl'. I loved it when he praised me telling me, "I'm proud of you being able to say how you feel." That put an end to that conversation – my questions never asked, answers never given.

Suzie didn't let the matter drop. I shall always be grateful to her for the fact that she continued to probe and dig. She'd seen Mum and me together so many times; she'd seen the close bond between us and now she couldn't believe what I was saying. She encouraged me to think about seeing my mum again. "It wouldn't hurt to go along with Jonty, just for a little while. What harm could it do? You'll probably start getting loads of stuff." I was tempted, well more than tempted. I did want to see Mum but I couldn't tell Dad that. How could I? My head was bursting with confusion and nothing made sense except when I was snuggled up to my dad each evening. Then I felt warm and safe in his arms until this niggling ache for my mum reared its stubborn head again. Yes, I did want to see her, maybe just a bit wouldn't hurt, would it? That wouldn't stop Dad loving me, would it?

I made several attempts to talk to Dad over the next couple of weeks. Then one night when he was tucking me up in bed, I formulated exactly what I was going to say. 'I tell you what, next time Jonty goes to see Mum…' But I just didn't manage it, so instead I hatched a plan with Suzie. She came for tea and it was she who said to Dad, "Mr Taylor, Hetty and I have been talking and you know she really wants to see her mum again at the Contact Centre with Jonty."

It all came rushing out. Dad looked in amazement and turned to me and said, "Is that true? Do you really want to?"

I could feel myself blushing, my cheeks blazing like beacons. I couldn't look at him and sort of mumbled, "Yes, I reckon I do."

"Fine, I'll arrange it, you can go on Saturday with Jonty." And that was it. When Saturday came, all my confidence had ebbed away.

"You don't have to go you know," said Dad. "It's entirely up to you, your decision. I'm keeping out of it."

Chapter 4

In spite of that, I went. I remember walking across the cobbled yard and through the big front doors of the Convent in the centre of Shrewsbury and saying goodbye to Dad in the hallway and being greeted by a smiling lady and a man who showed us where Mum was sitting at the far side of the room opposite the wide-open door. Mum stood up with a big smile on her face, her arms outstretched. Jonty ran to her. She looked up and smiled at me and held her arms out. I wasn't having any of that but then I looked at her and I just couldn't help myself. I ran to her and she put her arms around me and Jonty together and held us both. Thoughts were whirring around my head. A little voice nagging away 'you're not supposed to want to see her, Dad won't like it. Dad's your hero, Mum's bad, you know she is, she'll hurt you, you know she will Dad said so'. But equally insistent was 'you used to love being with your mum – go on, she's waiting for you, she loves you'.

Mum had brought Jonty's favourite game of pick up sticks and suggested that we all joined in the fun. She had also brought a huge bunch of black grapes and bottles of apple juice and a packet of our favourite chocolate orange biscuits. I was relieved that she didn't ask me loads of questions. She just simply let me say what I wanted to say. I guess I was fairly quiet. I kept wanting her to hug me and hold me close. I had forgotten how soft and gentle her hands were and what it felt like when she stroked my hair. She jumped at the opportunity to put my hair up in a French pleat. Aunty Nicky tried but really anything beyond a ponytail was too much for her. I could do that myself, but Mum had a special way with hair. I was so proud when she had finished doing it.

Our two hours together went quickly and one of the ladies came across to remind us that it was time to say goodbye. Mum gave us both a book and then 'see you again'. I didn't answer. I didn't know how to. She just squeezed my hand and gave me a big kiss. Jonty and I walked back together to Dad waiting in the hallway. He caught my hand as we got there and suddenly it was like old times again. Jonty and me together. Me, Jonty's big sister.

I thought Dad would just want to know if we had had a good time. His endless questions took me by surprise. He asked about how she'd been, what she'd said, what she wanted to know, what she told me and what I had told her. "She's even forced you to have your hair up – she's always forcing her views on you, Het. I'm surprised the supervisors didn't stop her." My eyes filled with tears but I kept silent. How could I say how much I loved her doing my hair? He and Aunty Nicky were hopeless at hair. I wanted the questions to stop so that I could keep everything separate. Dad and Mum, not get them all muddled up together in one huge mess.

That night in bed, I cried. Everything was so difficult. I loved my dad so much I just didn't want to hurt him, disappoint him, make him cross, but seeing Mum again had stirred up all those feelings I had for her. That night, I woke up screaming. Dad rushed in and held me close. "It's seeing Mum again, isn't it my love? It brought it all back to you, I'm so, so sorry. I pushed you in to it." Did he really believe that? Of course he didn't, but as always, he jumped at every opportunity to undermine my relationship with Mum. Oh how I wish I'd had the ability to see that then.

Two weeks later, I didn't go with Jonty to see Mum. I can't explain why I suddenly didn't want to go any more. Dad had let her know and said that it was just too difficult for me. That was true, but not because I was scared of her. I just didn't want to lose my dad too. When Jonty got home, he had an envelope addressed to me from Mum. As he was passing it to me, Dad took it. "Better to let me have it first, I don't want you getting upset again." He shoved it in his pocket. As usual, Jonty's visit to see Mum wasn't mentioned and on Sunday,

Aunty Nicky took us to the cinema. I was able to push the thoughts of Mum and the letter to the back of my mind.

Aunty Nicky picked us up from school the next day and as usual, I rushed upstairs as soon as I arrived home. As I went past his room, I could hear Dad's raised voice. He sounded angry and I stopped. Of course, I was twelve years old and I wanted to know what was going on. He sounded really angry. At first, I couldn't make out what he was saying but then, "When will you get it into your fucking head, they're not your kids any more, not after what you've done, can't you see they hate you." My heart was thumping as I ran into my room. I slammed the door and threw myself on the bed, hot tears springing to my eyes. With fists clenched, heart pounding, clutching at the duvet, I tried to make sense of what I had heard. So, Dad must have been right, he wouldn't get angry unless Mum was really bad. Of course if she was that bad, I couldn't love her and Jonty shouldn't either. I had to stop him, I had to stop him going to see her, it just wasn't fair on me or on Dad. Dad was only protecting us, doing what was best for us. I had to work it out. I had to work out a strategy of how I could convince Jonty he shouldn't be going on Saturdays to see Mum. Not any more, not now.

I picked my time carefully, when Jonty wanted me to help him find out about pirates for his school project. I even offered to lend him my best colouring pencils. Then, "Jonty, you know Dad's right, you really shouldn't see Mum, she's bad, he's trying to protect us. You shouldn't go, it's just not safe." He looked at me open mouthed. At first he resisted, then as I put my arms around him, he began to see that I was right.

He still protested though, "But when I'm with her, she's really nice."

"Yes, but that's not what she'll stay like, you've forgotten how horrible she was, it's not safe, Jonty."

Later in the week, I told Dad that I didn't think Jonty wanted to see Mum but was only going because he thought he had to and why didn't he arrange something good for both of us to do on Saturday – like a trip to the ice rink? Sure enough next Saturday, Dad, Aunty Nicky, me and Jonty all went off to the ice rink in Telford. I guess that Dad must have told Mum that neither of us would be coming to the contact centre. I never did see Mum's letter to me – maybe if I had, it would have been too difficult to let her go.

It was that week when another letter with a solicitor's frank across the top arrived for Dad. Again, he made light of it, reading it before folding it up and shoving it in his pocket, but I'd noticed, I'd seen it and I'd seen the angry look on his face. His silence confirmed just how furious he was. That evening, he told us that Jonty and I would have to talk to someone about how we felt about Mum. He reassured us that we didn't need to be scared and we could just tell the truth and say that we didn't like her and we didn't want to go any more; nobody would try to make us. "I don't want to talk to anyone," I protested. "It's not fair, I don't want to see Mum, but I don't want to talk to anybody about it. Just tell them to go away."

I thought it had gone away but a few weeks later, it was Aunty Nicky who told me that Mr Richards was coming to see Jonty and me and to talk to us both. "I don't know what to say!" I screamed. "Can't you just tell him to go away and tell him I don't want to see Mum?" It was Wednesday breakfast time when Dad told us that we would have to miss our clubs after school that night because Mr Richards from CAFCASS was visiting. "I can't miss choir," I protested. Jonty had started going to chess club and he didn't want to miss that either. Our protests fell on deaf ears.

Dad reassured us that nobody was going to make us see Mum, and it was quite simple, we had to tell Mr Richards how we felt and that we didn't want to see her any more. "Can't you see no one will believe me? It has to be you two saying how scared you are. Surely, you can do that for me – it's not too much to ask. I thought you loved me."

If it was that easy, why did all those horrible feelings surface again? I couldn't concentrate at school during the day and then I fell out with everybody during break time. Jonty and I held hands in the back of Aunty Nicky's car on the way home. We both dashed off upstairs as soon as we got in. Dad was nowhere to be seen which was unusual. I wanted his support, but where was he? At 4.15, sure enough there was a knock at the door and Aunty Nicky greeted Mr Richards. Jonty came in to my room and we both crawled under the bed and waited to hear Aunty Nicky calling us to come down. Eventually, I heard her footsteps coming up the stairs, of course she found us within seconds. She wasn't cross and seemed to really understand how difficult it was and how we didn't want to talk to anybody. She said she would stay with us whilst we talked to Mr Richards. With that, we meekly followed her down the stairs.

Mr Richards was old, well at least as old as my dad. He had sort of sandy coloured hair and a nice smile. He looked friendly and talked to us about school; what we liked to do, where we liked to go and all about our friends. I breathed a sigh of relief, well that's okay then. But then, everything changed when he mentioned Mum and how she was looking forward to seeing us at the Contact Centre and hoped we would go again on Saturday. He reminded us that the volunteers there would make sure we were happy and quite safe. Jonty burst into tears and I just clammed up. I remember that I just couldn't speak, I kept shaking my head. Aunty Nicky explained for us, "They've got such bad memories, it upsets them both so much; they're so much better when they don't see her. Isn't that right?" she asked us. Mr Richards, or Clive as he urged us to call him, tried to encourage us to speak for ourselves. Jonty couldn't stop crying and all I could do was to nod in affirmation to what Aunty Nicky said. He didn't stay much longer. He and Aunty Nicky were talking in hushed voices in the hall but I heard him saying that he would come back on another day and maybe we would be willing to talk to him then.

Dad made bedtime routine extra special that night. We got two chapters from an old favourite Horrid Henry book. Then as he tucked me up, he sat on my bed, held my hand and stroked my fingers. "I know it's difficult my darling, I know how painful it is, I'm really proud of you. We need Mr Richards to understand just how bad it was with Mum. It's so hard for you I'll have a chat to him and I'll explain just how scary it was and he'll see that there really isn't much point in coming to see you again." I didn't protest, I didn't argue, I just felt really safe and secure and so pleased that my dad was proud of me. I couldn't let him down, not now.

Dad explained that he had talked to Mr Richards. He was annoyed that Mr Richards had been in touch with my school but relieved that the teachers there had explained that it had been really difficult for Jonty and me. Dad had told Mr Richards that he was so worried that if we started being forced to see Mum again that it would bring back my nightmares and upset nights that we had both had experienced. I remember Dad explaining to me how he and Mum were talking to a judge at the Family Court and that Mr Richards would help to explain to the judge that it was better for us not to see Mum and then hopefully, she would understand and stop pestering us.

In spite of Dad's reassurance, Mr Richards did come to see us again but although he suggested that Aunty Nicky left us and went into the kitchen, I grabbed her hand and pleaded to let her stay. Mr Richards wanted to reassure us that boys and girls coming to terms with their parents' separation usually felt differently after life had settled down and when that time came, Dad would ensure that arrangements were put in place for us to start seeing Mum again. In the meantime, Mum would hear how we were getting on by getting our school reports and she would be sending us a letter in the post each week. It was hoped, well expected, that Jonty and I would write back to her. I felt so relieved and so nodded my head in agreement and at the same time wondering if Dad would mind if I wrote. I guessed he might but maybe I could ask him just in case letters were okay.

When Mr Richards had gone, Dad told us that he and Mum would be going to court the following week and hopefully, the judge would agree with what Mr Richards was recommending. Dad sounded happy again. Good old Dad, it was great when he was his usual jovial self. I was so pleased, I'd made him proud and happy and I just wanted him to stay that way.

Chapter 5

Bonfire Night loomed. We had always gone with Mum and Dad to the big family event at the West Midlands Showground on the other side of Shrewsbury to watch the huge firework display and the massive bonfire with the guy on top. It would mean hot dogs and jacket potatoes oozing with cheese. "Of course we're going to the 'West Mid's Showground' – we always do," Dad said.

"Can Suzie and Jenny come too?" I asked Dad and was delighted when he said yes, he would arrange it with their mums, we could all meet up at the showground car park. It was a short walk from there. It was a super evening. The fireworks were spectacular and I gazed in awe at the amazing colours shooting across the sky. Dad bought us all hot dogs and all too soon, we were walking back to the car park. I walked on ahead with Suzie and Jenny when all of a sudden, we saw her. It was Mum. I froze. She was walking straight towards me. I grabbed Suzie's arm. "Don't let her see me, please, please." And yet a bit of me wanted to see her. I wanted her arms around me, I wanted her, I wanted her so much.

Then Dad was there, his big, strong arms engulfed me and I heard him saying, "Just go, just go, don't cause any trouble, just go. Nobody wants you here."

Mum just vanished into the night. I didn't say anything on the way home. I ran upstairs when we got in, I was just so upset and of course that reinforced Dad's belief about just how much I hated Mum. How could he know how confused I was? I did hate her but I'd got opposing feelings too, feelings which were so big I just couldn't explain them. I tried to make sense of those whirring emotions churning in my stomach, a mishmash of feelings which were tearing me to pieces. As I lay sobbing, the realisation that it was all my fault slowly dawned on me. I must be such a horrible person to cause so much trouble for my lovely family, to make my dad so unhappy. What could I do? I'd try anything to put it right for my dad, anything, but exhausted I fell into a deep, troubled sleep.

For the next week or two, there were lots of whispered conversations between Dad and Aunty Nicky. I caught snatches of them, but it was clear that I wasn't meant to hear. And indeed Dad just didn't mention Mum to us so of course Jonty and I didn't bring her up either. In the build up to the end of term and Christmas, I was able to push thoughts of Mum aside, and the fact that Dad and Aunty Nicky were especially attentive clearly helped. Jonty and I were excited when Dad explained the plans for us to spend Christmas in the Cotswolds with his younger brother, Uncle Paul, and Aunty Zoe and their ten-year-old twins, Jess and Danni. Aunty Nicky and Uncle Colin would be there too and of course, there would be no chance of us bumping in to Mum.

Chapter 6

The school carol concert was always something which I really enjoyed. I was in the choir so of course I had a special place. I had been persuaded by Mr Douglas the music teacher to sing the first verse of *Once in Royal David's City* on my own. It was a pretty nerve-wracking ordeal in front of all those people, but I managed fine during the afternoon performance in front of the rest of the school. Then it was the evening performance and I remember eagerly scanning the audience for Dad and Aunty Nicky and returning their smiles. Then the lights went down and the concert began. My solo was the last item before the interval. I listened to the opening bars, tensed up and froze. There sitting on the third row from the back was Mum. It was like everybody around her just melted away, all I could see was my mum, she smiled that lovely smile especially for me. I opened my mouth but no words came out. There was silence. Realising the situation, the choir rescued me and started the first verse. I doubt anybody in the audience was really aware of what had happened, but I was. The curtains closed on the last lines of the carol. My friends turned to me and immediately, "What happened? What went wrong? What's up with you?" I couldn't speak. I just couldn't. I ran sobbing and there was my dad. I was engulfed in his arms. Those big, strong arms. Then he saw her and realised what had happened.

"It was just like her to come and spoil everything for you, she only thinks about herself, never about you." He must have had a word with Mr Douglas, the music teacher, because nothing more was said to me the incident just simply vanished.

Everybody enjoyed the rest of the concert, but I didn't. I just wanted to go home and push it all out of my mind and forget about it. The rest of the term was a sort of blur, I didn't really engage with my friends any more. It was only when school was done that Jonty and I could start to get really excited about our Christmas plans – a Christmas far away with no reminder of the mum who so often dominated my thoughts and overwhelmed me with such sadness and longing that I thought I'd burst open.

Whether or not Mum sent anything for me and Jonty for Christmas or wrote any of the promised weekly letters, I just don't know. Certainly, Dad never told us and, well I'm ashamed to say I didn't ask. At the time, it was another opportunity to reinforce my view that she really didn't care about me and I guess that helped me to not want her quite as much, although so much of me did. I just couldn't afford to let those thoughts in.

I went back to school in January full of determination that things were going to be different. I was going to be the old me again, enthusiastic about everything and have lots of friends. I was not sure how I thought I was going to achieve that but that was certainly the plan. I didn't realise that Dad had been to court again. He told Jonty and me that he needed to talk to us both. I thought at first it was because we were going to have a special holiday, perhaps we were going to go to Disneyworld, I don't know, but I wasn't prepared for what he did tell us. "It's your mum, she won't give up. She can't see how much damage she's doing to you. This other woman has to come and talk to you both. I guess you're going to just have to convince her that you really, really don't want to see your mum. It's entirely up to you two, I can't convince her, only you can."

Jonty did his usual thing and burst into tears. I just felt this anger welling up inside me. I shouted and screamed, "I don't want to see her, can't you understand, I don't want to, I don't need to see any woman and tell her that! Dad, why can't you tell her?!" Dad alternated between being really kind and gentle, holding me and stroking me and getting quite cross. I got even more confused.

A couple of days later, a letter arrived addressed to me and Jonty. 'Dear Hetty and Jonty. My name is Carol. As you know, your mum and dad have been finding it difficult to talk to each other about you and they have been to the local family court for some help. The judge there has decided that it would be a good idea for you to talk to somebody not really connected with Mum and Dad and so I am coming to see you. I look forward to meeting you both after school on Wednesday. Regards, Carol'. "That's only the day after tomorrow!" I screamed. "Can't you say I'm busy that I can't be there, that I can't see her?"

"I guess she'll be really nice. Just tell her, tell her how it is for you," said Dad. "Help her to understand how scared you've been and that you just don't want to see your mum." Jonty didn't seem to be particularly bothered, I don't think he had any idea.

Wednesday dawned and somehow, I got through the day, twice I got told off in class for not paying attention and my classmates told me I was in a mood. But I did confide in Suzie. As always, she was so wise and understanding. "If I was you, I'd keep an open mind, just talk to her, tell her how you feel and she may be able to help you to work it all out. Just trust her." That sounded easy but I wasn't so sure.

34

Chapter 7

Carol had this really big, warm smile and I instantly felt surprisingly comfortable with her. She explained she wanted to get to know me and Jonty, to spend time with both of us on our own. She was emphatic that she wasn't there to try and force us to do anything that we felt really uncomfortable with but to help us to unravel some of the confusion that was going on inside our heads. But first of all, she just wanted us to relax and so we sat and chatted about the holidays and Christmas fun with our cousins – all pretty safe and not scary at all. Then she suggested that perhaps she could spend a little while chatting to each of us individually.

Whilst she and Jonty were talking, Dad came and gave me a big squeeze and a hug. "Don't worry, my love," he said, "I know I can rely on you to say how it really is, not to pretend it's better than it is; just tell her the truth, how badly it's affected you and how upset you've been." Of course, I can see now what he really meant was 'don't rock the boat – don't forget your loyalty is with me'.

Carol seemed to be genuinely interested in hearing about school and about my friends, what I liked doing, how far I could swim, which books I liked best. I just felt so relaxed and comfortable with her. I heaved a sigh of relief and willingly agreed to see her the following week. She suggested that if Dad and Aunty Nicky didn't mind, she could pick me up from school, we could have a milk shake at McDonald's before coming home. She arranged to see Jonty on a different day saying it was important that we were both made to feel special and weren't just lumped together as 'the children'. She seemed to respect that we might have different ideas and views about things. I think in those early days that Dad liked her and indeed, he jumped at the idea of me meeting her after school. He was so sure that I wouldn't let him down – I was his – a helpless fly in his spider's web – sticky and cloying, impossible to break free.

The following Wednesday, I felt a bit panicky in case my friends saw Carol arrive. Suzie once again came to my rescue and suggested I simply said it was a friend of the family. She assured me that nobody would be really interested. She wouldn't be coming in to school to see me, but would be waiting with everybody else outside. Of course it was fine, just as Suzie said my fears had been unfounded.

Carol and I chatted in McDonald's. As I slurped my milk shake, I felt this enormous sense of relief, I can't explain why or how, but I felt different, more relaxed. I guess this explains why I suddenly heard myself telling Carol that I wanted to see my mum but at the same time I didn't, and how muddled up that was and how difficult and that nobody understood and that I didn't want to hurt my dad and that my dad was right and my mum, well she must be bad because Dad says she was and I remembered all those bad things she'd done when we lived there. It all just came rushing out and Carol just sat there and patiently listened. Then she put her hand on mine and said, "Sometimes people change. Sometimes we have to see for ourselves whether they have changed. Sometimes our memory isn't quite accurate and we get muddled. I wonder if it might help if you saw your mum and then you could make your own mind up about her, because I guess at the moment what you're doing is just remembering bits of what happened in the past and how your dad's feeling about her now. I guess there's lots of stuff between Mum and Dad that you don't even know about which hasn't been resolved and that's all getting in the way." She explained that she could come with me and we could see Mum together. It didn't have to be at home, it could be anywhere I would feel comfortable. If during the meeting I wanted to leave, then I could. It sounded so simple. But how could I tell Dad that? He just wouldn't believe it and I'd feel such a traitor, a traitor to Dad. Dad, the one who had looked after me, kept me safe. Carol suggested we told him together. "You'd really help me tell him?" I couldn't believe it.

Sure enough when we got back to the house after a bit of chatting with Dad, Carol broached the subject. "Hetty feels very confused about her mum," she said. "I think it would help if she met with Mum, but that I was with her so that she could work out how she feels now."

"Right." Dad looked surprised. Well dumbstruck really, but then he turned and that winning smile of his flashed across his face as he said, "Yes, of course, if that's what she'd like." But there was always a 'but' so that he could reiterate his concerns about Mum. "But I am worried you know. Every time her mum's appeared, it's brought on these awful nightmares and upset and it takes ages to get her sorted out and settled down again. I don't want that blowing up."

"Don't worry, Mr Taylor. Hetty and I have a plan that if it's all too much for her, she will just give a secret sign and we'll be gone within seconds. And I will be visiting Mrs Taylor prior to the visit to ensure that she understands that she's not to put Hetty under any pressure. It will just be a causal laid-back meeting at a venue for you and Hetty to choose." Dad had no response, Carol had everything covered. A flicker of annoyance crossed his smiling face.

We planned for the visit to take place the following Saturday afternoon. On Friday, I was in bits. I couldn't think straight, I was bad tempered, bit everybody's head off. On Friday night, I tossed and turned and just couldn't sleep. When I did, I woke up screaming with Dad stroking my forehead. "It's okay my little one, if it's too much for you we'll just ring Carol and tell her you can't go."

"I want to, I want to, let me this time, Dad." I don't think Dad really understood what I meant, I couldn't put it into words. A bit of what Carol had said to me about people changing, about me not remembering accurately that sort of stuck in my head and I just wondered. Maybe Mum was different; I wanted to see.

Our meeting was to be in the café in the park in Shrewsbury. I don't know why I'd chosen that, but I guess it was the openness and perhaps memories of happy times playing on the play equipment with Mum joining in was significant. Carol came to collect me. I spent ages getting ready. Dad got impatient and kept shouting up the stairs, "Aren't you ready yet?!" Eventually, I willed my feet to walk down the stairs. I felt sick. I looked at Dad's face. I wanted him to tell me that it was all right, all right to see my mum. But he wouldn't look at me, not really look at me. He had a big smile on his face, but somehow it didn't feel real. He just said, "Have a good time, my dear." I could tell that he didn't want me to know that he really didn't want me to want my mum but I knew the truth. I recognised that look of disappointment in his face – I'd let him down, but no – I couldn't think that – I pushed those thoughts away.

Carol held my arm and off we went to the park. My feet just seemed like they were lumps of lead. They didn't want to walk but Carol was so cheerful, so smiley and encouraging that I followed her through the café door. Mum was sitting at the table with her big smile on her face. I had to hold back the tears and the urge to run and fling myself into those arms, those arms which had wrapped around me so many times in the past. I held back, somehow, 'cos there sitting on my shoulder was Dad and his persuasive voice was nagging in my ear. 'Careful my dear, just be careful, don't trust her, don't trust her, she's not real, she's not real'.

"Do you want a milkshake?" said Mum. "A flapjack as well?" And I nodded and breathed a sigh of relief, as Mum walked towards the counter. I was panic-stricken, but Carol just smiled and put her arm on mine.

"It's okay, don't worry." And somehow when Mum sat back down with the tray of goodies, the tension between us just melted away. I found myself just chatting to her and telling her about school and my friends and Christmas and what we'd been doing. It just all came spilling out. I didn't mention Dad or Aunty Nicky, and Mum didn't ask me about them. She was just really, really interested in me, wanted to know all about me and I forgot to ask her about her. The meeting came to an end and I knew I wanted to see Mum again but I didn't know how to say it. Carol saved the situation by saying, "Let's not make any plans today. It will give me a chance to have a chat with Hetty and work out what's best for her." Mum was fine with that, just fine. We'd been holding hands as I talked to her, and it just seemed quite natural to put my arms around her and give her a kiss before I left. I saw the tears running down her cheeks, she quickly wiped them away and a big smile lit up her face. It was her winning smile that I took home with me and could still see as I fell asleep that night.

As we walked back across the park, Carol seemed to sense my need for silence. I remember that she came in with me and surprisingly, Dad wasn't there. Aunty Nicky had a friend around. Carol and I arranged a meeting and then she went. I felt exhausted as I battled with my whirring emotions. The euphoria and how fantastic it had been to see my mum, her lovely smiley face and soft gentle hands was at war with the drumming in my head constantly reminding me of how she had been or rather how Dad had said she was. He'd always insisted she was a threat to my safety and to Jonty's. He wouldn't say that if it wasn't true, my little voice insisted. Perhaps my memory was playing tricks and I'd forgotten how weird and scary she'd been.

I didn't know what to believe. Dad was firmly back on my shoulder, the repetitive parrot, oh so persuasive. 'I thought it was me you loved. Don't trust her, she's not what she seems, you'll get hurt' it screamed in my ear. His warnings were reinforced when he came home. He put his arms around me and twirled me around. Jonty and I were soon laughing as he tickled us. He pretended to be a hairy monster chasing us around the kitchen. Funny Dad, safe Dad. Nevertheless when I went to bed that night, it was my mum's smile which illuminated my thoughts. Her tender arms wrapped around me as I fell asleep. Dad just didn't mention Mum and my visit or the fact that Jonty had seen her either.

Chapter 8

I felt a buzz of excitement mixed with a sense of relief to see Carol later in the week. She picked me up from school and we went to McDonald's again. It was so easy to explain how I felt, the words tumbled out and as always, she listened carefully and then, "I wonder if meeting up with your mum has helped you to remember some of the good times and the special things about her?" We talked about nobody being all-bad; that most people had attributes that we weren't keen on however much we liked them and then she asked what would make me feel more comfortable about seeing Mum. I knew straightaway that I wasn't ready to go to our old home, I wanted to go out to places, for Mum and me to have good times together and for Jonty to come too, not always, but some of the time. "Carol, surely Dad knows that I will have a good time with Mum and he won't mind?" She asked me what Dad would need to know to support me. "I guess he needs to know that I feel that I'm safe. I guess he's likely to prefer us to go to places rather than to be at home." I panicked, would I ever tell Dad that I felt good with Mum, that I'd changed my mind, I wasn't scared of her and she didn't upset me. Carol and I worked out a strategy. She would support me and together we would tell Dad. She knew that Jonty felt the same but she would help him on a separate occasion. She felt that it was important that just as we each established our own individual relationship with Mum so we needed to make that clear to Dad.

I was excited when we went back home but quickly deflated by Dad's total lack of enthusiasm. He didn't seem particularly pleased to see Carol. She gave him one of her winning smiles making it very difficult for him to be anything other than friendly. Between us, Carol and I explained that I wanted to see Mum regularly for a few hours at a time each week going out to places. His response surprised me. "Oh, you want to give her a second chance? That's what's so remarkable about you, Hetty, you always put everybody else first. The trouble is that you can get hurt doing that in this tough world. I can't say I'm happy about it, but if it's what you want, we'll give it a try."

I fought back the tears. I wanted Dad to be happy for me. He stood there with his arms folded across his chest; he didn't seem like my dad any more. I started to panic; perhaps I'd made a mistake. Perhaps like Carol had said, I didn't know everything and perhaps it really wasn't safe. Carol saw my panicked look and stepped in explaining to Dad, "I'm not going to be there all the time but I'm going to pop in unannounced when the children are with Mum. I'll talk to Hetty and to Jonty in between the visits to ensure that things are okay for them. Don't worry Mr Taylor, if anything is untoward, I'll make sure you know but Hetty and Jonty need a chance to re-establish their relationships with their mum and they need your support. Surely, you can do that for them."

Put like that what could he say but. "Of course, but well, I know her in a way you don't, Carol. She's a masterclass in deception and I don't want Hetty and Jonty hurt. I'll pull the plug if I need to." Carol smiled.

"Don't worry Mr Taylor, Jonty and Hetty will be quite safe." And as she was leaving, she said, "Some children find it easier when their Mum and Dad don't get on having two separate boxes; when you are with Dad, have him out of his box and shut him away when you see your mum and put her back in her box when you go back again. Have a think about it; it does help sometimes."

I agreed that it sounded like a good idea but there wasn't much chance of it actually happening. Dad seemed to take every opportunity during the next week to check that meeting up with Mum was really what I wanted and it wasn't just Carol persuading me, convincing me of something that I wasn't really sure about. "I know how you like being with her but can you trust her? She's a good actress – your mum – it's all designed to win you over." He was so convincing and just threw me into a state of confusion.

Chapter 9

The Saturday when I was to see Mum again loomed and on Friday night, I couldn't sleep. I tossed and turned and Dad came in and stroked my head. "There, there my angel, I'll ring Carol and tell her it's just too much for you."

"No." I panicked, I didn't want that. "Let me go with Jonty and see how it is."

"Oh my dear, I don't want you to have all this upset. She's not worth it – you've got me. I've lost my little girl, I want her back."

"It's all right, Dad. We're going ten pin bowling and then for something to eat. There will be lots of people about; she can't get angry with me."

"Be careful," sighed Dad. "I don't want her to upset you. You know what she's like; she'll just fly off the handle if you do anything she doesn't like." But the funny thing was that I actually couldn't recall Mum ever doing that with us – it was when she and Dad were arguing that sometimes she'd scared us when she got so angry and upset.

At breakfast time, Jonty and I fell out and between us ended up knocking the milk over. "If this is what going to see your mother does, you won't be going that's for sure." Dad was really cross. It took me ages to get ready. I didn't know what to wear and then I had butterflies in my tummy. I just wanted Dad to put his arms around me and tell me that it was all right, but he didn't come anywhere near me.

I shouted at Jonty because of this ridiculous toy dog that he had started to carry everywhere. "You're not a baby, you can't take that bowling, you stupid child!" I yelled at him. Jonty promptly burst into tears and was comforted by Aunty Nicky.

43

"Come on, Hetty, there's no need for that."

"What do you mean, why me? Why is it always my fault?!" I shouted, as I flung my bag across the hall. Aunty Nicky looked horrified; it was so unlike me. "Sorry," I muttered. Aunty Nicky gave me a quick hug. Then Carol was knocking at the door, and it was time to go. There was still no sign of Dad, where was my dad? Why wasn't he saying goodbye to me?

Bowling with Mum was fun. Carol simply dropped us off and disappeared. She came back to pick us up three hours later. Mum was relaxed and attentive and just my lovely mum. She made Jonty and I both feel so special and so wanted. I knew I had made the right decision. Yes, of course I wanted to see my mum.

When we got back, I burst through the door ready to tell Dad how good it had been. "Whoa, there!" He swept us both off our feet together. "My word, it's great to have you two back, it's been so quiet." I wanted to tell him about Mum, about bowling but somehow it just didn't happen. Dad and Aunty Nicky never mentioned her.

And that became the pattern. Jonty and I would go off every other Saturday and spend a few hours with Mum and when we came back, we would pick up our lives with Dad and Aunty Nicky again. He never saw us off, never told me to have a good time and in the preceding week, he would always ask me on several occasions if it was what I really wanted. He constantly reminded me that I could always back out, I could just say the word and he'd sort it.

It was a while later after Carol had talked to Jonty and me about seeing Mum and we'd said we'd like the visits to be for longer that there was a subtle change in Dad's demeanour. As he kissed me goodnight, he wasted no time in reminding me. "She's been on her best behaviour, just seeing you for short visits but remember all those times when she snapped and lost it and how scared you were. Once Carol's not around, that's what's going to happen again, she can't help herself. You won't feel safe then. If you start going back home to see her, it won't be the same as when you've been bowling and swimming and out for meals and walks. She'll be up to her old tricks again. She'll be drinking. You know what happens to her then, how nasty she gets, how scared you were and all that yelling. Think on, Hetty, it's not what you really want." Then Dad would cuddle me and hold me and tell me how safe I was with him and how he'd always look after me. I was his princess and he'd win me over again.

In spite of that, Carol must have talked to Dad and to Mum because arrangements were made for Jonty and me to spend longer with Mum and to go back to our old house for lunch on those days. It was five months since we'd seen our old home and we were both looking forward to rooting around our old stuff in our bedrooms. Mum had delivered all our really important things to Dad long, long before but there were bits and pieces still at home that we'd almost forgotten. I knew that Carol had spent ages talking to Mum and Dad and then she explained to us that she wouldn't be taking us to meet Mum on Saturday morning but when it was time for us to come home, she'd be there to pick us up.

A sense of panic overwhelmed me at the thought of Mum and Dad meeting. This couldn't happen. They'd start shouting and it would be horrible again. But in her calm, gentle way, Carol encouraged me to think of what would need to happen to make me feel more comfortable, what would Mum and Dad have to do, so I wouldn't be so scared that it would just blow up between them. That was the thing about Carol, she never expected me to make decisions and she listened oh so carefully to what I said, what worried me, my hopes and my expectations. I know now she used a solution focussed approach to make sure I felt included and felt part of deciding whatever arrangements were then put in place but without the responsibility for how other people felt. Somehow, she always seemed to know how I would feel and she encouraged me to identify what I needed to happen to take away all those panicky feelings. It didn't matter that she was old, well as old as Mum and Dad at any rate. I just trusted her, I trusted her like a friend, a friend who would never let me down. My panic about Mum and Dad meeting gradually subsided. I felt reassured by Carol's assurance that she would talk to Mum and Dad and stress to them the need for them not to argue or to discuss anything in front of me and Jonty but just to say 'hello' and 'goodbye' to each other. It couldn't be much simpler – well, that's what I wanted to believe.

Chapter 10

A few days before that first Saturday, I felt quite excited when at breakfast Dad said, "There's a really good film on at the cinema on Saturday and we could all go." Then he added with that beaming smile of his, "Oh gosh, I forgot of course you're meeting your mother. Well never mind, I expect we'll get another chance." His smile vanished and a look of disappointment crossed his face so in spite of fighting it hard, I just couldn't get rid of those guilty feelings nagging away at me. 'He's the one that saved you, he's the special one, she'll let you down, don't trust Mum, don't trust Mum'. They went on and on burning away in my head but I didn't say anything, I just got snappy with everybody instead. Then on Saturday morning, Jonty and I were ready ages before we were due to set off. It was only a ten-minute walk to the supermarket where we were meeting Mum. Aunty Nicky seemed to have disappeared.

"Dad," I whined, "can't we go now? I don't want to be late."

His snappy response surprised me. "There's plenty of time, stop fretting." Then when we did set off, he insisted on going to the newsagents to get himself a paper. It was three minutes after ten when we actually arrived at the car park. I anxiously scanned it for Mum's car, as we walked across towards the entrance of the store. I saw Mum in the distance and tugged eagerly at Dad's arm. "She's there, she's there!" Jonty started jumping around excitedly.

"Okay, if you're sure you want to go, off you go," said Dad. He stood there with his arms folded and wouldn't look at me. My heart was thumping wildly – tears pricking my eyes – he was making me choose, either her or him. I felt like a spring ready to snap, my heart started to thump even faster and then as Dad put his arms around me and whispered in my ear, "I always knew you didn't really want to go, my love. What about if Jonty goes now and you go another time?" It was all so easy. "Go on then," he said to Jonty, "off you go. Hetty's not coming." He gave Jonty a little push and he ran across to where Mum was standing and I watched him and Mum embracing, looking around as he held her. Even from that distance, I could see she looked puzzled – she gave a little wave in my direction and then she and Jonty were hugging each other.

Dad put his arms around me and pulled me close to him. I couldn't really see her any more. The next moment, Mum was there and Dad was shouting at her. "Get the message you idiot, she's not coming, don't try pressurising her, just get out!" His voice was cold and emphatic. "Just go," he repeated. I'm sure if Mum had stayed, a scene would have erupted, but she turned and went with Jonty trotting eagerly by her side.

Dad insisted that we caught the bus into town and he took me to Costa to choose what I wanted from the menu. Hot chocolate, with marshmallows and lashings of cream on top, things Dad would never normally let us have, to tempt me. I made a half-hearted attempt to look as though I was enjoying it. "You're so brave especially when you're put under that much pressure from your mum and Carol too. I can see how difficult it is for you, I've got you safe now," Dad reassured me.

There was an 11.30 showing of the film Dad had suggested earlier in the week and of course, we went to that. At the time, I fought back tears and the muddle that drummed inside my head. I felt so confused, so sad, I knew that Dad must be right because he always was. He was the one that kept me safe but I couldn't even concentrate on the film, my eyes wouldn't focus, they kept welling up with tears. I hated myself, I hated Mum, I loved Mum I felt so wretched and so sad. I couldn't go with Dad when he went to collect Jonty from the car park where Carol was dropping him off later that afternoon. I couldn't bear it. Aunty Nicky turned to me and said, "I thought you were really excited about seeing your mum, what's happened?"

"I wasn't really that bothered," I muttered, but I must have sounded unconvincing.

Aunty Nicky came and put her arms around me. "It's hard my love, isn't it?"

I dreaded seeing Carol later in the week. I didn't really know what on earth I was going to tell her. I felt such a coward – a traitor, such a bad person. I couldn't think why I hadn't wanted to see Mum on Saturday. But then, I just told her what had happened, how Dad had made me chose, except I couldn't and true to form, Carol was lovely. She put her hands on mine and said, "I think if I was you, I'd find it just as hard as you do. What if we try and work out a way in which you won't feel you have to choose between your mum and dad. I wonder if there's anything your mum and dad could do to make it easier for you?"

"I don't think he really wants me to go," I blurted out. "I think he thinks I won't be safe."

"Mmm," said Carol, "that's a hard one for you then, isn't it? Do you feel safe when you are with Mum?"

"Yes, I do. She's just lovely as long as Dad's not with her. I used to get scared with Mum and Dad arguing and screaming at each other – it was horrible – she was horrible," I added, not wanting to be disloyal to Dad.

"Let's get this right. You feel quite safe with Mum and quite comfortable with her? You enjoy spending time with her? But Dad somehow doesn't think it's the best thing for you and puts forward all sorts of reasons why you shouldn't go, why contact shouldn't happen and you feel that you have to choose between them. And that's impossible if you love both of them. You feel loyal to Dad because he's been especially nice to you over the last few months, he's been the one who's kept you safe. I wonder if you feel like you're letting him down." She was right. That was it – exactly – but nothing will ever change, will it? I sobbed.

"Well, I wonder can you think what would have to change for you to feel that it was okay for you to see your mum. To be able to spend time with her and not to feel guilty like you were letting your dad down?" That was what Carol always did, she didn't tell me what I was thinking, what I ought to think like so many grown-ups but encouraged me to work it out for myself, and in that way I felt in charge. I didn't feel like it was all running away with me. I felt empowered. It wasn't easy though. In fact, Carol had to ring Dad and tell him that we would be about half an hour late. But eventually, I blurted out that I just needed Dad to be pleased that I was happy with Mum and I wanted him to be really glad and not to pretend 'cos that made it all worse.

Carol wanted to make sure she really understood what I was saying. "Let's get this right. Dad tells you that he's quite happy for you to go but his language and his actions don't always match that so you don't really believe him. Is that what you are telling me?" I nodded. A bit of me felt really disloyal to Dad for saying those things but it was the truth. I was just so unhappy. I wanted to make it better. Carol reinforced to me that it was not my responsibility to keep Mum or Dad happy. She needed to see where I was hurting and do something about that, for me. It made sense, but how was that going to work? Dad hated Mum and really didn't want me to go and see her. But why did he say that he didn't mind? It was a lie, wasn't it? Carol went on, "What you're saying is that you don't want to have to choose between Mum and Dad and you need Dad and Mum to stop their dislike of each other getting in the way of you loving both of them. Is that right?"

I nodded and whispered, "Yes." Carol thought for a moment or two and then said that she needed to talk to Mum and Dad separately and really get them to understand how hard it was for me and Jonty and how their adult stuff was getting in the way. I wasn't to worry and in the meantime, it would perhaps be best if she picked us up and then Mum dropped us off at the supermarket so we could go home with Dad at the end of the time. I breathed a sigh of relief, it sounded so much better, much easier, well for me at any rate and for Jonty; Mum and Dad together, it was just too much. Carol was right, we were the important ones. It was getting it right for us that mattered. I couldn't take responsibility for Mum and Dad and how they felt. It was so easy to feel like that when I wasn't with either of them but when I was back with Dad, it got a whole lot more complicated.

Later in the week, Dad told me that he had met up with Carol. I could tell by his face that he wasn't happy. They had gone for a coffee together in Welshpool. He'd been flabbergasted when she had told him how guilty I had felt when I hadn't gone to see Mum. Why on earth was she saying that, it wasn't what we had talked about, it wasn't what I'd said. He looked at me in disbelief. "What game is Carol playing? I tell you what Hettie, she's not here to help you, she's on your mum's side and is trying to cause a rift between the two of us. I certainly think that every other Saturday is far too often," Dad said. "She knows what a strong bond we have. Once a month maximum, otherwise there's no time for us to do things as well. At the moment, I feel so squeezed out and you're so miserable worrying about getting it right for a mother who doesn't deserve you that you don't enjoy our time together either," said Dad. I nodded in agreement. I just didn't know what else to say, I didn't know how to disagree with him. The confidence that I felt when I was with Carol, it just ebbed away when I was with Dad. I hated what I was doing but Dad just won me over every time and I couldn't risk losing him so I didn't have a choice. I argued with myself trying to justify dumping my mum. I screamed silently trying to drown out Mum's gentle 'oh Hetty'.

When Carol and I next met, she must have detected a difference in me. I was reticent whereas usually I had loads to say I wouldn't look at her or engage with eye contact. Of course she sensed that there was something wrong and her characteristic, "Mmm, I wonder what's gone wrong, Hetty? What's bothering you?"

That helped me to blurt out, "What you told Dad." And I recounted what he had told me.

Her response, "You see, Hetty, sometimes people hear what they want to hear and mums and dads in particular can sometimes either deliberately or accidentally misinterpret things because they find the truth quite difficult to manage. I wonder if that's what's happened here?" She gave me time for that to sink in.

"You mean Dad's lying?" I whispered.

"No," said Carol, "I'm not saying that, I'm saying that maybe he interpreted the conversation that we had in a way which fitted with how he feels about you and your mum. Do you want me to talk to him again and to help him to really understand how it is for you and for Jonty?"

I almost forgot to tell Carol that Dad had suggested only seeing Mum once a month. Her response when I did 'is that what you want?' encouraged me to shake my head and whisper. "No, but I don't want to tell Dad that. Please don't tell him I said anything different," I begged her.

"I understand completely," Carol said in her reassuring way. "Having to be the one who decides everything is really tough and just not fair on you. Don't worry, I'll talk to him and to your mum too. I'll come and pick you and Jonty up on Saturday so and you can see your mum, okay?" I couldn't help it, I just flung my arms around her. She patted me on the shoulder. "Come on let's get back home to your dad, he'll be wondering what's happened to you."

Chapter 11

Carol

My head was banging. I'd spent the morning with Jeremy in an interview room in his Welshpool office and most of the afternoon with Ceri in the former family home. Hetty and Jonty's mum and dad weren't the easiest people to work with. I drove back to Shrewsbury and parked my car down by the river close to the weir. It was a beautiful, crisp winter's day. A walk along the riverbank away from other people would clear my head and give me an opportunity to try and make sense of what was going on for Hetty and Jonty.

Jeremy, an affable bloke whose big presence matched his rugby playing stature, had been true to form on every occasion I had seen him – articulate, witty and charming. I had observed him with Hetty and Jonty and seen what a loving, tactile dad he was. He was hero worshipped by his children. In fact, more than that, for Hetty had elevated him high up on a pedestal, in her eyes he was perfect, the best and always right; although more recently, she'd been struggling with the dilemma that created for her. Jeremy clearly revelled in her loyalty and devotion to him and seemed to have a need to take every opportunity to reinforce how much she depended upon him, in particular to keep her safe from her mum. There was no doubt that it was Hetty, rather than Jonty that he centred his attention upon. But why? Was it that she was more susceptible to his charms, more easily manipulated? More willing to be taken in by him?

Ceri had initially been shy and reserved. She seemed to be scared of saying something to me which might incriminate her or encourage me to judge her as a bad mum. There was no doubt that she wanted me to like her whereas Jeremy simply assumed I would join his fan club and had attempted to charm me and convince me that his version of events was genuine, that Ceri's thought processes were so twisted and confused that she was a stranger to truth and reality.

I had observed Hetty and Jonty with Ceri and was not really surprised that there was no evidence of the fear that Jeremy was so keen to tell me about at every opportunity and to reinforce to Hetty and Jonty. She was attentive, genuinely interested in Hetty and Jonty and sensitive and receptive to their needs. In so many ways, the children's love for her just brimmed over. They had of course shown initial reticence, but once they had a chance to experience positive times with her, they had so readily and naturally reassessed their views of her.

Ceri's Story

It was hard to get my head around the very different versions of events which Jeremy and Ceri presented. Ceri had been overwhelmed by loss of her family and bewilderment at the speed that had happened. The separation had been abrupt and had apparently been imposed by Jeremy without any warning or any discussion. "Oh yes, they'd been going through a tricky patch, but equally…" Her voice had trailed off – so much remaining unspoken. In the following difficult and lonely few weeks when Ceri had not seen the children, she had had time to sit back and reflect on what had happened to her and why her relationships with Jeremy and with Hetty and with Jonty had gone so badly wrong. In spite of her pain, she had forced herself to work out what had happened. She felt undermined and demolished by Jeremy's caustic comments and constant criticisms of her in front of the children. She explained, "It always seemed to be my fault." She elaborated, "Everything that went wrong was turned around so that it would be me who got the blame and the children would see me in a bad light. I began to believe that I was useless, my self-worth, my confidence, they just ebbed away. You know I began to think the children no longer cared about me." She admitted that on occasions, she had as she put it 'lost it'. She'd got angry and banged things around and screamed and shouted. Yes, now she felt ashamed, well aware that the children must have been terrified of seeing their mum out of control. She had cried as she recalled those awful occasions but emphatically denied that she had ever shown any signs of violence towards Jeremy or the children. He had hit her once and since then she'd backed off if arguments had got too heated. She half-heartedly laughed, "I'm half Jeremy's size, I wouldn't last five minutes." The separation, although painful had at least brought relief from the barrage of emotional abuse, but she was utterly devastated. She loved Hetty and Jonty, but did she still love Jeremy? She didn't know, she didn't think so, but she certainly grieved the loss of him and the family life she had felt so secure in once upon a time. She had fond memories of times when things were very different but were they genuine? Or was it only when she complied with Jeremy? Now she wasn't sure if she ever really loved him. "I needed him and he made sure that continued."

She told me, "He was a very demanding husband, someone who always expected lots of attention and oh boy, that's what I gave him. I idolised him. When we first met, I knew I'd met my soulmate. I'd just do anything for him, I always put him first, he was the most special person in the universe, my hero. I was proud of him. He loved me to dress up and look glamorous so he could show me off, so I always made a real effort to please him."

"We were surrounded by a group of similar aged couples and some singles left over from school and uni days whom he had always hung around with. On reflection, I can see that they were in fact all his friends and that most of my special long-term friends, the ones I had made during my childhood in the Welsh valleys and then in the Newcastle area had somehow got side-lined, and I rarely saw them. I hadn't really realised that was happening but now when I think about it, I can see that my friends weren't quite so admiring of him, they were down to earth and they were the ones who used to warn me that whilst on the surface he was the life and soul of the party, he would use people, he'd manipulate so called friends, making them believe that of course they agreed with him. I chose not to listen but I realised early on that criticising Jeremy just wasn't on. I remember trying it once before we were married, sort of light-heartedly. I told him that he was getting a bit pudgy around the middle – forties' spread come early I'd laughed. He just flipped – yelled at me that if that was what I thought of him, he knew where he stood and stormed off leaving me gobsmacked and very embarrassed. All of our friends were equally nonplussed. Jeremy's reactions were so often completely over the top. I didn't want to be the target of his anger, I admit it now. I just backed down in the future and let him dominate me, and in the process, I'm ashamed to say that I lost my own sense of identity and my sense of self-worth. The real me got lost."

"I loved being a parent, but it was different for Jeremy. I can see that the novelty of being a dad 24/7 soon wore off. Oh yes, there was no doubt that he loved Hetty and when Jonty came along, he adored having a son, but he seemed to expect us both to be able to switch off from them and to enjoy adult time together. He hated the fact that I was always on the alert for Hetty and Jonty; that 'cos I'm a mum that I always put their needs first – it was instinct. I realise now he was jealous. Jealous of the bond I had with both Hetty and Jonty which didn't include him."

"As the kids got older, I tried to return to my career as a physiotherapist but I soon realised that shift work wouldn't work for us. Jeremy just couldn't be depended on, so I gave up the idea and went to work regular hours in a bank in Shrewsbury and that seemed to trigger more arguments with Jeremy and he and I began to drift even further apart."

"I'd always done everything for the children and that continued. I'd been the one who'd taken them to dance classes and swimming. I was the one who stood on the cold side-lines of the rugby pitch waiting for Jonty to play a game which he wasn't really that interested in, but which his dad had insisted that he ought to play 'cos that's what all the other lads from school did. I did everything for the children. I juggled my work hours and didn't resent not having any me time. The kids were the joy of my life."

"Admittedly, Jeremy worked long hours and made a lot of money. Materially, we could have everything we wanted but he never seemed prepared to swap anything around so that he could do anything with us all as a family. He just seemed to be unavailable and I guess that he may well have chosen to interpret that as him being marginalised and pushed out rather than him choosing to spend the free time he did have with his mates on the golf course or having a drink. If I'm truthful, I know he didn't really make much of an effort. But I'm equally guilty. I didn't make any effort to encourage him, convincing myself that there was no point. He needed to be the one at the centre of my attention not the children and he couldn't cope 'cos he wasn't number one a hundred per cent of the time."

"And then suddenly, all that changed in what proved to be our last twelve months together and he began to show far more interest in the children. Not by engaging with us all as a family but by undermining me. Like I'd say 'come on kids, it's time for bed, it's school tomorrow' and he'd say 'oh, go on you can watch just one more programme, your mum's such a meanie'. And when I said 'no, you're not having another ice cream, you've already had one today'; he'd say 'well, you're only kids once, go on, get another, enjoy yourselves'. And perhaps worst of all if they had misbehaved and I grounded them and they understood why and accepted it, he'd say 'well go on, I won't tell' and he'd let them go around to a friends' house. Of course they loved it, they lapped it up. He was Mr Nice Guy and I was the one that was always nagging them. I felt them slipping away and struggled trying to keep hold of my family. But I felt so alone, so isolated, so worn down and I suppose I gave up and stopped fighting. I had friends but like I said they'd drifted away 'cos Jeremy discouraged them and my two sisters and their families are all in Montreal in Canada, so I can't burden them. My Dad and Mum both died a long time ago."

Ceri had spent so much time delving into her past and her insight and willingness to explore those painful times and to begin to see how the children were affected was impressive and no doubt gave her the strength to fight to regain her confidence as Hetty and Jonty's mum, but she knew as well as I did that that would be an uphill struggle.

Jeremy's Story

In contrast, Jeremy laid the blame for the family breakdown upon Ceri. He painted a picture of her as an unstable, cold, unpredictable mother who showed little regard for her children and insisted he had always juggled work and home to be their main carer. "The children naturally came to me to share any troubles or concerns they had. Ceri was always sort of distant, detached, she never got down to their level. Of course work commitments meant that Ceri managed the day to day practicalities but when it came to being there for the kids, it was me. I was the one that they trusted." Jeremy had been very keen to tell me how on occasions he had had to restrain Ceri, convinced that she may attack him or the children. He elaborated with apparent relish. "The kids would be cowering under the table and she would be like some sort of mad creature, foaming at the mouth with rage, spitting venom at me and lashing out. No, she never sought any medical help. I guess as a family we were pretty ashamed of her behaviour and we wanted to deal with matters in house. When we left, we had all reached the point where we had had enough. We just had to get out. The kids were desperate for normality. You know what's so sad is that there's absolutely no sign that she's changed, not really. Oh yes, she puts on a good front but she pressurises the kids so much. Look how often Hetty has backed off from seeing her, poor kid, all those sleepless nights she's suffered and Jonty, well he seems to have lost his childlike innocence and become silent and moody, much more like a timid five-year-old than a ten-year-old out there ready to take on the world why he even cowers on the side-lines at rugby. I think Ceri encourages him to be a baby – maybe she thinks she can influence him that way. I don't want my son being a wimp, it's a tough world and he needs to shape up."

Separated parents invariably have a very different take on life before and after separation. It was the intensity of Jeremy's hatred of Ceri that was so marked in this family. Everything was presented in a negative way. He couldn't recall Ceri having one single positive attribute and no doubt his negativity encouraged his belief that she had little or no significance for the children and indeed that if they never saw her again, if she disappeared from their lives, the only impact on them would be one of enormous relief. No doubt this was the message he either deliberately or unwittingly burdened the children with. I pondered – was he really afraid for the children or were there other deep-seated adult reasons which triggered what seemed to be his burning need to embroider and elaborate events prior to separation and then to perpetuate stories describing the children's ongoing distress and fear and their reluctance to see Ceri? There hadn't been one scrap of evidence which supported his persistent complaints, either in my meetings with them or times that I had observed the children with Ceri. Jeremy's theory just didn't weigh up that they had contact just to appease her.

The Family Dynamics

Whilst the discussion and exercises I had completed with the children didn't in any way collaborate his story, they did suggest that his involvement had increased during the year before separation and at the same time, parental arguments had become more visible to both children. There was no doubt that on occasions they had been scared. Hetty had described in painful detail hiding under the duvet willing the shouting to stop and how those 'secret' arguments had escalated into nasty rows on almost a daily basis. Nothing as dramatic as Jeremy described but scary nevertheless. "It was like Mum just couldn't do anything right and she'd get mad and shout and bang things and Jonty and I were scared, we just wanted it to stop. Dad kept blaming her and telling her she was rubbish and calling her nasty names." Hetty and Jonty understandably had been relieved when Jeremy had taken them to their aunty's. "The shouting stopped, Dad made us safe." At least initially that had satisfied both Hetty and Jonty and there was no doubt that Jeremy had not envisaged Ceri's feisty recovery.

During my earlier meetings, it was clear that Hetty had been convinced by Jeremy that Ceri posed a risk and that only Jeremy could keep her safe. The failed attempts to establish contact at the Contact Centre had of course reinforced Hetty's belief in Jeremy's version of events. Assisting the children to reassess their experience of Ceri had been an important step forward and had begun to show Jeremy in his true colours. I had witnessed a regular pattern of him undermining progress since then at every opportunity and of continuing to regurgitate well-rehearsed stories of when Ceri had 'lost it'. Without doubt, he'd discouraged any positive memories the children had either of Ceri or of family time together. Ceri certainly wasn't blameless and prior to seeking counselling, she seemed to somewhat naively assume the children could just move between the two homes in spite of graphically recalling how difficult she found it to disagree with Jeremy.

My role was to help Hetty and Jonty to begin to unravel the confusion they were experiencing. When the time was right, I would need to encourage their independent thinking, help them to weigh up different versions of events before and after their parents' separation. I was pretty sure that twelve-year-old Hetty was capable of separating her own reasoning from that of Jeremy and Ceri and with that would come her budding ability to make judgements about her parents and then she would begin to apportion blame where it was due. But if she feared the consequences of doing that, she would resist, she would block those thoughts out and in her desperation she may be encouraged to choose one parent or the other simply as a way of minimising her own pain. Jonty was much more likely to sway between favouring one parent over the other, but he would be unable to shake off those overwhelming feelings of guilt, because no matter how hard he tried, he just wouldn't be able to get it right for either of them.

After parental separation, children invariably feel disempowered and a huge sense of loss and bewilderment. The family life they have always known has suddenly gone and they need time to grieve that loss and make sense of the changes demanded. Children often do have the resilience to come through the experience remarkably unscathed, but – and it's a big but – only if parents work together and begin to see the situation from the children's perspective rather than allowing their own pain and resentment to dominate. That's easier said than done. Parents have to find the strength to make arrangements which avoid their children being plunged in to the painful dilemma inevitably generated by divided loyalties and having to choose between one or the other parent.

Immediately after separation, both parents and children experience a myriad of emotions. Anger and bitterness can blind both parents from making the right choices. In time when emotions are less raw, the majority of parents, believe it or not, manage to prioritise their children and life settles down into a pattern where many children are able to maintain a reasonable relationship with both their parents. Some parents need help and some expect the impossible. If for example the child-parent bonds weren't strong prior to separation it is often nigh on impossible to establish a relationship once parents have split up. But for those families where parent-child bonds were well established, a solution focussed approach often assists them to move on. By that, I mean prompting each parent to identify what they want to achieve for their family and what steps they personally can take to achieve that aim. It encourages parents to listen to their children and then to take responsibility to make arrangements which work and empower each family member rather than denigrating the ex. It is a remarkably simple way forward and encourages parents to recognise how they, not the other parent, can take certain steps towards establishing harmony within the family. At the same time, children have an opportunity to express what they want, but are relieved from making inappropriate choices between their parents. Sadly, that approach just doesn't work with some families and I have spent hours cogitating, wondering and exploring 'what goes wrong in those cases?' Invariably, I have come to the conclusion that so often one parent lacks the capacity to empathise with other family members, is wholly self-centred and thus jeopardises the whole family's future happiness. I am not a psychologist, I can't diagnose or make assessments about people's personalities, but I am all too frequently aware that the presence of certain traits appear to sabotage any progress.

I considered Jeremy. It would be very hard for any child to dislike such an outgoing, bubbly, big personality. However, I detected that underneath that brash extrovert lurked Jeremy's huge need to be wanted and needed by his children. His behaviour in the months prior to separation suggested he had attempted to monopolise them. I guess he had realised that the children were Ceri's priority and he was jealous of their bond with her. He needed Hetty to idolise him and for both children to hang on to his every word convinced that whatever he said was right and in this case, he was the only one who could keep them safe. Almost certainly, he had felt threatened and undermined, as they had rebuilt their relationship with Ceri. The tactics he employed demonstrated how troubled and fearful he was of the children's budding relationship with their mother. Whether knowingly or not, he had put the brakes on progress, perhaps not realising (or maybe he did) just how damaging it was to his children or that the love he offered them had strings attached and couldn't match the unconditional love Ceri gave them.

Jeremy's initial protests of the children's reaction after seeing Ceri may well have been generated from his genuine concern for their well-being but as time progressed, his lack of enthusiasm and support had accelerated. He had shown a determined reluctance to accept that they enjoyed spending time with Ceri and felt safe with her and he had encouraged Hetty to share his fears. Poor Hetty experienced a positive time with Ceri and was then left bewildered and convinced that her dad genuinely wanted to keep her and Jonty safe and believed that her mum threatened their safety. Hetty's vivid description of a parrot on her shoulder constantly nagging and reminding her of the danger that Ceri posed was particularly poignant. She longed for her dad's support and approval to love her mum, but was thrown into turmoil when his occasional assurance that she could go if she wanted was accompanied by closed body language giving a powerful message of disapproval to her. It was those contradictory messages, together with his subtle attempts to undermine any progress of contact as their time with Ceri became more established and regular and to encourage Hetty and Jonty to question their trust in me that led me to the sad conclusion that Jeremy was never as he put it 'going to let the other side win'. For him, this was a battle and about him winning or losing his children. They were trophies to be lost or gained. His constant need for admiration and approval, his lack of empathy or even any understanding that his children might feel differently from him. I recall him earnestly telling me that he doubted that other people had valid opinions which differed from his own, he made no attempt to disguise his disdain for Ceri and that intense negativity intensified as she began to rebuild her confidence and feelings of self-worth and to challenge him. From my discussions with experienced psychologists, I knew that somebody like Jeremy would find any criticism from me abhorrent. His instant reaction would be to belittle, ridicule or dismiss any alternative viewpoint that I may have and to undermine my trusting working relationship with Hetty and Jonty. Nevertheless, I had to find a way of challenging him that left his grandiose feelings intact. Without doubt, current family circumstances meant that he had the greatest influence on Jonty and Hetty's lives. He was the parent who was with them for most of the time. Understandably, he shaped their views about people and about events within and outside the family. The party line within Jeremy's family was that Ceri was a danger, the bad one, she posed a risk, could not be trusted and would cause trouble if given the opportunity. If Hetty and Jonty opposed this view, they would be risking exclusion from the family they loved, something which of course would be unthinkable for either of them at their current stages of development. Re-establishing relationships with Ceri had brought enormous satisfaction and pleasure to both children but at the same time, it had created a whirlwind of emotions for both of them. Jonty, although concerned about both his parents and their well-being, was on the whole able to compartmentalise his time with each of them and as a consequence moving between the two was just that bit easier for him. Hetty with more developed cognitive skills was constantly balancing and counter balancing her relationship with each parent. Her parrot was permanently nagging and reminding her of the danger that he had insisted Ceri posed. No matter how positive her experience with Ceri was, there was that persistent doubt in the background. She was terrified of displeasing Jeremy – she had clearly sussed that his love for her was conditional.

I had encouraged Ceri to seek counselling. She had initially presented as a brow beaten hesitant woman, a victim, someone who had been ground down by her domineering partner and who had in that process forgotten how to voice her own views. But underneath, I could see that there was a strong, feisty woman, just longing to get out. Ceri made remarkable progress with the counselling that she arranged and funded herself. Within a short time, she was able to put her own emotions aside and to concentrate on what Hetty and Jonty needed, and this encouraged her to have patience to move at the pace which was right for them and not to pressurise them or burden them with the additional responsibility of choosing to spend more time with her and consequently less with Jeremy. She appreciated just how difficult it was for them and how fearful they were of upsetting Jeremy – just as she had experienced. As she re-established her relationships with Hetty and Jonty, they were encouraged by their new mum as she emerged more assertive and confident and in turn became more relaxed and was more fun to be with. But this threw Jeremy completely. He couldn't cope with the new challenging, questioning Ceri who dared to stand up to him. The feistier she became, the more belligerent and obstinate he was. He constantly criticised her and expressed his fears about her, but cleverly couched these in such a way that it was as though it was the children who were experiencing ongoing fears and nightmares. He insisted that contact with Ceri rekindled their memories of terrifying times. He was equally certain that he had successfully overshadowed those by the safe and secure home life he had created for them and the last thing he wanted was for that to be sabotaged.

I am totally convinced that child centred arrangements carefully thought out by parents after family separation are far more likely to work than those imposed by a judge or, often even worse, prepared by one parent but not really approved of by the other. Hetty and Jonty needed a swift but satisfactory conclusion to the current court proceedings. Research suggests that long drawn out litigation has a detrimental effect on children's welfare and in addition, I didn't want Hetty and Jonty to become too dependent upon me. My role needed to be fleeting, to enable them to express how they felt, what they feared and hoped for in the future and to encourage both their parents to listen and to understand and to be motivated to craft their own arrangements which could work for everybody. Sadly, that approach wasn't infallible and I needed to accept that at times, however skilful it is, that negotiation doesn't achieve the objective. I needed to weigh up how important it was for the children in this family to maintain a good relationship with both parents. If parents can't or won't work together, it can, on some occasions, be far more damaging to pursue the relationship with the 'other parent'. Just occasionally, it may be better for them to have one and not the other, but this is rare because inevitably one day children will decide themselves how to apportion blame and their relationship with the resident parent may then be irretrievably lost or damaged.

I wanted to avoid falling into the trap of labelling Jeremy because I know full well that compartmentalising anyone can never truthfully depict the whole complexity of them as a person. However, I knew that it was essential for me to consider what encouraged his behaviour and thought patterns and how that could trigger clues to the way that I could best work with him. I realised that sadly, he may well lack the capacity to compromise regarding arrangements or to empathise with the children's pain and confusion or even recognise and accept Ceri's true and meaningful place in their lives. However, my role was to encourage him to see that regardless of what had happened in the past, there was now no valid reason why the children should not pursue a relationship with Ceri.

The only so-called evidence of problems was his insistence that they continued to have nightmares triggered after contact, but this was not backed up either by my observation of the children with Ceri or by discussion with them, or reports of their performance and progress at school. Without doubt, Hetty and Jonty were troubled children but that may well be generated by their confusion surrounding contact with Ceri and the mixed messages they received from Jeremy. The level of responsibility that he heaped upon them – their constant feeling that if they chose Ceri, they were disappointing or displeasing him and risked losing his love for them. Of course time with Ceri had to guarantee their safety and therefore if contact was to take place, it was better for Jeremy to at least initially retain control over those arrangements rather than risking him digging his heels in and a regime being imposed upon him by the judge. It was just possible that he would begin to see that part of the package would be that he would have to give the children genuine permission, support and encouragement to bond with Ceri and that if he didn't, the court case would drag on until eventually the judge would run out of patience and impose his or her own solution. It was a long shot but the alternative would be to criticise and to demolish his faulty thought processes and damaging behaviour and in doing so to completely alienate myself from him. He would, as I had already surmised, dig his heels in and seek some other 'expert' who would – at least initially – support his blinkered view. He would assume that eventually Ceri would realise that she couldn't win and back off. If standing up to him and challenging his views was a scary prospect for me to consider, how on earth could Hetty and Jonty be expected to do so? Of course they couldn't, he was their dad, they loved him to bits however destructive he seemed to be.

Chapter 12

Carol must have met with Dad the following week. He came home on the Wednesday night and was all sweetness and light with me. He had told Carol that of course he didn't mind me going to see Mum but he had to make sure that Carol completely understood how it had been with her. He went on 'to know the history and how it actually was'. Carol, she assumes that Mum is genuine but 'we all know she isn't what she seems'. "If you're really sure, Hetty, that you can handle this, then of course I'll support you." Then he added, "Carol may be taken in by Mum but we know she's always so nice, so convincing to people when they first meet her. We have to be careful and watch out for signs of your mum beginning to lose it. If you're not happy, you must tell me and I'm warning you, Hetty, Carol's on Mum's side so don't tell Carol everything, be careful, Carol twists things so everything sounds good. She wants Mum to win this battle and she's using you, Hetty, so watch out or it will be me, your good old dad who gets pushed out." My head felt like it was bursting. How could all that be true – I trusted Carol, but Dad hated her just like he hated Mum. I had to be careful or he'd hate me too.

In spite of my fears, Jonty and I had a really good time with Mum the following Saturday. Carol took us and then Mum dropped us off at the supermarket and we went home with Dad. We had sort of got used to him not really saying anything about how we had got on, just a casual 'okay kids' and then him telling us how he missed us and how quiet it had been. During the visit, Mum had mentioned February half term and said that she had wondered if we would like to stay over for a night and what did we think? We had been back to the house that day and that had been sort of funny, it felt like stepping back in time I suppose. Mum must have seen the look of panic that crossed my face and I guess she mistook it for me worrying about it being our old house, my old bedroom, but no it was about asking Dad. I could imagine just how he would rant and rave about us being with Mum overnight. Good old Mum, she didn't pressurise us but instead she suggested that Jonty and I thought about it and then she would talk to Carol so that she could set it up. I worried all the way home. Then, I just took the plunge and said, "Dad, you know half term…"

And quick as a flash Dad interrupted with, "Yes, and I've got a super surprise for you two. Guess what, we're going down to the Cotswolds to stay with Uncle Paul and Aunty Zoe. We had such a great time at Christmas. I knew you'd be thrilled to bits to see your cousins again." And that was that, a fait accompli, nothing more was said, how could I spoil Dad's happiness?

I bit my lip and fought back the tears. I'd really wanted to spend some time with Mum, and I guessed that Jonty did too, but at least I didn't have to choose one or the other and I sort of breathed a sigh of relief that it was all sorted out for me. I pushed away any thoughts of it not really being fair. I knew we would have a fantastic time in the Cotswolds, we always did so much with Uncle Paul and Aunty Zoe and with our cousins there too, it would be great. I thought wistfully of the times in the past when both Mum and Dad had taken us to stay there and how super it had been. I'd only been little then and I thought that my life would never change – well how wrong I'd been. The fairy tale was over and I had no idea of what was going to happen in the future. My world was falling apart and the more I tried to patch it up, the worse it got. Carol was a real friend, but like she said she didn't have a magic wand. Mum and Dad just couldn't get on and I didn't think they ever would so I'd always be like a ping pong ball in a fast game of table tennis – wham, wham, wham – just hurting and hurting.

That night, Jonty crept into my room. "Hetty," he said, "can I have a cuddle?" He didn't often ask for one but looking at his earnest little face, I held back the bed covers and let him climb in. "I really think Dad's cross 'cos we go to see Mum," he said. He'd just started to think about how complicated our lives had become and was beginning to see what was going on with Mum and Dad. I pressed the light on and looked at that little worried frown. "Oh Hetty, I'm so scared," he said, as his face crumbled and tears ran down his cheeks. I put my arms around him and held him tight. "It's okay Jonty, I'll always be here for you even when you're a pesky little brother and you know I can't stand you." I stroked his hair just as Mum used to stroke mine, and his. "If we both tell Carol that we want to stay overnight at Mum's, we'll go there one weekend instead and we wouldn't upset Dad by saying anything about half term." That must have satisfied Jonty because by then, he had fallen asleep and rather than wake him up, I crept into his bed and slept there.

Carol suggested that all three of us could talk to Dad about staying over for a weekend at Mum's. She must have seen the look of panic cross my face. She would help us but Dad needed to hear from us that that was what we wanted to do. That was what was so special about Carol, being there with us when we needed to tell Dad something just gave us the confidence we needed. Sure enough telling Dad that Jonty and I would like to stay at Mum's overnight for a weekend wasn't half as difficult as I had feared. But I had not anticipated his reaction. He snorted and a look of complete surprise filled his face. "That Mum of yours, she's just so clever, so bloody devious," he blurted out. "She's convinced the pair of you and you Carol, the supposed professional, that everything's fine and that you're quite safe, but you mark my words, she'll get her claws into you kids, you'll be hooked and then everything will change and she'll be back to her old tricks again. Yes, you can stay overnight if you are prepared to risk it but I want safeguards in place. It's up to you Carol, to convince me that those kids are going to be safe." He stood up, his chair scraped across the kitchen tiles, he looked cross, really cross and with a shrug, he walked out of the kitchen.

Jonty promptly burst into tears. "I want to stay with Mummy," he bleated. I just felt scared. I didn't know how to handle this. Carol put a reassuring hand on each of ours. She checked with us that there was nothing that we were worried about before assuring us that she would talk to Mum and to Dad and would work something out for us. She wasn't going to leave us with that responsibility. A bit of me worried what Dad would say to me later when Carol had gone. In fact, he didn't say anything, it was like it had never happened. That's how Dad dealt with tricky stuff; he just wiped it out. We saw Mum on alternate Saturdays and I guess that in that intervening time, Carol must have spent ages with both Mum and Dad. On the Wednesday before Mum's weekend, she told Jonty and me that if we still wanted to, we could stay over on the Saturday night and go back home for ten o'clock the next day, but we had to phone Dad and he insisted it was dead on 7 pm and again just before we went to bed. We had to promise that if there were any problems at all that we would ring him and he would come and fetch us home. Well, that sounded simple except I knew from bitter experience that it wouldn't be.

Jonty and I packed an overnight bag between us and of course, Jonty wanted to take Zobo his dog, the one that he always slept with, but for some reason, Dad wouldn't let him. "You might forget to bring him back and then what would we do on Sunday night?" he insisted.

"I want him at Mum's!" shouted Jonty but Dad was adamant that Zobo wasn't going.

Carol picked us up as usual on the Saturday morning. "I wonder if you're both a wee bit nervous about staying over?" she said, as we drove along to the supermarket where we were meeting Mum. We were early so as we sat waiting for Mum to arrive, there was time for us to explore that with Carol.

"I'm worried about not phoning Dad on time," I blurted out. "Then he'll get cross and maybe he won't let us go again. Or he might come and force us to go home with him." Carol explained that Mum knew the conditions that Dad had put in place and it would be up to her to be the timekeeper, not us.

We didn't have to talk to Dad for long, just simply to reassure him and tell him that we were okay. I'd had this niggling doubt that it would be tricky, it was this trying to get it right for Mum and for Dad that was just so, so difficult. It was only Carol who seemed to understand that. Mum just didn't have a clue, and Dad, well he just assumed it would be a horrible experience for us.

I knew that we'd have fun with Mum – we went swimming and then back home and it was Jonty's turn to choose the evening meal. The chicken and jacket potatoes with lots of melted cheese was just what we both loved. Then we had great fun making pancakes and taking turns tossing them up to the ceiling. We had a really good time together. It was like old times – the memories I'd forgotten were coming back – happy, carefree times with Mum and Dad together except that it was now one or the other, never both of them, and I had to juggle my time and my feelings.

Mum made sure that we had finished our evening meal well before seven o'clock so that we could ring Dad. That was easier said than done. Mum got him on her mobile and handed me the phone switched on to loudspeaker. He answered immediately. "Hi kids, how is it?" His voice sounded sort of anxious, I just clammed up and didn't know what to say. Jonty said hello and then ran off and left me with the phone. Dad took my silence to mean that there was something wrong. He kept on repeating, "Do you want me to come and get you? Is it that bad? What's she done? What's she saying to you?" In the end, I just flung the phone back to Mum and ran upstairs. I could hear Mum repeatedly offering reassurance that we were all fine but clearly, Dad was taking a lot of convincing.

Mum came up to Jonty and me afterwards. "Come on," she said, "if you're going to do that it makes it really difficult because your dad just doesn't believe me when I tell him that you're having a good time."

"I don't want to talk to him when I'm here," I said and Jonty nodded in agreement. "It's just too difficult, can't you see that?!" I screamed, really wound up.

Mum said, "Yes, my love, I can see, but sadly your dad can't and we need to help him to understand how it really is for you. Otherwise, he's just going to go on imagining, it's how he believes it will be, in other words, that it won't work."

I couldn't help it. I just started to cry. Of course that was the truth, but I just couldn't change how Dad was. Mum put her arms around me and Jonty too and held us both tight. Although she seemed to understand how hard it was for us, it didn't really make it any easier. I was still meant to ring Dad later that evening before we went to bed. I put a brave face on for Mum and said I'd try.

At nine o'clock, Mum rang Dad again, she pressed loudspeaker and I immediately said, "Night, Dad."

Jonty shouted, "Night, Dad!" and pressed the end of call button. Mum snuggled us down into bed and switched the light out and kissed us both good night.

It was sometime later when I heard voices from downstairs. I got out of bed and opened the door, crept on to the landing to listen. It was Mum in the lounge, talking quite loudly. She sounded agitated and I heard her emphatic 'they're my kids too, they're not just yours'. I instantly knew that she was talking to my dad. I crept back into bed, buried my head in the pillow and sobbed.

Chapter 13

I felt deflated when I came downstairs the next day. Somehow hearing that conversation between Mum and Dad the night before had taken the joy out of the weekend with Mum. I didn't know what I wanted any more, but why did I take it out on her? I just didn't know but I heard myself snapping at her when she asked me what I wanted for breakfast. "Come on, Hetty, that's not like you," she said.

"I don't care, I don't know," I retorted. Jonty was playing on the floor with a Lego model he'd constructed and looked at me in surprise. "What are you staring at? You don't know anything." I snapped at him. "That toy is rubbish." Mum tried her best to placate me but I was having none of it. I chased my cereal around in the bowl before pushing it away and saying I didn't want it. We were due to meet Dad at twelve o'clock and it was only nine, three more hours. The day before we had talked about going swimming in the morning, but now I just seemed to drag my heels, I wanted the time to be over – to go home. The worst of it was I just didn't know why.

"Come on hurry up and get ready," said Mum, "or there won't be time."

"I don't want to go swimming!" I screamed at her, "I just want to go home, I want to go back to my dad. I want to go now. I don't want you – it's like Dad says – you're horrible." The words blurted out from nowhere. Mum looked horrified, really shocked. She came over to me and put her arms around me, but I pushed her away. "I told you!" I screamed, "I want to go to my dad, why do you have to shout at him like that, why do you have to be so horrible?! He's my dad and I love him!"

"I know you do my dear, I know. But when you're here. I just want us to have a good time and then you can go back and see your dad and have good times with him." I knew Mum was talking sense but I didn't want to listen, I couldn't stop the turmoil in my head.

Jonty burst into tears. "But I want to go swimming, I want to have a go on the floats and they'll have the great monster one out. It's not fair; Hetty always spoils everything." It was half past ten before I had managed to get ready so there wasn't that much time. But yes, we did go swimming and once I was in the water, I had quite a good time, a good laugh as we splashed around and for a brief spell the demons in my head were quiet. Mum always had good fun in the water with us. She was a good swimmer and she liked to dive to the bottom and tickle our feet. But of course, my fears returned when we got out of the water. I kept glancing at my watch. I was so worried that we were going to be late and knew that would make Dad cross with us as well as with Mum. It was the thought of displeasing him that upset me. I couldn't bear to see that look of disappointment on his face. I knew Mum could tell that I was anxious; she bought us both a drink at the machine rather than going to the café as we had planned. And then, it was five to twelve and it was time to go around the corner and meet Dad on the car park. It was only a few minutes' walk from the swimming pool. Why did Mum walk so slowly? As we walked, I suddenly felt this terrible longing to stay with Mum. I held her hand tight until we turned the corner and I saw Dad's car. I felt a wave of panic – I couldn't let Dad see me holding Mum's hand, I felt like a traitor. I let Mum give me a quick kiss but then I pushed her away and ran across to Dad. I don't know what Jonty did, I expect he gave her a hug as well but then he followed hot on my heels. I glanced back and saw Mum standing there. She gave a little wave, but I couldn't acknowledge it. My dad's big arms were wrapped around me. "Oh I've missed you so much," he said. "It's been so quiet. You know I didn't think I could manage without you." He just heaped on the guilt that I was already bursting with. "I was so worried that you weren't having a good time and I know Mum made it difficult for you to chat on the phone. We need to get that sorted so we can talk properly whilst you are at Mum's, especially if you're planning some more overnight stays."

Jonty blurted out, "Hetty was crying."

"Oh Hetty, I knew it would all be too much for you," said Dad, as he hugged me. I couldn't argue with him, I just couldn't, I wanted to but the words just wouldn't come out, so of course he interpreted my silence as confirmation that Jonty was right and I had been unhappy away from him. In the past, Dad had hardly mentioned anything about our time with Mum; he just never showed any interest. But this time, it was different, he wanted to know everything. What we had talked about, where we had slept, what time we had gone to bed, what Mum had said. Yes, he was particularly interested in that. What had Mum asked us? Was she trying to find things out? Had she asked about him? He just went on and on – I wanted him to stop, but I guess he just wanted to be sure that we were safe; well, that's what I wanted to believe.

It was great being back with Dad. I felt so safe with him but I had to block out all those thoughts about what it had been like with Mum because otherwise I just got so muddled up. Yes, I did miss her, I missed her like crazy, but there were all these buts and I thought my head would explode. I talked to Suzie the next morning at school. She listened as I told her all about our visit to Mum's and how it had all got spoiled because Mum had been shouting at Dad and how lovely it was to be back with Dad and how much he'd missed us. "You know, Hetty, you can see your mum and your dad. You don't have to choose between them." I shook my head.

"I don't think that's right, I don't think I can, I think it's too hard, I think I can only really have my dad 'cos if I have my mum too, then I think I'll lose my dad and I couldn't stand that." The tears streamed down my face. I'd got a lesson in ten minutes. Suzie dabbed my eyes with a tissue and gave me a big hug. "Why don't you talk to Carol about it, she'll understand, she'll help you to work something out. Your mum's so lovely; don't give up on her."

Of course, she was right. I did love my mum but I couldn't work out how to have her and Dad. That was impossible, but I hoped that Carol would understand. I wasn't seeing her for a few days but I guessed that she would know that there was something wrong without me really saying very much and then she'd help me to say it 'cos that's just what she always did.

Carol didn't let on that she had already talked to Dad and she'd probably had a word with Mum as well. She asked me how the weekend had been. I told her how good it had been to see Mum and spend time with her and staying overnight, but how it all got spoiled because of having to ring Dad and then me panicking and not being able to say anything and then Mum and Dad shouting at each other on the phone and how it was all my fault and I didn't think I could do it anymore. But I loved my mum. And then, I just dissolved in floods of tears. Carol patiently listened and then said, "You know mums and dads don't always get it right, they sometimes make mistakes just like everybody else does and we have to help them to understand how it is for you. They sometimes get a bit bogged down about the grown-up stuff still going on between them."

"But Dad just wants to protect us and he really believes that Mum's going to hurt us and says she will be 'up to her old tricks' and I just don't know, I don't know if that's true or not. And Dad misses us and I just don't like being away from him." Carol helped me to unravel my confused thoughts, so I could begin to make some sense rather than spinning round and round faster and faster.

"Tell me about these 'old tricks' you keep mentioning," she said.

"Well, Dad says she'll lose it and well, I think he thinks she will be dangerous and might hurt us," I floundered.

"Is that what *you* think, Hetty?"

"Well no, but Dad says. He must know more than us – he must be really scared for us."

"Mmm, I understand that's how Dad thinks it is, but unless I've got it wrong, you and Jonty have got on fine with

Mum just as you both get on fine with Dad. What didn't work was Mum and Dad together."

I agreed yes that was it, but separating them in my head was impossible, they kept getting all muddled up together and well, I believed Dad. I was sure he was really worried Mum would upset us.

"What would make it easier for you?" Carol asked me. "Anything you could do?"

"I wish I could talk to Dad and – you know – tell him that I love Mum too, but I can't, I can't do it." Carol responded by giving another 'mmm' and then paused, looking thoughtful.

After a bit, she said, "You see if you don't ever tell your dad that you want to see Mum, it reinforces what he wants to believe and that is that you really aren't enjoying yourself with her."

"But he either says nothing or else I get drowned by all these questions, so half the time I'm just wanting him to say something like he cares and then I just freeze and clam up and I can't speak – the words won't come. I just panic."

"I know," said Carol, "you see mums and dads sometimes make things very difficult. They often don't intend to but they can't see how it is for anyone but themselves. I know it seems unfair but you know often it's the children in a family who end up helping their mums and dads to see sense."

"Okay then, I can see I'll have to phone him when we're at Mum's. But if I can just ring and say goodnight to him and Jonty does the same and he doesn't start asking loads of questions, then…" I trailed off. "Can I do that, please?"

Carol could see how much I was struggling – as I fought back the tears and as she laid her hand on mine, I knew she'd fight for me. She said, "Okay, so we've got to get your dad to agree that he won't ask any questions and he will accept that you are having a good time if you say you are, and Mum needs to make sure that you make the phone calls at the agreed time so you and Jonty don't feel responsible for it. But if you want to ring Dad at any other time, then Mum has to agree that either you or Jonty can. Is that okay?" She made it sound really simple. She carried on reassuring me and insisting that it wasn't my fault, that it was up to Mum and Dad to make things work, it wasn't my responsibility to get everything running smoothly – Jonty and I had a right to spend quality time with both Mum and Dad. I knew she was right and it helped so much, I felt like this huge black cloud had moved away. I was on cloud nine but then Dad brought up about the phone call from Mum's a few days later. "So you don't want to chat to your old dad?" he said. "Oh well, I know when I'm not wanted."

"Dad, it's not that, it's just that…"

"Oh come on, I know, when you're with your mum, you haven't got time for your old dad. Okay then, just a quick call but don't forget that I want to hear both of you saying goodnight to me. I'm not going to be able to sleep without that."

Why did I always feel so guilty whenever Dad said anything to me about Mum, it just felt like it was all my fault again? In spite of what Carol had told me, I had this nagging voice 'traitor, traitor, traitor' booming in my ear. That bloody parrot.

Chapter 14

Two weeks later, Jonty and I had a fantastic weekend with Mum. We stayed until four o'clock in the afternoon on the Sunday and the phone call to Dad on Saturday night went okay. He didn't ask questions so it was literally, "Yes, we're having a great time and goodnight, love you, Dad." And Jonty and I were all smiles. I listened carefully after we'd gone to bed but there were no phone calls between Mum and Dad, I breathed a sigh of relief and thought, *Maybe it will be all right. Maybe from now on we'll just come and see Mum and have a great time.*

I knew that Dad had already arranged for us to go to our uncle's again for a few days during the Easter holidays but then as we were having tea one evening, he said, "Oh so I hear that you want to come back early from Uncle Paul and Aunty Zoe's so that you can go to your mum's. Well, that's a shame, isn't it? Cutting short our holiday. Can't you see your mum some other time?"

"But it's Mum's weekend," I blurted out.

"Yeah, and this is a special extra holiday with your dad, so what's more important?"

I could feel the colour rising in my face, my heart was thumping, a thousand pulses throbbing all over me. I looked down at my plate, pushed it away across the table spilling carrots and cottage pie everywhere. I stood up knocking my chair over and stormed out. "I hate you all!" I screamed, as I ran up the stairs.

I lay sobbing on my bed so I did have to choose. I had to choose between Mum and Dad. No, no, no. A bit later on, Dad knocked and came in with a big smile on his face. He put his arms around me. "Oh, Hetty, I don't want it to be so difficult for us but your mum makes you feel so guilty – I know how hard she tries to win you over. We've all been looking forward to a fun time with Uncle Paul and Aunty Zoe and your cousins, we had such a lot of fun at half term. You can see your mum the following weekend instead, she'll just have to lay off pressurising you." I sniffed and nodded. Anything would be better than choosing. It wasn't until afterwards when I realised that it would mean that we would go three weeks without seeing Mum. "So you've dumped your mum – you're a coward, Hetty." That little voice droned on and on and I knew it was the truth.

In spite of all that, the Easter break with the family was enormous fun. I loved spending time with my cousins and Jonty and I just had a fabulous time. I guessed Dad and my uncle and aunty talked at night when we were safely out of the way and supposedly asleep. It was hard to hear but if I crept on to the landing, the sound floated up from the kitchen and I could just make out most of what they were saying. Of course, I wanted to hear. Jonty crept out of his room to listen too. It was quite late and our cousins, Zac and George, were fast asleep.

"I don't know what we're going to do about her," I heard Dad say. "She's a real bitch, screwing up the kids' minds, twisting everything I do and say. It would be far better if she just disappeared." My uncle seemed to be agreeing with him and then there were chinks of cups and glasses and I couldn't hear what they were saying. It struck me then just how much my dad hated my mum. Nobody in the family seemed to like her and that made it so hard for Jonty and me. It just seemed so unfair. I hugged Jonty tight and took him back to his room. "Give Zobo a cuddle, you'll be okay," I told him reassuringly. He was my little brother and I had to look after him. If it was hard for me, I couldn't imagine how confused he must be. At least I had my best friend, Suzie; he didn't have anyone but me. I knew he'd pretended to his school mates that we all lived happily as a family. I guess that's why when he went bowling or swimming with friends, he never asked if anyone could come home. I'd never thought about it before. Poor

Jonty, he was living a lie – that's the only way he could survive. I felt so guilty 'cos I knew I was often horrible to him, pushed him away when really I was all he'd got – the only one other than Carol – who realised how hard it was when your dad hated your mum and you loved your mum and your dad.

Chapter 15

That conversation between my dad and my uncle and aunt stayed with me for a long time. It niggled me and I guess it was the first time I'd actually begun to question what Dad said and thought. It felt really uncomfortable but I couldn't let him know how I was feeling. His reaction if I stepped out of line was too scary to even contemplate. I had to push doubts about Dad to the back of my mind, forget about it. Contact continued on alternate weekends and somehow we managed the nightly phone call to Dad. Dad didn't put too much pressure on us. I guess in a way, I was able to compartmentalise my time with Mum and Dad, just as Carol had suggested might help. I felt a sense of relief but deep down, I knew it wouldn't last, something would change, I just knew Dad didn't just give up, he always won.

Sure enough a few weeks later out of the blue whilst we were sitting having tea, Dad said, "I bet you didn't know that your mum's got a boyfriend, did you?"

"Well," as he saw our surprised faces, "she has and something else you didn't know was that the new fella has got two children. Let's see now, one's seven and one's probably about five, and guess it won't be long before he'll be moving in with your mum and those children will be there with her full time. What do you reckon about that then, kids? You're going to get pushed out, they'll have your bedrooms, your stuff and your mum. I guess they'll call her 'Mum' and they'll have more of her than you do." I couldn't take in what he was saying.

In a state of panic, I screamed, "Of course Mum hasn't got a boyfriend!" I was furious but at the same time terrified. "Why do you say that, Dad?" As I fought back the tears, my heart was thumping like crazy. "No, no no, don't let it be true!" my head screamed at me.

"You ask her, but then again, she might be a bit wary about talking about him, but aha, rest assured, my words will come true." He smiled, nodding his head. "Just you see." And then, the conversation was over. Dad had a meeting to go to and I was left with his voice whirring around my head.

"It's not true, it's not true," I told myself, but then this nagging voice 'Dad's always right, you know he is'.

Next time we saw Mum, I asked her. It just blurted out and I realised then it was much easier to bring things up with Mum than it was with Dad, I didn't have to sort of um and ah and worry about how she'd react, I just came out with it straight. She looked surprised and then she put her arm around me and said, "Where's that come from then? Yes, of course, I've made some new friends and I do have a life when you're not with me, I go out with people. I don't want to be all on my own all the time, but no I haven't got a serious boyfriend and if I did have, I'd certainly talk to you and introduce you to him at the right time. Maybe one day I will, but I'm not ready for a new relationship yet." She talked to me in a really grown up way and I respected that. She understood how worried I was, how threatened I felt and she wanted me to understand that whilst one day it might be right for her to have a new relationship, just as she said it would be right for my dad to find somebody else she wouldn't do it behind my back and no one would ever replace Jonty and me. I felt reassured, much happier. I knew then that Mum's love for Jonty and me was unconditional and forever, no strings attached, she'd always be there for us. Why was it always so much harder to make sense of what was going on when I was with my dad? Why did I always feel so confused about Mum when I was with him?

The following week, I was due to go to Suzie's house after school but then her mum met us saying, "I'm really, really sorry, Hetty, but Suzie's brother has got a sickness bug and has had to come home from school and I can't possibly take you to our house tonight. I'm so sorry. Will your aunty be in or your dad or anybody if I drop you off at your aunty's?" I knew that Aunty Nicky was having her hair done; she'd told me so in the morning. She wouldn't be back until about half past five, but I knew where the key was, we kept a spare one, it was hidden under a flowerpot in the conservatory. I assured Suzie's Mum that I'd be absolutely fine and so she dropped me off at the entrance to our cul-de-sac and I ran off down the road.

I was surprised to see Dad's car parked on the drive. Odd, he should be at work. I can't explain why I didn't ring the bell but instead I went around and found the key and let myself in through the back door. I stopped dead. There was Dad's jacket hanging on the bannister, but on top of it, there was another coat, a pink fluffy one. It certainly wasn't Aunty Nicky's and there was a pair of high heeled boots on the floor like they'd just been kicked off. They weren't Aunty Nicky's either. Cold water ran down my back; my heart thumped, what was going on? I don't know what I expected and I don't know why I didn't just shout out 'Dad' but I didn't. I crept up the stairs. It was very quiet, but then I heard sort of moaning noises coming from Dad's bedroom. I stopped, rooted to the spot. The door was open just a chink and I could see… I covered my eyes and then opened them again… I couldn't believe what I saw. It was my dad, he'd got his shirt on but he didn't have any trousers and there was his pink bottom waving up and down and there was somebody else there. It was a woman I didn't know with long blonde hair. He was straddled over her and she was moaning. I'd had sex lessons at school, I knew what they were doing. It was gross, it couldn't be happening. They were having sex. My Dad was having sex. I felt sick, I felt ill.

I crept into my bedroom. Somehow, I still managed to keep quiet. I pushed the door shut very quietly and I threw myself on the bed and covered my head with the duvet and sobbed. I cried my eyes out. How could Dad possibly do that when he'd been the one to scare us so much with the thought of Mum having a boyfriend? I hated him. I really, really hated him.

I must have been there about half an hour before I crawled out from under my duvet. I glanced in the mirror and saw how blotchy my face looked. I needed to go and sort myself out before my aunty came home. She'd ask me all sorts of awkward questions otherwise. I listened, all was very quiet. I crept onto the landing. Still silence. Dad's door was closed. I crept across the landing to Aunty Nicky's bedroom. It was on the front and I peeped out of the window. Dad's car had gone. So, they'd left. I splashed water on my face and got some books out and strewed them across the floor so it looked like I'd been working and then lay on the bed. I couldn't concentrate, I just lay there thinking. Well, trying not to think really 'cos it was too painful to see the truth about my dad.

When Aunty Nicky came back, she shouted up to me. I went running down. She looked at me and as I was explaining about Suzie's brother, I could tell that she was wondering what else was up but she didn't say anything. She just gave me that quizzical look that grownups have when they think they know and you can't keep secrets from them.

Later on, it was just before tea time I heard Dad come in with his usual cheery greeting. He ruffled my hair and flung his arms around me. I froze, a panicky feeling spreading over me. I loved him like anything and I didn't want that vivid image of him and that woman filling my head. During tea, he asked me about my day like he usually did. "Cor! Lucky you finishing at four o'clock, I've been slaving away, tied to my desk all day." I stared at him, I couldn't quite believe what I'd heard, but then of course he wasn't going to tell me. It was his secret, his dirty little secret. A bit of me wanted to shout, 'that's a lie, you had that woman here' but of course, I didn't. I pushed it to the back of my mind and I knew that I never would challenge him. I couldn't tell a soul what I'd seen. And why not? Because if I did, he'd be so angry that I might lose him. He wouldn't want me just as he hadn't wanted Mum, not if I wasn't his little girl, his angel. And that was so scary I couldn't contemplate it, so of course his secret was safe with me.

However, something changed after that day. It was like I had another parrot on my other shoulder. A parrot sitting there saying 'don't trust him, don't trust him, he's a liar and a cheat'. It felt like I was on a giant seesaw. I'd slide down and there I'd be with my mum having a fantastic time with her and Jonty and then it would bang down the other side and I'd be with Dad and I'd love to feel his protective arms around me and I relived all the fun times we had and how much he cared for us, how much he wanted to keep us safe. I just didn't know where I was. I felt like I'd been squeezed out of myself, like toothpaste that wouldn't go back in the tube. I just didn't know what to do but I know the strongest feelings I had were that my dad's love was conditional. I had to love him completely or he'd stop loving me, and that was unbearable to even contemplate. Somehow, I lost my sparkle, sort of went flat. I just went through the motions each day but the bright, sparkly, little girl that used to be there had somehow melted away.

I heard Dad talking to Aunty Nicky one night after I'd gone to bed and he seemed to be suggesting that my low spirits meant that I was suffering from depression brought on because it was all too much for me being forced to go and see Mum and how for her sake I'd put on a brave face and pretended I liked it. "She always wants to please her mum and get it right for her. Poor Hetty." But that wasn't true, I knew it, they'd got it so wrong. I loved my mum, I loved her so much, but I didn't know how to. But I was even surer now that Dad really didn't want me to even see her. He must still be convinced it wasn't safe with her. Perhaps…well, I didn't know. I felt safe, but perhaps Dad knew the truth and just wasn't telling me. My head felt like it was bursting with confusion.

My friends at school began to comment. "What's happened to you, Hetty, you just don't seem interested in anything anymore?" Then they'd wander off because I wasn't much fun to be with. I was quiet in class and I think all the teachers must have noticed it. But when I went to Mum's, then somehow I became bright and cheerful, sinking back into deep despair when it was time to go back to Dad's.

Then out of the blue one morning, Dad suddenly announced, "I'm going to take it all back to court. Remember a few months ago, I talked to a judge about you and Jonty, well the arrangements have just got out of control and I know it's all got too much for you, Hetty. I want it sorted properly; I really think that your mum's visits, well, they need to be limited now. It's all too much for all of us and, Hetty, you've changed so much it's painful to see and I can't let it go on." I just stared at him. I couldn't respond. The words were stuck in my throat, no sound would come out. I just hoped that maybe Carol would come and talk to us so that... But even my thoughts were a jumble – would I say anything even to her? I didn't know, I just didn't know. All I did know was how desperately sad I felt – a sadness like I'd never experienced before, a lonely aching wretchedness.

Chapter 16

Before that could happen, there were changes which I never envisaged would spark off such a chain of events. We were at Mum's for our usual alternate weekend, chilling out together after tea. Out of the blue, she said, "I've got something important to tell you and Jonty. It's about work. They've asked me if I'll go to their Aberystwyth branch for four weeks. It would be really good if I could do it. It would stand me in good stead to get the promotion I'm in line for and now that Dad and I aren't together any more, I want to make a go of my career." Then almost as an afterthought, she added, "I'm sure your dad will agree to swap weekends so there aren't long gaps. I'll have a word with him. What do you think, kids?" On one hand, we were pleased for her, pleased that she had got a chance to get on at work but of course we both knew we would miss her like anything. The long gap in seeing her after she and Dad had split up was still vividly imprinted on both my mind and Jonty's.

"You mean we won't see you at all during those four weeks?" Jonty blurted out, blinking hard to stop the tears.

"Yes, of course I'll come back up and see you but I'm hoping that your dad will be willing to swap so that I can see you for a bit longer before I go and then when I come back." That sounded fine but a huge black cloud hovered above me. I'd got used to nothing working out how I wanted it to and somehow I knew Dad wouldn't make anything easy for Mum.

I guess deep down, we weren't keen on the idea of Mum going, but there wasn't anything we could do so we left it up to Mum to chat to Dad. A few days later, Dad brought it up. "So your mum's gallivanting off to Aber then, is she?"

"I think it's work, Dad," I quietly retorted.

"Aha that's what she tells you, is it?" His laugh was loud and he had a big grin on his face as he said, "Remember that boyfriend I told you she had? Well, I bet he's going to be in Aber too – just a coincidence of course. Anyhow, sorry kids it really isn't possible to do any swapping or adding extra days – it's far too messy. No, we need to leave arrangements as they are till the court gets them properly sorted. So, you're going to have to get used to not having her around for a while. Never mind, I expect she'll ring you. That is if she remembers and has got her phone and a signal where she's staying and of course if she isn't far too busy with work." He gave a little snigger and a shrug of his shoulders.

But of course he'd done it again. He'd sown those seeds of doubt in my mind. Why did he have to mention Mum's boyfriend? She'd told me that he didn't exist and yet Dad was so certain she was lying, so certain that he was around and that he'd be going to Aber too and like that was the real reason that Mum was going away. I felt bad about it, I didn't want to doubt Mum but Dad was so convincing. I didn't really know what to believe. I had a go at Mum when we next saw her. "Mum, why are you really going to Aber?"

She looked surprised. "What do you mean, Hetty? Why am I really going? It's for work, I'm going to the branch there like I told you."

"Well, are you sure it's really for work? You're sure you're not just, like, going away? Dad says –" But then I stopped, Mum looked so sad and so surprised, Dad must have got it all wrong. I hated myself for doubting her.

She put her arms around me and hugged me. "Of course it's for work, Hetty, but look, if it's really that difficult for you, I'll just tell them I can't go."

"No, no, no, don't do that, don't do that." How could I possibly have the responsibility of stopping my mum getting on in her job, that just wasn't fair. She couldn't ask me to do that and I couldn't be so mean. But I don't know, I just had this niggly, niggly feeling. It just wouldn't go away. Dad was so, so convincing and, well I couldn't, or was it wouldn't, believe that he'd lie to me so blatantly.

She was going to be away for the second half of April and part of May and the Saturday before she was due to travel on the Sunday soon came around. I guess we were both a bit clingier than usual and snappy with each other, but Mum couldn't conceal her excitement so we both tried to hide our sadness. "Look, I'll ring you during the week, I promise and then I'll be up, not next weekend but the one after that because that's our weekend together. It's a shame that Dad can't swap but he says he's got something really important arranged that day for you and it would be a bit unfair for that to have to be changed." I looked in surprise. I didn't believe that Dad had got anything arranged. Then it dawned on me, or rather it hit me like a sledgehammer, Dad wasn't going to do anything to make it easier for Mum. I'd always suspected that but I knew for sure now. We had lots of big hugs and then Dad was there and Mum had gone.

I was pretty miserable all the following day. It was Sunday and it should have been when I was with Mum, but instead of that, she was driving to Aber to get settled in before work the next morning. I consoled myself with planning the next weekend together even though it was two whole weeks away. But then, there was another surprise. Dad came home really excited the following Wednesday. "Guess what kids, you know you've been waiting ages and ages, Hetty, to go horse riding again?" I looked up with a big smile on my face, Jonty and I had loved riding when we were younger and Mum and Dad were together but since they had split up, there just hadn't been any opportunity. Now, Dad had sussed out a riding stables not far from where Aunty Nicky lived and they had got some spaces and I was going to go on Saturday mornings from 9 till 10.30. Yippee! I was so excited!

"And Jonty, you've wanted to do Tae Kwon Do for so long? Well, I've found a club that you can start at on Saturdays too. It's from 1 till 2 each Saturday. How about that then, mate? We can go and get your new kit ordered. And Hetty, we'll have to make sure your riding gear still fits or whether you need anything new. I bet those jodhpurs are far too small and maybe your head has got bigger too and you will need a new hat." I was over the moon and so was Jonty – I just loved Dad to bits. Of course, it never dawned on me then that he knew exactly how to win me over and oh so surreptitiously erode our time with Mum.

At the time, such thoughts were far from our minds. We were so excited, so thrilled about the new activities that we sort of forgot all about Mum. It sounds awful now but that's how Dad worked. He whipped up our enthusiasm so there was no room for anything else. We ordered some new jodhpurs because I'd grown loads over the last few months. My riding hat did still fit all right so I guess my head was still the same size. Jonty was very proud to get his kit. He kept putting it on and showing us all. Dad got him a book so that he could begin to see some of the moves he would be learning. He seemed really keen, happier than I'd seen him for a long time. And I was over the moon. I couldn't wait to tell all my friends.

Mum had promised to phone on Wednesday evening and Dad explained that she would ring his mobile in case we were out – we never went out on Wednesdays so that was a bit odd. I listened out all evening but no call came and in spite of my protests, Dad insisted on bed at our usual time. "But Dad," I started, "Mum said she'd ring."

"Well, she hasn't, has she?" said Dad with a smile. "I guess she forgot or she's too busy – never mind."

"But Dad…" He wouldn't have it and packed me off to bed. I felt sad, let down, disappointed. Had Mum really forgotten? Were we so unimportant? Those thoughts just rattled around my head.

Mum phoned on the Friday night, this time she used the home phone and Dad answered. "Hey kids, it's your mum. Do you want to talk to her?"

"Of course we do." We both dived on the phone together, trying to talk at once. She was so pleased to hear about the Tae Kwon Do and about the horse riding. We forgot to tell her when it was, just that we were so excited about it. Mum told us a little bit about work and how challenging it was but what lovely people they were there and that she was staying with somebody who worked at the office so it was far better than at a hotel. She had walked along the seafront and nearly got blown away but most of all, she was really missing us and was looking forward to coming up the following Friday and to seeing us on the Saturday and Sunday. She wouldn't need to drive back until Sunday lunch time so we'd have plenty of time together. Then I blurted out, "Mum, why didn't you phone on Wednesday like you promised?"

Her immediate response hit me full on. "I tried all evening but your dad's phone wasn't on, Hetty, he must have accidentally switched it off." I wanted that to be true but a bit of me knew that Dad's phone was never off.

The next week and a half were difficult. Dad and Aunty never mentioned Mum. They certainly didn't acknowledge that we might be missing her so Jonty and I kept our 'Mum thoughts' to ourselves. I was dead excited on the Saturday morning when Dad drove me off to the riding stables. I wanted to get there really early. It was absolutely fantastic. Maria, the owner of the stables, took me around to see all the different ponies and showed me the one I would normally be riding. Her name was Blossom. She was a beautiful roan. Because I'd been riding before, she wasn't one of the staid, plodding ponies, but had a bit of life and spirit about her and I was going to join the second group, not the novice group. We spent that first lesson in the indoor riding school. I was surprised how much I could remember. Our teacher, Jodie, was really, really nice. She was quite strict and made sure that we rode exactly as she told us. She didn't want us to get into any bad habits.

I'd rather hoped that Dad would have stayed to watch but he disappeared. I guess he was busy. Anyhow, he was back just before half past ten and as I was saying goodbye to Blossom and telling her that I would see her again the next week, Jodie shouted me over. "Hey Hetty, have you heard about Pony Club?! We meet on Friday nights, just wondering is that something you'd fancy doing? You just pay once a year and then it's one pound a week. We go to the gymkhanas in summer and do lots of things together and it means that you can come and help then and take part in some of the events.

What do you reckon? We could ask your dad if you like."
Well, I was over the moon. Absolutely ecstatic and when Dad
sauntered over, I couldn't wait to tell him.

"Hey, hey, whoa, wait a minute! Let's go and talk to Jodie
to see what it's all about." I was surprised how quickly Dad
agreed to sign me up for the Friday nights so there it was
Friday nights and Saturday mornings – how exciting! My life
was suddenly fantastic.

Jonty came back from his Tae Kwon Do absolutely
ecstatic. It had been great, he loved it and there were lots and
lots of opportunities for him to go in for competitions and
enter for grades which awarded different belts. He was really,
really excited about it. A couple of boys he knew from school
already went so he had been able to pal up with them. "So
that's a definite then, Jonty? You really want to go every
week?"

"Yes, please," he said, with the biggest beam I'd seen in
ages across his face.

"And you, Hetty? Saturday mornings and Friday nights –
that's fine for you?"

"Yes, that's great," I said.

"Okay, I'll let your mum know."

Well, it was like my world just shattered and I was
spinning towards a bottomless pit. My heart started thumping.
Grief! I thought. *What have I done?* It's Mum's time and I've
gone and arranged all these things so there won't be any space
for Mum. I looked at Dad just wanting him to reassure me and
say something that would make it better. But he just smiled.
"I'll have a word with her next time she rings and make sure
she understands it's what you want. Okay, kids?" And with
that, he'd gone.

"Oh, Jonty, what will Mum say? It means we can't ever
do anything with her 'cos we've gone and taken up all her
time now."

"I'm not swapping my Tae Kwon Do, I've waited ages to
go to that, it's not fair if I can't go any more!" screamed Jonty
in a real strop. I was torn to bits. Of course I wanted to do my
pony riding, I'd missed it like anything over the last few

months and I'd always wanted to join a pony club group. But I wanted my mum and I just didn't know what to do – Dad somehow seemed glad that it was all such a mess.

All the elation that I had felt about going horse riding again, it just sort of like evaporated and when the phone rang a few days later, it was with bated breath that I waited for Dad to say something to Mum. He took the phone out of the room, so I couldn't really hear what was said. A few minutes later, he came back and thrust the pone in my direction. "Here, have a chat to your mum, tell her that it's what you want, both of you, it's not what I've chosen. It's your choice entirely, nothing to do with me except of course I'm paying." So he was dumping it all on us. It was all our fault. I knew all this was my fault. I knew that I was to blame. I knew that I was the cause of all the trouble. I must be such a horrid, horrid, horrid person. I didn't deserve anybody to love me. Those thoughts just flashed through my mind.

"Oh Mum, Mum, I've missed you so much," I sobbed down the phone. She was really lovely. She didn't even mention the Friday or Saturday to us and so of course, I was unbelievably relieved.

When we saw her the following weekend, we were really excited. Dad had arranged for her to meet us both after Jonty's Tae Kwon Do. Mum suggested that we went out for a meal that evening in Shrewsbury. It was a real treat for us. "Can we go to Pizza Hut *please*?" said Jonty.

"Oh go on then, all right, Pizza Hut it is." So off we went, although I would personally have preferred to go to the new Zizzi's restaurant in town.

It was whilst we were eating our chocolate sundaes, another special treat, that Mum brought it up. "So you've got horse riding and Tae Kwon Do arranged now each weekend? That's really good, but maybe it would have been better if we'd all discussed it first because it does mean that we haven't got very much time together."

"But, Mum, you could come and watch." I felt a wave of panic, why was she making it hard?

"Well, yes of course I could and I'd love to do that, but I meant if we wanted to go out or go away for the weekend or do something altogether, it's going to make it a bit difficult."

"Well, I'm not missing Tae Kwon Do for anything," said Jonty glaring at his chocolate sundae.

"No Jonty, I'm not saying that, I'm just saying we need to work out how we can manage it all." I didn't say anything; my heart was thumping so hard and I just stared at my chocolate sundae too.

In spite of that, I enjoyed the time we did have with Mum, it was really, really good and I just knew how much I loved her, how much I missed her. I was so sorry to have to say goodbye to her Sunday teatime. Usually at weekends, she'd drop us at school on the Monday morning, but of course she had to get back to Aber. "It's half way through now kids, so it won't be that long before I'm back and then maybe your dad and I can to sit down and sort something out so we can have more fun time together and you can do pony riding and Tae Kwon Do as well." Once again, my heart dropped, I just somehow knew that Dad wasn't going to arrange anything with Mum, he just seemed to be so gleeful if it meant that she didn't get as much time with us. I hated thinking that but a bit of me knew it was true. Somehow, it felt like it was a competition with us as the prizes, like at a fairground, throwing the hoops to see who could hook us first.

A few days later, I was snuggling up to Dad watching a film, Aunty Nicky was out and Jonty was lying across the other half of the settee with his feet on Dad. "You know kids, it's because I love you so much that I arrange these things for you, activities that I know you both really, really like doing. It's just what any mum or dad who really loves you would do. They don't mind that you do all the things you want, they don't start talking about my time and your time, but just what makes you two happy, when you have fun. It's about knowing the right things to arrange for you, that's why I set up the Tae Kwon Do and took the opportunity for you to go riding again, Hetty, because I know that's what you really wanted. It's a bit of a shame if your mum sees it as me taking her time away from her, it's not like that at all. If she really loved you and it wasn't just about her, if she really loved you, she'd see that and she'd be absolutely delighted for you just like I am." It sort of made sense what he said. But I couldn't quite get my head around the bit about Mum not loving us as much as Dad did.

Dad kept on with the same theme over the next few days and it seemed as though he really wanted to make sure that we understood what he meant. It certainly worked as far as Jonty was concerned. "I am going to tell Mum I really don't care what she says or what she thinks my Tae Kwon Do is most important and I'm going to it. Right?" It was so unlike Jonty, he just wasn't usually so emphatic. I guess when I thought about it, I knew that there was no way that I wanted to give up the Pony Club or horse riding, but somehow I wanted to make it better between Mum and Dad. Of course if I was honest, I was equally sure that wasn't likely to happen. Mum never said anything nasty about Dad, but Dad just seemed to be happy if Mum was sad or disappointed about something and that something usually involved me and Jonty.

Chapter 17

It was a few days before Mum was due to come home from Aber, this time home for good and wasn't I glad. I'd really, really missed her even though I still had this niggle about what Dad had said about maybe she didn't really love us if she didn't want us to do all the things that we enjoyed doing. Then Dad suggested that we went with him to the new sports club that had just opened up. It was only about ten minutes from home and they had a free open evening with trials of different activities and sports. So, we went along. I don't know how it happened, I really don't know but before we left, somehow Jonty and I were signed up to the new junior tennis club which was starting in a few weeks' time, indoors at first and then moving to the outdoor courts, and guess what – it was at six o'clock on Sundays – six till seven. "Your mum will take you, it will be really good, won't it? I'll just send her the details." I felt cold water running down my spine. How had we got ourselves into this now? It had just happened so easily, one minute we were chatting about tennis and how we both liked to play and the next minute we were signed up and… Oh, what had I done? How could I possibly tell Mum that… Oh I don't know, I just didn't know any more. But what I did know was that usually on Sundays, we went out somewhere and we'd get back during the evening and have a meal together and then a lovely relaxing time just chilling out and she would take us back to school the next morning. But now, we'd have to dash back from wherever we were and have our tea early or else have it late when we came back from tennis. Dad patted us both on the head. "I'll have a chat to your mum and tell her about all these things and just make sure she understands what's arranged." That smile of his hovered across his face.

All thoughts of tennis went out of my mind, I was so pleased to see Mum that weekend and have a proper weekend with her instead of what seemed like a small amount of snatched time. On Friday evening, she came along to the Pony Club and of course Jonty came too, although he moaned about having to hang around waiting for me and was even crosser when he had to come along to the riding lesson the next morning. There wasn't really time for Mum to go back home again and then come back so once again, they hung around whilst I was doing my lesson and this time, it was partly inside and then we went on a proper ride. I guess Jonty got bored. He was quite grumpy when we came back. And then we had no sooner got home than we had to have an early lunch because he was off to his Tae Kwon Do. At least that was in town and Mum and I could have a bit of a wander around the shops but we were clock watching so we couldn't really enjoy ourselves.

I guess it was convenient that tennis wasn't starting right away, I don't know how I could possibly have told her about that. As it happened, I didn't need to because sure enough during the week, Dad announced that he was going to give Mum a ring. "Just to set her straight on what's organised for you both," he told us. But he somehow looked, well, like he was looking forward to upsetting Mum. Anyhow, after I'd gone to bed that night, I heard him in the hall. I guessed he was going to ring Mum from there. I crept out of my room so I could hear, well at least I could hear some of it. I think he started by telling her what we'd got arranged. I don't know what she said in response but he sort of laughed, a nasty sort of laugh. "Well, what do you expect?" I heard him say. "The kids don't want to be with you, of course they don't. They couldn't wait to fill up your time." So he was making out it was all our fault, that we'd chosen not to be with Mum and that just wasn't true and it wasn't fair. But what could I do about it? Nothing, really 'cos I couldn't say anything to Dad, I couldn't disagree with Dad, 'cos well, it just wasn't possible.

But Mum, she'd be so disappointed. Perhaps she would stop loving us, perhaps she would get a boyfriend who'd got kids and like, replace us, have somebody new. Perhaps it's true what Dad said, perhaps that was what she went to Aber for, perhaps it was 'cos that's where she's going to go and live, Perhaps she's just going to leave us, perhaps she doesn't want us.

I talked to Suzie the following day. I hadn't had a really serious talk with her for ages, I knew that I had sort of drifted away from all my friends a bit but Suzie was still always there for me. She put her arms around me and said, "You know your mum loves you to bits and you love her to bits and she knows that. Of course you love your dad and your dad loves you, but you're not going to lose your mum, not in a million years is that going to happen. She'll understand about the pony riding and the tennis and it's not like you've got to go with your dad, your mum can take you."

I guessed it was sensible but... "It's just that we can't sort of do anything with her, like special stuff because there's never going to be any space anymore." Of course Suzie didn't have the answers but she just reassured me.

"Look, don't worry. I think when grownups don't love each other anymore that they sometimes do stuff to get the other person really upset and angry, it just seems to happen and I think grownups are often quite childish," she said.

"Gosh, you're so wise Suzie, you just know so much. How do you know so much?"

"Well, I don't really but I guess I can see what's happening 'cos I'm not stuck in the middle of it like you are. You'd probably be just as helpful to me if it was the other way around." I doubted it!

"What do you think I should do, Suzie? How can I make it feel okay with Mum? I've just got this horrible feeling that I'm going to lose her, 'cos she'll think we don't love her."

"Of course you won't lose her. Don't be silly, Hetty," said Suzie. "Why don't you and Jonty think of something that you could do with your mum on Sundays during the day? So that would be your special time with her?"

"I can't really think of anything," I said.

"Well, try," said Suzie. "It's hard for your mum too, you know." I could see that but I was hurting so much I couldn't think straight.

We hadn't seen Carol for some time and then out of the blue, she sent us a letter saying that she would like to meet us after school. She had clearly already told Dad because he didn't seem surprised when I said that I wanted to meet her and she was going to take me to McDonald's and that I'd be home at about half past five and was that okay?

"Well, I suppose so, if you must. I can't really see why she needs to talk to you again though. Just be careful and remember we stick together. Don't let her wriggle her way between you and your old dad. Trust me, not her. She's on your mum's side. Don't forget when she's all sweet and smiley." I couldn't understand why Dad didn't like Carol. She wasn't a bit like he said, and I really trusted her.

When Jonty told me that Carol had arranged to see him at a separate time, I was quite relieved because I wanted Carol to myself, somehow it was much easier to talk when there was nobody else there, just me and her. She sort of just made it right for me to talk and she just listened. She nodded thoughtfully as I explained about the riding, the Pony Club and the Tae Kwon Do and now the tennis and the quandary I felt that I was in. And how it felt like it was all my fault and that I was getting blamed for Mum getting squashed out. She didn't agree or disagree but asked me what I thought could happen to perhaps make it feel easier for me. It was then that I blurted out that Dad reckoned that it would mean that Mum didn't really love us if she didn't want us to go and do those things. Carol looked sort of surprised. "Mmm, I wonder if that's what you think?" she pondered.

"Well, I just don't know. Dad's always been right. It just seems like he wouldn't have got it wrong this time."

Carol nodded. "You know mums and dads don't always get it right, sometimes when mums and dads are too busy fighting each other, they sort of get muddled about what's best for their children. Of course you want to do your riding and of course you'd like to do tennis, but I just wonder whether maybe tennis could perhaps be on a different night, one that isn't a night that you're seeing your mum? Whether that would perhaps make it a bit easier?"

I nodded but then… "I don't think that Dad would like that. He'd never agree."

"Mmm, maybe it's something I could have a chat to Dad about rather than you doing it?" said Carol.

"Yes, but I don't want Dad to think that I've been complaining, 'cos…"

"Just trust me," said Carol. "I'm not going to promise anything but let's just see if there's any room for a bit of a wriggle around, eh?"

"Dad says it shouldn't be Mum's time and his time, but it should just be our time," I blurted out. "Like it shouldn't matter when things are arranged, but we just want to have some time to do special things with Mum and Mum had been talking about us going away like some weekends and now I've gone and messed that up, so that can't happen."

"There's the holidays, you get a holiday every six weeks," said Carol.

"But we never seem to have much time with Mum because Dad gets something organised and then the holidays all go."

"It seems to me that we need to get something a little bit more definite in place about holidays so that Mum and Dad don't need to argue. Do you think that would work better?"

I knew, or perhaps hoped, that Carol would get it sussed for me. "Yes, a million times better," I whispered.

I don't really know what went on between Mum and Dad and Carol over the next few weeks. Dad seemed to be in quite a grumpy mood so I guess Carol had talked to them both. I held my breath hoping that something would change but nothing happened. And then, he announced one day. "Like I said kids some weeks ago, we're going back to court to get this sorted out once and for all. We can't have your mum messing everything up, demanding her time and stopping your fun."

I looked surprised. "What do you mean, Dad?"

"Oh never mind, I don't want to be talking about that now," said Dad. "Talking about her gives me a thumping headache." I looked startled. "Come on, let's go and kick a ball around the garden for a bit."

Chapter 18

Of course, Carol came to see us again. She saw us by ourselves and then together. I don't know why but I just cried when she arrived, I just crumbled, I didn't know what was happening. I didn't know how to sort it out any more. It just seemed so muddled up. "I just want it all, well just running smoothly and Mum and Dad to get on and I don't want it like this. I just feel like there's a war going on all the time and I don't know which side I'm supposed to be on," I sobbed.

Carol understood, of course she did. She smiled at me and said, "I wonder what we can do? How you would really like it to be if you could just wave a magic wand?"

"Well, I want to see Mum and I want to have time with her and now we've got all these things arranged, well I want to do them, but they're always in Mum's time and there's never any chance to see her just on her own and I get sort of sad and then Dad says Mum's got a boyfriend and he's got children and she's going to not want us anymore and –"

"Hey, whoa, whoa let's take one thing at a time, shall we? Of course your mum and dad will both probably meet somebody else one day, but from what I've heard and from talking to your mum and your dad, they're not ready to do that at the moment, they just want to get it right for you. Yes really, Hetty, that's what they both want – the trouble is they aren't very good at working together to get it right for you. They both think that they have the perfect answer."

I looked at her and gave a sharp intake of breath, should I say about Dad's girlfriend? Of course not, I couldn't say anything bad about him; it would be disloyal, it would be unfair, 'cos, 'cos… I pushed the vivid memory of his bottom waving in the air out of my mind, I couldn't think about it, it was too horrible. I felt a tiny bit reassured by what Carol was saying and then I heard myself responding, "Well, what I'd really like would be to spend a couple of nights in the week with Mum, staying over so it isn't always such a rush. That is as well as alternate weekends' otherwise it's such a long time before I see her again. And then in holidays, I'd like some proper time with both her and Dad. He arranges really good things for us but he doesn't give Mum any chance at all."

Carol looked thoughtful as she said, "I guess what I'm hearing is that you want to get it fair for everybody, but this is about what works best for you, Hetty, and what's right for Jonty, whether you two always want to be together or whether you think you want to have some time on your own with Mum or with Dad." She made it sound all so sensible and easy and talking to her that was easy too, but the reality was that Mum and Dad would never ever agree and I was just so no, I couldn't think of it – this nagging doubt, this other parrot on my shoulder that, if I didn't please Dad, he might stop loving me. I couldn't contemplate that it would be worse than anything, worse than dying.

I don't know how Jonty's meeting with Carol went but he was certainly in a bad mood when he came back. He banged and thumped around, "I'm not going anywhere," he said, "why can't this all stop? I hate them, I hate them." Then he burst into tears; I put my arms around him. I knew exactly how he felt but I guess because I was that bit older at least some of the time I could see that there may be ways out. For Jonty, it just felt like this Mum and Dad stuff got in the way of everything else, no one could ever get it right for Mum and Dad and his way of dealing with it was to be cross and thump around and shout at everybody.

Carol wanted to talk to us together and Jonty, quite unusually for him, snuggled up to me. He didn't really say much and when he did, he looked at me before he answered any of Carol's questions, insisting, "I want what she wants." We both agreed that we preferred to go together to see Mum and to be with Dad together because that's what we had always done. Yes, Dad took us both to different things and that was good but I didn't want my time with Mum to be separate and deep down, I know I was scared – I didn't want Jonty to be with Dad and I to feel pushed out. I always had this fear that unless I was with Dad, he'd forget about me and not want me anymore.

Carol said that she would talk to Dad about us staying overnight with Mum, each Wednesday and Thursday. My heart started to thump, I could feel a panic coming over me, my ears were burning, my cheeks were burning, I bit my lip, I could taste blood in my mouth. I blurted out, "But Dad'll be so cross, he won't love me anymore."

"Hey, now, now," said Carol. "I'm not going to tell your mum and dad what they've got to do; I'm only going to suggest to them that quite often children find it easier if there's a fairer division of time between them. I'm not taking you away from your dad. But let me talk to your dad and then we will see, you don't need to say anything to him, let me do it. Okay?"

I felt a bit reassured but I got this uneasy feeling that it would all go wrong and I guess I waited over the next few days for there to be some sort of explosion and for Dad to come storming in, being really angry, angry with me. But it wasn't like that at all. Dad obviously had seen Carol 'cos one evening before tea at his suggestion, we went and kicked a ball around on the 'rec' with him, he seemed a bit quieter than usual and then as we walked back home, he came out with it. "I'm really disappointed and sad to hear that you don't want to spend as much time with me. I thought we had such a great time together." Why had he twisted it around like that? It wasn't like that at all, it wasn't that we didn't want to spend time with him, but that we wanted to spend more time with Mum, couldn't he see that, why did he have to make me feel so guilty? I burst into tears and Jonty kicked the football very angrily. Dad shouted at him because it went on the road. Nobody said anything until we got back. I desperately wanted my dad to put his arms around me. I couldn't bear it if he stopped wanting me because he thought I'd chosen Mum rather than him.

"It doesn't matter," I blurted out. "It's just that we thought it might make a change, but we can tell Carol we'd rather leave it like it is."

"Too late now," said Dad. "The damage is done. She's off to court armed with her report and what you two have said. It'll be a walkover, the judge will just give her whatever she asks for and you'll be saddled with Wednesdays and Thursdays at your mum's, forgetting your stuff, not having the right things with you, are you even sure that your mum's going to pick you up, will she even manage to get out of work on time? Oh, I can see it all unfolding into complete disaster and then you'll want to stop and for me to rescue you. You'll see I'm right. All this messing around isn't any good for you, Hetty, or for you, Jonty. Your school grades are going to plummet and Hetty, you need to do well this year. In September next year, you're off to senior school. Sure, they've accepted you but if your grades slip, they may not be so keen."

I looked at him in amazement, "But, but –"

"No, no no more buts, let's leave it."

I didn't have time to tell him how much I loved Mum and how much I loved him.

When we went to bed, Dad came in. He was like his old self again. He gave me a cuddle and kissed me, told me he loved me and that I was his little princess. I breathed a sigh of relief but still heard that little niggling voice in my head 'only because you've done what he wants, only because he thinks he's got you on his side, it's not real, not real'. "Go away!" I screamed at that pesky voice, "go away and leave me alone."

Mum was in a good mood when we saw her that weekend although as usual, it was all a mad rush and we didn't get much time to talk together. She did say that Carol had been to talk to her and how pleased and hopeful she was that arrangements would be fairer so that we could spend more time with her. "Dad's not happy," blurted out Jonty. "He thinks it's a rubbish idea. I do as well. I'm never going to have the right stuff, I'm going to get into trouble at school 'cos I'll forget things."

"Come on," said Mum, "we can be a bit more organised than that. We've got your timetable and we know what you need. If necessary, we'll get some more PE kit so that you can't possibly forget it." That perked Jonty up a bit. "Yes, and we might even have the chance to have some of your friends around for tea, we never get a chance at the weekend with all your activities on." That really won Jonty over 'cos we never had anybody around when were at Aunty's. Dad always said that it was too difficult.

Later, Mum chatted to me on my own. "I guess it's really hard for you my love, isn't it? Trying to get it right for everybody?"

"It's just all so muddled up, Mum. I just never know what to do and I feel like I'm the one who has to sort it all out. It always feels like it's all my fault."

"What's your fault?" she asked.

"Well, just because it's so difficult. Dad doesn't seem to understand that we love you just as much as we love him. It's like we're being disloyal to him to love you. I can't tell him that." I was surprised I could tell her, but Mum listened, put her arms around me and hugged me.

"Don't worry love, this is for the grownups to sort out, we're the ones that have got to get on with things and make it best for you two. I guess at times it's easy for both of us to be selfish and want what we want, but I think your time with me has been squashed out and that doesn't seem fair to you. This way at least we get a bit more time and proper holiday time together, so that we can plan and do things."

I knew that was fairer, much fairer, 'cos when Mum put it like that it seemed really sensible; it was just that when Dad described it to us, it just seemed an even worse mess than it had been before. Is that what he wanted me to think?

However, my confidence that Mum was calm and rational – the good parent – was shattered on Saturday afternoon after Tae Kwon Do when we had gone into Welshpool and on our way home, we popped in to our favourite café for a milkshake. Mum's friend, Jan, joined us, her son, Billy, who was in between Jonty and me was with her and we both liked him so we went to sit at another table together whilst Mum and Jan had a natter. I wasn't intending to listen but I couldn't help hearing Mum say, "The bastard, that f***ing bastard, he wants to take the kids completely away from me. Well, I'll teach him, I'm going to go for full residence if he's not careful and see how he likes that." I sucked hard on my straw although I could hardly swallow the milkshake in my mouth. I could feel the tears in my eyes. So Mum was just as bad as Dad really, she wanted us all or nothing. Maybe she'd stop loving us too and then I wouldn't have anybody. Perhaps I'd have to go to one of those children's homes where they treated you really badly. Perhaps I'd never see either of them again. Perhaps they just wouldn't want me and Jonty. Those thoughts all came zooming around my head crashing and thundering – why, why was life so horrible?

"What's up with you then?" said Billy and gave me a big prod. I smiled and made a big show of being the life and soul of the party again but I couldn't help that nagging anger towards Mum and a very real fear of losing her too.

Chapter 19

Neither Mum nor Dad said anything further. I knew from what Carol had told us that the court date was looming. She had explained to Jonty and me that she was suggesting that we shared our time between Mum's house and Dad's house but that we would in fact be spending more time with Dad and just two days in the week with Mum and alternate weekends. It seemed perfectly reasonable and if I could have got those nagging doubts about both of them out of my head, then it would be okay. But I was dreading the court date. Both Mum and Dad told us when it was and reassured us that we didn't have to worry about it. I could see that Mum was quite edgy and Dad was quieter and more moody than usual.

The day of the court hearing came and I was expecting Dad to come home really angry but he didn't. He completely took the wind out of my sails when he sat down and said, "Well, the court has decided that you are going to live with both of us and this is how it will be." He explained that we would see Mum on alternate weekends and that on Wednesdays and Thursdays, we'd be living with her too and spending the rest of the time with him. We'd be spending holiday time with both of them. He seemed unexpectedly resigned to it. "Well, we'll just have to see how it works," he said. "We'll give it our best shot."

Why didn't I quite trust him? There was something that wasn't quite right, it didn't quite make sense. Why was he being so nice about it? What was going on? I tried to push all that out of my mind and just to enjoy the sense of relief that washed over me, delighted that he wasn't going mad about it. The arrangements were due to start the following week, so on the Wednesday and Thursday, we'd be staying at Mum's. I was excited and spent ages making sure that Jonty and I had both got the right stuff with us. Of course, we talked to Mum on the phone and we knew that she was definitely going to pick us up from school so I didn't have any concerns. I knew that she must have made arrangements at work, as she'd never been able to collect us, Dad had always been much more flexible with his work hours.

It was good to have Wednesdays and Thursdays with Mum although it was only the evenings we seemed to have time to just to relax and have a laugh together and do whatever we felt like doing without Dad watching. We chatted about commitments we had and she didn't mind that we had after school clubs on Thursdays, she said that she was pleased she could be part of what we were doing at school and she hadn't had that chance before. It all seemed fine and indeed, it was for the next couple of weeks. But then came the bombshell.

Dad dropped it completely out of the blue. "Well kids, you know I'm always trying to be fair. I don't want to be hard on your mum, I know how difficult it is for her, she's really struggling to keep up with the mortgage payments and maintain the house now that we're not here. Of course, it's pretty big and she doesn't earn much so I've done a deal with her. I've told her that I'm buying her out." And he went on to explain what that meant and that we would be moving back into our old house. "So that's good news, kids! That's fantastic isn't it, we'll have everything back like it was. It's not been right for you to be turfed out of your own place."

"But, but where will Mum go?" I looked at him in utter disbelief – "Where's Mum going to go?"

"Oh Mum will get a little place of her own and you'll all be fine there. You may find it a bit cramped and you and Jonty may have to share a room, it just depends what she can afford."

"But, but, but..."

"Never mind love, this is for the best. I'm being really generous to your mum and trying to help so she'll have a bit more spare cash. As you know, she's struggling and she can't get you the treats and those little extras that you like."

111

Jonty didn't speak. He stormed out and slammed his way up to his room. I just didn't know what to say. Dad was jumping around as happy as Larry. He flung his arms around me and danced me around the room. He didn't seem to have any idea about how upset I'd be. How worried I was for Mum. Did she even know? Well, she must know but what would she do now? Why had she agreed to Dad's plan?

We soon found out when we went to Mum's that weekend. She had clearly been crying. She looked upset and seemed irritable and not her usual self. She tried to make the best of it though and laughed and said, "Oh yes, we'll get a really nice place and I'll include you in choosing somewhere good. I might have to rent to start with because I think your dad wants it all to happen very quickly and I might not have time to buy a new place."

"I'm not living in some poxy rented place," said Jonty. "I don't want to move twice. I'm going to live just with Dad, I don't want this." I stared at him and so did Mum. I don't think either of us knew quite what to say. She clearly went and had a chat with him later 'cos he seemed quite sorry and contrite. But I knew exactly how he'd been feeling. It was all messed up, with all this chopping and changing. The little niggling voice was telling me that it was just what my dad had always said – he said that it would all get too difficult.

Just as Dad wanted, it all happened quickly and within a few weeks, Mum was packing boxes and sorting her stuff ready to leave and we were doing the same at Aunty's. I would be sorry to leave her, she had been a good sport and she had understood me at times when I had been upset and Dad didn't quite get it. It would be a bit weird just being us and Dad together. I worried what would happen when he went out, whether it would be hard for him to juggle his hours 'cos he had relied on Aunty quite a bit to look after us although she had been only too pleased to help out.

Of course, I worried about Mum as well. Like she said, it had been too quick for her to arrange to buy another house so she had rented a flat over a hairdressers in the centre of Shrewsbury.

It was quite fun really 'cos she was right amongst the busy shopping streets and you got the smells of the hairdresser wafting up. It had a big living room, a tiny kitchen and a tiny bathroom and two bedrooms. Mum explained Jonty and I could have the bigger one, but when we moved again to a proper house, she would make sure there were three bedrooms. I wasn't that impressed having to share with Jonty. It made it a bit better because a friend of Mum's had some bunk beds she didn't need and she let us have them. At least I wouldn't have to sit looking at him. I bagged the top bunk so that I could have more privacy.

At first, it was quite good fun. It seemed like being on holiday. But the novelty quickly wore off and there just seemed to be stuff everywhere. Neither Jonty nor I were the tidiest children in the world, we'd been used to a big house. Jonty, in particular, just dropped everything where he was when he came in from school and his PE kit, shoes, rugby kit, homework, bags and stuff were just dumped in heaps. Now there never seemed anywhere to put all our stuff. I could see it got on Mum's nerves a bit. The kitchen was so minute we couldn't all get in it together. There wasn't really anywhere very suitable to do homework. Of course, I made the huge mistake of telling Dad. I suppose his response was predictable. "I've been thinking, perhaps it's better to suspend your Wednesday and Thursday overnight stays until Mum gets a proper place of her own. We don't really want to go back to court. I'll have a chat to her and see if we can sort something out, she's bound to agree. It'll be better my way," he said.

Somehow, Mum and Dad came up with a compromise. We were to go to Mum's on Wednesdays and Thursdays after school for tea but we'd come back to Dad's, well our old house, to sleep. It was only meant to be for the time being, but why did I just wonder – would it ever be any different again? Is this what Dad wanted all along? Because Mum had moved into Shrewsbury and we were back in Welshpool; we had to meet half way in the car park at the Windmill on the Shrewsbury to Welshpool road so that cut the evening short.

Somehow, it hadn't felt weird with just Mum and us in the family home, but it did with just us and Dad. For a start, he bumbled around in the kitchen and I realised that he had actually relied on Aunty to cook most of our meals. Now it was mainly convenience foods, ready meals from Marks and Spencer's or Tesco, which Mum never did. It wasn't that Dad couldn't cook, he just didn't have the time, or perhaps the inclination. Everything in the house was a bit muddled, a bit messy, not like Mum kept it. I tried to stop comparing the two but a bit of me resented the fact that Mum was living in this really cramped flat and Dad messing up our old house.

I knew she had been looking at houses but as she said, it took time to get something which was right. She wanted it within easy reach of school but at least on the way to our Welshpool home. All this uncertainty unsettled me even more and I went through a time when I just felt really sorry for myself. Why did this have to happen to me? Why did Mum and Dad have to screw it up for me? It wasn't fair. I looked at Suzie. She was such a good friend. "Come on, it's not the end of the world. This happens to lots and lots of kids not just you and Jonty. You're lucky, your mum and dad live within a few miles of each other, for lots of kids one parent lives miles away or goes abroad even and then you're really screwed."

I could confide in Suzie but not completely, I had my secrets. There was that little bit which I was too afraid to even voice – that my dad would stop loving me unless I was 'his little girl'. I knew it was like he owned me, controlled me, managed me but it was a small price to pay. I kidded myself if in return I had this wonderful, wonderful relationship with him, this love and affection and all this fun and everything I adored about him. But a bit of me realised that this meant that I had secrets about Mum too; how I felt about her, the love I had for her. It made me sad and of course if Dad saw me sad, he thought it was because I couldn't manage the arrangements with Mum. He had already reduced my time and knocked off the two nights. Mum had agreed so it hadn't meant going back to court but I don't suppose she had had much choice, she knew how difficult he could be.

Jonty and I argued like mad even at weekends when we were staying there. It wasn't easy having a pesky little brother staying in your room. It was like I couldn't even have any private thoughts any more. I had to get dressed and undressed on my bunk, it was really difficult and inconvenient. A bit of me wished that Jonty wouldn't come to Mum's that he would stay at Dad's. But I knew that wouldn't be fair on either him or Mum.

The following week, Mum was really excited. By chance, she had found a house to rent that she liked and she wanted to take us to see it. Jonty and I were thrilled. She told us it where it was and gave us the address in Meole Brace in Shrewsbury. Dad Google Earthed it. He laughed, "Well, it will be pretty roomy and I guess it's got a reasonable garden. It's an ex council house, it looks as though it's on the edge of a council estate. Still I guess a lot of them will be privately owned now so it won't be quite as rough as it used to be." Talk about pouring cold water on us – he was the world's best at that.

The following day was Wednesday and after school we trekked around to see this house. I loved it. I thought it was really nice and Jonty did too. But then, he turned to Mum and said, "I'm not living on a pesky council estate, I can't have my friends around here, can I?" Was he trying to be loyal to Dad or was that what he really thought?

Mum looked horrified. "Jonty, that's not a very nice thing to say. Your friends come to see you, not your house or where you are. And it's a perfectly respectable neighbourhood. That's a really terrible thing to say. I haven't brought you up to think like that."

"It's what Dad thinks. He thinks it's a rubbish place. It's not just me, so don't blame me," said Jonty. I'd never seen Jonty like this before, he was really cross and he sort of put a black cloud over the visit.

I squeezed Mum's hand and said, "But I like it Mum, I think it's lovely. And it's got three bedrooms so we wouldn't have to share Jonty, so stop being so mean and horrible." He perked up a bit and insisted that in that case, he had to have the bigger bedroom and I could have the poky little one. I didn't mind that – anything to keep the peace.

Mum was only renting and as nobody was living there, we had moved in within a couple of weeks. That's one advantage of having a Mum who works at a bank I guess. She could pull a few strings and get things done quickly. Jonty had come around because Mum said we could both help paint our rooms the colours we wanted. He wanted navy blue and surprisingly, she let him but she did insist on rolling up the carpet before he started to paint.

In the end, we all helped but Mum did the major share of the painting and Jonty's room looked really smart – navy blue with stars and his posters. My room was in pale turquoise. I had chosen some material from the market and Mum had made some curtains and Jonty had had a roller blind like he had always wanted. The carpets were already down and they weren't bad and with Mum's furniture in and some new things she had bought, it looked nice. But clearly, it was nothing like the house that we were living in with Dad which was an old four bedroomed detached longhouse with a big garden down a private road. Dad said it had the 'right' address so that's where Jonty got his snobby ideas from – it was from Dad.

I surprised myself when I found that I was being a bit more critical of Dad more recently, not that I'd actually say it to his face, of course I wouldn't but I had this sort of inner conflict going on. It wasn't very easy to manage. Until recently, I'd batted away any negative thoughts about Dad and now the good and bad thoughts got tangled up in one horrible mess.

Chapter 20

Things changed dramatically over the next few weeks. Mum was excited to be in a property she could feel settled in but it was the other side of town so it meant further to go to school and to our other activities. It was clear that Jonty wasn't impressed.

He started moaning about staying over on the Wednesday and Thursday which Dad had begrudgingly reinstated. Mum was clearly disappointed. "I thought you liked staying over," she said, "now that you've got your own bedroom and we have time together. It's so busy at the weekends." But Jonty had become sullen and miserable.

"I don't want to stay," he said but he wouldn't talk about it.

It was the following week and I unexpectedly saw Dad in school. It was a Monday – what was he doing there? I looked quizzically at him. "I've come about Jonty," he said. "I'll see you at home." And that was it. Well, it all came out later, Jonty had apparently kicked another boy and bruised his shin and then sworn at him. It seemed as though the attack had been totally unprovoked. I heard Jonty crying that night and Dad talking to him. The next day, Dad broached the subject with me. "What's this about Jonty saying that Mum's shouting at him and being unkind?"

"What!" I said looking amazed. "I don't know what you're talking about, Dad."

"Well, Jonty reckons that it's been really difficult the last few weeks and that Mum has been particularly nasty to him and that he is actually scared of going."

"Scared? That's ridiculous"

"Well, Jonty's certainly upset about something; it's not like him to go hurting people at school, is it? I'm going to get to the bottom of this."

I guess he and Mum talked but whatever they said didn't make it any better. In fact, it made it worse. Jonty became downright rude to Mum and when he was there the next weekend, every time she asked him to do something or to go somewhere, he'd turn around and say, "I don't have to, I don't have to even come if I don't want to, Dad says." What had happened to my lovely brother? I hated him, why was he being so horrible? Mum just looked so upset, she hadn't lost her temper or done anything but she was clearly bewildered and it was hard for her to fight back her tears.

Things changed at home with Dad too. I couldn't help noticing how close Dad and Jonty had become. Jonty had always been somewhat separate from everybody else and it had always been Dad and me. I'd been his 'little princess' but suddenly, I felt like I was being pushed out. I tried not to be jealous, but to be honest I was. There were these odd remarks like: "How's my mummy's girl then?" It hurt, I'd see Jonty cuddled up to Dad in fact it became that he wouldn't let Dad go out of his sight. He started saying that he didn't want to go to Mum's and stay overnight at all. He didn't mind going sometimes in the day but he'd really rather that Dad took him to Tae Kwan Doe because it was more Dad's sport than Mum's. And he didn't want to come to watch horse riding because it was boring. He just seemed to constantly find reasons why it was better for him to be at home with Dad. I expected Dad to challenge him and encourage him to go to Mum's but he didn't, he seemed to just lap it all up. A little smile would appear on Dad's face, hardly there, but I'd notice. Whenever Jonty criticised Mum, Dad said, "Tell me about that, Jonty, I can see how upset you are." And of course Jonty just revelled in that attention. His descriptions of how awful Mum was became more and more graphic and fanciful. I couldn't make it out. A bit of me wanted to just be with Mum but I couldn't face the thought of losing Dad. I would do whatever it took to keep Dad, I knew I would. Dad was my idol, Dad was always there for me, Dad was always right, I couldn't lose that and if it meant that I had to be more critical of Mum then, horrible as it was, that was what I would force myself to do.

On Wednesdays, Jonty would often come and find me at school and tell me that he had decided that he didn't want to come to Mum's that night after school and would I tell her. "No," I'd say. "You tell her yourself."

And so when Mum came to collect us, he'd mumble something like, "I don't really want to come, I don't care," and then storm off. Of course Mum got upset and didn't really know what to do but in the end, she'd have to ring Dad and ask him to come and collect Jonty. Dad clearly wasn't impressed with that.

Sometimes Jonty would do the same again on a Thursday and it got that over the next few weeks, he rarely came at all in the week but Mum still tried every time. She'd meet him after school and she'd talk to him but he'd shake his head and say 'no'. She was just at a loss to know what had happened, why had he changed? I tried to talk to Jonty to try to make sense of what he was saying about Mum. "Why are you saying those lies about her? It's just not true Jonty, she's not horrible to either of us, she's lovely. So why do you keep telling Dad she's horrid? He just believes everything you say and that's not fair on Mum."

"I don't think it's fair on me at all," said Jonty. "I tell you, Hetty, when your mum and dad split up like ours, you can't have both of them, you have to choose one or the other and it's easier for me to have my dad. So that's it. I can't do it anymore."

I could see he was upset but I didn't know what to say. I couldn't talk to Dad about it because he seemed to be on Jonty's side, perhaps that was what Dad wanted, for us both to choose him and for us just not to bother with Mum. I talked to Suzie at school, she listened and then said, "Well, I reckon that you're going to have to talk to your dad and tell him that you don't want to have to choose between him and your mum, that you want both of them."

"But I don't want to lose him Suzie, I don't want him to think that I don't want him."

"Your mum loves you too, you know. I guess you don't want to dump her either." Suzie always spoke the truth. She seemed to understand and she made it all so clear. Of course, I wanted both of them. But it was easy for her, she had a normal mum and dad, I knew that my dad was different and that I had to totally agree with him or I knew he wouldn't want me.

I don't know whether Dad thought that Mum would just roll over and accept that Jonty didn't want to come any more but that's not like Mum, she loved us both to bits, she'd do anything for us and she wasn't going to let Jonty just disappear like that. Every time I went and he didn't, she'd give me a note to take home to Jonty and sometimes a comic or a magazine or a bag of sweets – just some little thing to let him know that she was still there. He'd snatch the note from me and take it upstairs. I must admit that I sneaked into his room one day and it didn't take me long to find the note that Mum had sent a couple of days earlier. It was screwed up and in the bin. I read it, it was bright and cheerful. 'I miss you, little chap, it will be good to see you soon. I'm sending you some pictures of Man United, they did well in the last match, didn't they? Love you – Mum'. And then there was a picture of a smiley face. Why had he screwed it up and thrown it away? It didn't make sense. I smoothed it out and took it back with me, maybe one day he would want it.

The next time that I handed him a note, Dad was there and he turned to Dad and shook his head. "She writes horrible notes to me Dad, I just don't want to read them anymore. I get all upset."

"What!"

"Now now, don't get all upset, I'll take that." Dad snatched the note from me.

"But Dad…" I could hardly say that the notes were nice because nobody knew that I'd actually read one.

Later Dad had a chat to me. "You know I'm really worried about Jonty. He's clearly seen a side of Mum that she's perhaps hiding from you. A leopard doesn't change its spots you know, you know how unpredictable she was when we were living there. My fear is that that's going to be how she'll be with you soon. We'll just have to be really, really careful and if Jonty doesn't want to go, then I'm not going to force him. Poor Jonty, I think he's just beginning to show how difficult it all was for him."

"But Dad…"

"Yes, I know it's hard for you as well, my love."

"But Dad…"

"Yes, I know. You don't need to explain. I understand completely. You are trying your best, aren't you? Giving Mum another chance. But it might be a losing battle you know." I looked at him wide eyed but the words just wouldn't come. I couldn't say anything because, because… I buried my head in his shoulder and sobbed. Of course, he took that as me being relieved that he understood how difficult it was for me to see Mum, he'd got completely the wrong end of the stick; it wasn't like that at all, I was so scared of losing him. It was all so very muddled up, such a mess.

Chapter 21

When we'd been living with Aunty Nicky, she had sometimes realised there was something up and she'd come and put her arm around me and I could talk to her, but now it seemed like I'd got nobody. There was this barrier that was coming between Dad and me, a big solid wall that I couldn't break through. I could feel this anger welling up inside me and I didn't know what to do with it. Then one night, I heard Jonty in his room, he was making quite a noise and I went in and asked him what on earth he was doing and he snapped back, "Oh shut up!" I screamed at him, "you stupid little boy!" He shouted something back and I don't know how it happened, I didn't intend to but I picked up a small metal car that was lying on the bed and threw it at him. It struck him just below the eye and almost immediately, blood was streaming down his face. I screamed and so did he. Dad came running up the stairs.

"Whatever's going on with you kids? Hetty, what have you done?"

"It's Hetty, it's Hetty, she hurt me!" yelled Jonty.

"Get out the way," said Dad and pushed me aside, as he swept Jonty up in his arms. He rushed to the bathroom and tried to stop the bleeding but it kept going. "I'm going to have to take you to A&E old chap," he said. "You'll need a stitch or two in that. Come on, Hetty, get your shoes and get Jonty's as well and your coats."

And so we ended up in A&E. Dad was quite cold towards me but he was all over Jonty hugging him and cuddling him. I looked on in amazement, I didn't know what to say. "I'm so, so sorry Jonty," I kept saying to him.

"And so you should be," said Dad. "What do you mean behaving like that?" It wasn't like Dad to go on at me. I suddenly felt awful. How could I possibly doubt my dad and then I knew it was Dad and Jonty that I wanted more than anything. They were my world. I couldn't bear to lose them. I knew then that I'd do anything. I'd sell my soul for my dad even if that meant betraying my mum.

And so that night when eventually we got to bed and Dad came up, I put my arms out. "Dad, Dad, there's something I need to tell you," I whispered. It was like this other bit of me was coming out, I could hear the words but in my head, another little voice was saying, "That's not true, that's not true, Hetty, why are you doing this? Your mum loves you." But there I was saying, "Dad, Jonty's right, you know Mum hasn't been herself recently she is quite nasty to both of us but particularly to Jonty. I can see now why he gets upset." A bit of me was horrified that I was saying those things. I fought back the tears, I knew really they were tears for my mum but I let Dad believe that they were tears for him. Then I'd be his little princess again; Dad, Jonty and me, I couldn't bear to be separate. I couldn't bear to lose him.

"That's so brave of you, Hetty, I know you've tried to be loyal to Mum but as I've kept saying to you, you don't need to protect her, she's the grown-up and she's the one who keeps on getting it wrong. Why do you think I took you away with me? It was because we couldn't trust her any more. You've given her so many chances. We'll sit down tomorrow and have a bit of a think and work out what's best. Of course, I want you to see her but we need to do it in a way that's safe and right for you and doesn't upset you anymore. Now you be especially nice to your brother, he's probably going to have a bit of a scar under his eye but I guess that'll just add character to his handsome little face so don't you worry about it. I know it was an accident and I know it wasn't your fault. You've had an awful lot to put up with lately and I promise you that you and Jonty aren't going to carry on suffering like this. Sometimes you know courts and social workers, they don't get things right, they make it worse, the main thing is that we stick together, okay?"

When he left me to go downstairs, I stared into the darkness my eyes filling with tears, I buried my head under the covers and I sobbed. Why, why, why was it like this? It was all so crazily muddled up and I'd just made it worse. I didn't know what to do, I didn't know how to manage it. Jonty was perhaps right when he said you have to choose, you can't have both. I didn't believe him when he first said it but now I reckon it was true. I tried to bat away the thoughts of Mum being sad, of being in her little house without us. I eventually fell asleep.

The next day was Saturday and of course with me busy with horse riding and then Jonty with his Tae Kwon Do, it was Saturday evening before we could have a chat. Dad suggested we got fish and chips as a rare treat and we sat around the lounge eating out of the wrapping, with fingers greasy from the yummy chips, savouring the crunchy battered fish. Dad got us a bottle of fizzy pop as well so by the time we'd finished all that, we were in high spirits.

"I think we need a plan of action," Dad said. I tried not to think about the night before but of course, it wasn't going to go away. Dad explained to Jonty that it was okay because I had told him that it was like he had described and Mum wasn't being fair to either of us. He again stressed how much he wanted us to spend some time with her and suggested that we perhaps had the occasional Sunday when we could go out for the day somewhere and maybe to go for tea one night a week. He explained that of course he would have to get Mum to agree otherwise it would mean going back to court, but with Jonty and me both saying how difficult it was going to see her and just how she'd been with us both, that that wouldn't be any problem. He'd soon get the court to understand how it really was for us and that she had been pulling the wool over the court's eyes and that social worker for too long. He made it sound all so easy, it was all Mum's fault and Mum was getting what she deserved. We needed to be rescued and he was the one who would do it. Of course, I knew that it wasn't fair and how cruel I was being but I wouldn't let myself have those thoughts. Dad had his arm around me and was giving me a cuddle with Jonty on the other side. "You two are the best things in the world," he said, "I'd do anything for you pair, you're smashing kids, I'm not going to have you hurt by anybody." Of course, my dad was right.

Chapter 22

True to his word, Dad must have spoken to Mum the following day. I was dreading Wednesday when we would be going around for tea after school. When Jonty came to me and said he wouldn't be coming, I said that wasn't on, he'd got to come. Mum would want to know why we'd changed our minds about staying with her. It wasn't fair to leave me on my own to tell her. Begrudgingly, he agreed to come.

There was a sort of damper on our spirits when we met Mum. Usually, I was jumping around the car all excited to see her but that day, we were subdued and she was too. She tried her best to be breezy and normal when we got back to the house, but there was this silence and awkwardness between us and in the end she said, "Why don't we all go and sit down and have a chat?" And so we did. "I just can't understand," she said. "Perhaps you can tell me what's gone wrong? I thought you loved coming here. I thought we had really good times together. Please don't tell me that I've got it all wrong." She looked so sad, so lost. I just wanted to hug her. I ran to her and put my arms around her.

"Oh Mum, we're not going to not see you, it's just that it gets, well, really complicated with school and stuff and…" My voice just tapered off. I didn't really have an excuse and my words sounded so empty and hollow, she knew I wasn't telling the truth. Jonty just sat there crying. He seemed to either have to do that or else he got angry. I can see now that he just didn't have the words to say how he felt.

"Oh well, your dad's coming for you at half past seven tonight, but Dad and I will have to do some more talking otherwise I won't have any choice, I'll have to go back to court and I don't want to do that," she said.

Of course, there wasn't another opportunity for me to talk to Mum and I gave her a hug and squeezed her hand as Dad pulled up at half past seven. Jonty just seemed anxious to get out of the door. Mum looked so sad, so alone as I turned and waved goodbye to her.

The new arrangement, apparently, was that we would go to Mum's on each alternate Saturday evening and stay overnight and the following day, Dad would collect us at 4 pm. Then I would go for tea on my own on Wednesday 'cos it was really clear that would be too much for Jonty. Jonty was cross. "I thought you said that I didn't have to stay overnight and now you're saying I've got to go on Saturday nights."

"No, every other Saturday," said Dad. "And it's after you've enjoyed the activities you want. It's not going to be until about eight o'clock and then I'll collect you back at four o'clock on Sunday."

"I suppose so," said Jonty. "But if I don't want to go, I'm not going and if I don't like it, I'll ring you and you have to promise you'll fetch me home."

"Yes, of course. I know it's really hard but if we don't go along with Mum a bit, then she's just going to take it back to court and we don't want to have to go through all that again. Talking to Carol and her twisting everything around. Just trust me; I'll make sure that it's okay for you. I promise you."

Of course I trusted my dad, he was always the big strong dad that I loved so much. When we went on Saturday, Mum looked awful, like she'd been crying for days. She seemed flat and sad although she made a huge effort to be really cheerful when we got there. There wasn't really much of the evening left. Jonty said he was tired and wanted to go to bed about nine o'clock. I stayed up for a while longer, although I was worried that Mum would want to talk and I didn't know how I was going to handle that. Of course, we did talk. "But Hetty, I don't understand why you had to agree with Jonty? I don't understand why you said I'd been horrible. When have I been horrible? When have I been horrible to either of you? It just doesn't make sense, I can't understand it."

I turned on her. "If you knew Dad, you'd know that I'd got no choice." She smiled and then held me by the shoulders and looked into my eyes. "Hetty, believe me I know your dad, that's why I'm not with him now. I didn't want to tell you, but I guess I've no choice."

"Tell me what? What do you mean?" I started to panic. I didn't understand. "Look, your dad's a lovely, lovely person, but and there's a huge but, only if you agree with him, only if you do what he wants, only if he's the centre of attention, the one everybody looks up to. If you take your eyes off him, then he can't stand that, he can't cope and he turns against you. That's what's happened to your dad and me. I got to the point where I just couldn't keep on being downtrodden by him. I guess I just stopped worshipping him. He wasn't my 'god' anymore." I put my hands over my ears, I didn't want to hear.

"Oh Mum, that's so cruel. That's not like Dad is." The little voice in my head said 'oh it is, Hetty, that's exactly what your dad is but you don't want to believe it. You know that's true. You know what your mum's saying is true'.

But instead, I just blurted out, "I hate you, I hate you. My dad is so special how can you possibly say such horrible things about him?" Tears were streaming down my face, as I ran upstairs and flung myself on the bed and sobbed.

A bit later on, Mum knocked and came in to me. She sad on the edge of the bed. "Hetty," she said very softly, "I didn't say those things to upset you. I was just trying to explain what's happened. I'm sorry, perhaps I've made a mistake telling you. Maybe you're too young to understand. Of course you love your dad, I know that." I let her stroke my hair, but I was scared, so scared. I really, really didn't know how I was going to handle this. I couldn't cut myself in two and be with Mum and with Dad. Jonty was right, just like he'd said the other day – you can't have both, not when your mum and dad hate each other as much as mine do. I fell asleep with Mum stroking my hair, my lovely mum, I didn't want to lose her, I really didn't.

The next day, we all got up reasonably early. I came downstairs and kept looking at Mum to see how she was. She sort of avoided my eyes. I knew we both felt awkward. Mum told us there was a jousting display on at Shrewsbury castle. Mum had seen it before and it had been really good so we packed a picnic and off we went. I was relieved 'cos it meant a distraction – no awkward discussions and we could at least seem like a normal family. In fact, it was a good day and Jonty especially liked dressing up in knight's armour and having a go at wielding one of the swords. We laughed a lot and had a lot of fun. We sort of forgot all the difficulties of the last few days. Then Mum looked at her watch and said, "Gosh, it's three o'clock, I guess we're going to have to get back."

Jonty started to panic. "We can't be late for Dad, we can't. We have to go back now."

"No, we don't need to rush," said Mum. "It's just that we need to watch the time. We've got plenty of time, don't worry."

"I need to go back now," insisted Jonty, pacing up and down and getting really wound up. "I don't want Dad having to wait, it's not fair. It's not fair on Dad."

"Hey, come on, come on," said Mum.

Jonty started to look really tense clenching his fists and through gritted teeth, he shouted, "I want to go home now! Can't you hear? Can't you listen you stupid woman? It's not fair."

"I don't know what isn't fair," said Mum, "but I won't have you speaking to me like that, Jonty." Jonty glowered at her.

"Oh please, please stop, the two of you," I interjected. I didn't want them arguing. It was just so pointless but Mum was upset and seemed so super sensitive and anything could trigger Jonty off. If anything wasn't fair, it was that I had to sort it all out.

Somehow, Jonty's outburst spoiled the day. We got back home and Jonty insisted on putting his stuff in his bag and standing by the window so that as soon as he saw Dad's car, he could give a quick 'ta ra' and ran off down the path. I looked at Mum and saw this sad, sad look across her face. She wiped a tear from her eye and put a big brave smile on and gave me a hug. Dad was tooting the horn and he clearly wasn't going to get out of the car and neither did he want to hang around. "I've got to go Mum, I've got to go. I'll see you on Wednesday." And I rushed off down the path. Dad was his usual bright and cheery self. But I don't know, somehow it all felt false. He wasn't at all interested in what we'd done that day, he was busy telling us about some friend of his who had got a new puppy and would we like one? But of course it would mean that we'd need to be there to take it out. Jonty immediately said, "Yes, yes, great, that'd be fantastic." But I don't know, something made me feel very wary. I wasn't sure. Yes, of course I would love a puppy, but what about Mum?

Later on, I told Dad that Mum hadn't seemed very happy about the new arrangement and that she had said that she would have to talk to him some more. He just smiled. "Well, she would, wouldn't she? You know secretly I think that she's really glad that she hasn't got you going around as much. It means she's free to lead her own life but she likes to pretend how sad she is. All this stuff about her not having a boyfriend, it's absolute rubbish. Of course she's got a boyfriend, she got one nearly as soon as we'd gone. She couldn't wait to see the back of us. She doesn't really want you, you know, she just wants to replace you. She's only trying to get at me by seeing you." Those words stung. They really hurt. But I couldn't say anything. I just gave my dad a big hug and of course he thought it was because I was pleased with the new arrangement and going to Mum's less often, not that I was just totally lost for words and felt such a traitor to my mum for loving him so much.

The next day at school, I just couldn't concentrate and twice Mrs Nicholls asked me a question in English and I didn't even know what she'd been talking about. "Now come on, Hetty," she said, "it's not like you not to be concentrating. Whatever's the matter?" I fought back the tears. This wasn't something that usually happened if a teacher was a bit sharp with me but I just felt like I was going to fall to pieces. Afterwards when the class had finished and I was walking towards the door, she put her hand out and caught hold of my arm. "Hey, Hetty," she said, "is there something wrong?"

"No, of course not, of course not." I shrugged her off – a wave of panic rising in me and Dad's voice drumming in my head 'it's our business.'

"Are you sure? Is it all right at home?"

"Yes, of course it is. Why wouldn't it be?" I snapped at her avoiding eye contact. "I need to go. I have to…" My sentence trailing off unfinished.

"It's just that you seem really sad and preoccupied and I just wondered if everything was okay. If you want to talk, I'm here and there are lots of other members of staff that would be equally happy to talk to you."

I pulled myself together and with a quick smile, I said, "I'm fine, I'm absolutely fine." Dad's words 'this is between us, we keep it in the family; we don't want everybody knowing our business' rang around and around my head.

Suzie caught up with me later. "There is something wrong."

"Of course there isn't," I snapped at her.

"Now look," she said, putting her hands on my shoulders and looking me straight in the eye, "I've been your best friend for goodness knows how many years. We're friends, we tell each other everything and now because something's really wrong, you're trying to block me out. That's not the best way to treat a friend, is it?" I burst into tears and she put her arms around me. "Come on let's go somewhere a bit quieter. Look, we can go to the back of the playing field; there's nobody else around there. We can have a bit of peace."

We'd both had lunch so we'd got plenty of time. I found it really hard to explain then I just blurted everything out. "You see, I love my mum but I think I'm scared to because if I do, then, I really don't think my dad will want me. It was so awful when he started to just be there for Jonty, it's like he was pushing me away, like he was taunting me. I can't stand the thought of losing him. My dad's everything. I just don't know what to do, because I can't bear to lose my mum either." Suzie listened.

She screwed up her face. "Mmm, that's a hard one, Hetty, it really is. Do you think…do you think your mum is perhaps right about your dad?"

"No, of course not," I said. But that little voice was there again 'she is you know, she is you know'. But instead, the words I blurted out denied that. "No, no that's not like my dad. He's just such a lovely, lovely man. It's not like him. He's never been horrible to my mum." 'Don't be daft. Of course he has. Don't you remember how he used to rubbish her and make her seem worthless? You saw him, you saw him when you all lived together'. That little voice thumping away in my head. I whispered to Suzie, "I guess sometimes he was horrible to her but I love him Suzie, I can't, I really can't bear to lose him."

"You mean it's easier to lose your mum?" was her response.

"No, of course not. I was horrified to hear Suzie voice my innermost fear. I want them both, but I don't know how to do it."

"Well, maybe you'll have to do like your dad says and just see her on Saturday nights and Sundays and Wednesdays after school. Perhaps that's best for the time being, Hetty."

"But I don't think Jonty even wants to do that and my mum doesn't want that. I just don't think it's true when Dad says that she doesn't want to see us and she's really pleased and she's got a boyfriend, I just don't think any of that is true. But I can't tell him, can I? I can't say anything because…"

"Because although your mum is right," said Suzie, "you can't disagree with your dad." I looked at her in amazement. She'd said the words I couldn't say. But then, it wasn't her dad. Although she was there for me, I realised then that she couldn't make it right, nobody could. But Carol, well she would be there, wouldn't she? At least I knew that she'd understand and make me feel so much stronger in myself. But even she couldn't make Dad change. She'd never get Mum and Dad to agree and Mum would do as she said and take it back to court and oh goodness – a thought flashed through my head – I couldn't lie there, could I? I couldn't say there that

I'd seen Mum be horrible to Jonty and she had been to me…could I? I don't know. I really, really didn't know. Suzie put her arm around me. "Look, I'm always going to be here for you but sometimes you have to fight your own battles. I guess this is one that you're going to have to do for yourself. Maybe you can't have the answer you want but lying isn't going to help anyone. In fact, just face it, Hetty – you've made it worse." She gave me a hug and then it was time for us both to go off to lessons. I hated myself, I really did.

Chapter 23

The next few weeks were really difficult. I just didn't quite know how to manage my see-sawing emotions. A bit of me wanted Mum to take it back to court, at least then I'd be able to talk to Carol. As it was, Mum and Dad had agreed arrangements at court to avoid a lengthy contested hearing so Carol wasn't on the scene and there was no way I could get in touch with her. There was nobody else who could understand.

What happened next was a bolt out of the blue. It was about three weeks after the new arrangement had started. It was a Saturday night and Jonty had come to Mum's and as usual was in a bit of a mood moaning that he didn't want to stay over. He brightened up after we'd had fish and chips with Mum. Mum seemed a bit edgy, so I guess I wasn't surprised when she said that she had something to talk to us about. I immediately felt the panic rise, what was it going to be this time? Please, please, let it be something that's not too dreadful. "Look," she started, "I'm finding organising arrangements about you two with your dad really difficult and I know you are struggling too. I've been trying to work out what's best. Should I go back to court and get the court to make a fairer arrangement? But then, I know it seems whatever is put in place will upset D –" She didn't finish the 'Dad' as I knew she had intended, but quickly added 'someone'.

I looked at her. Her eyes, they looked empty for a fleeing second and I realised how sad and how lonely she was. And then, she went on, "Anyway, I've decided that it's perhaps best if I'm not around."

"What, what! Whatever are you saying, Mum?" My voice came out like a shrill scream and I was overcome with a sense of panic flooding over me, drowning me. "Well, not around as much as I have been," she added.

"I don't understand. What are you saying, Mum?" I was scared; my heart was thumping like mad. Jonty just stared at her with his mouth wide open, his eyes huge.

"I'm not finding this very easy," said Mum, "but look, I've got the opportunity of having a transfer to Newcastle on Tyne. It's a long way away from here and it means, well, we'd be able to spend lots of holiday time together. There's a holiday every six weeks, so I think that might be easier than…" Her voice tailed off. I looked at her.

"I can't believe you're going to do that to us, Mum. I can't believe it," I said angrily. The panic had dissipated leaving a wild fury in its wake.

Mum just burst into tears. "What am I supposed to do, Hetty?" she sobbed. "Whatever I do, I can never win. Just face it, your dad isn't going to let me." She dabbed her eyes, sniffed and said, "Anyhow, that's what I've decided I'm going to do. After all, that's the area where I spent my teenage years. I've still got friends there, so we'll just have to work something out."

"Well, I'm not going to Newcastle 'cos it's hundreds and hundreds of miles away and I don't want to go anywhere during my holidays, I'm staying here, 'cos that's where all my friends are," said Jonty, clearly furious. "And we'll have a new puppy and I'm not going to leave my puppy not for anybody." He stormed out slamming the door as he stomped upstairs.

Mum just stared into the distance before saying, "Shall I make us a drink then?" Like the devastating last few moments had never happened. Was she completely mad?

I sat staring, thoughts whirring around and around my head. I couldn't make sense of it. So Mum was just going to get up and go, dump us, forget us. Maybe she had got a boyfriend, maybe she didn't really want us. Maybe all those things that Dad had said were true, they must be – it didn't make sense otherwise. 'That would be an easy way of thinking, wouldn't it?' whispered the little voice in my head.

I batted the thoughts away but they persisted. 'You know that's not really true, Hetty, it's just that you like to think it would be because that would make your dad right and that would make things easier for you'. I tried to dismiss the thoughts that were flashing in my head. I couldn't think straight and I didn't know what to do. If only Suzie was here, at least she would listen. She'd help me to make sense of all this.

It was much, much later in the evening when Mum came into my room and sat on the edge of the bed. "Hetty," she said in that lovely gentle voice that she has, "shall we talk?"

"I don't want to," I mumbled. Of course I really wanted to but I was scared; really, really scared.

"I think it's best if we talk," she went on, "I guess this all came as a big shock to you."

"Why are you leaving us, Mum? Why? I just don't understand. What have I done? Am I so horrible – do you hate Jonty and me?"

"Oh Hetty, it's not what you've done. You haven't done anything. It's that, well your dad and I we just can't work anything out, I'm so sorry. If I'm really honest, I'm pretty certain your dad isn't prepared to work anything out with me. He doesn't really want me around, Hetty. He wants you and Jonty all to himself."

"So you're just going to run away and leave us? How's that going to help?" I couldn't look at her so I kept my head buried in my pillow.

Mum persisted, "No, of course not. It's going to get properly decided. If your dad and I can't work it out, then yes, I will have to go back to court and get everything written down so that I know for certain that we'll see each other in the holidays."

"You mean I'll come and stay with you each holiday?"

"Yes, of course."

"But how's that going to work? What's Dad going to say? He won't let us, I know he won't."

"Well, that's for me to work out with him and for the court to tell him if he makes it difficult. I just wanted you and Jonty to know that that was my plan before I talk to your dad because somehow if it came from your dad, I'm not sure you'd have got the right message. I'm not going because I've got a boyfriend, I'm going because it's too painful for any of us to carry on like it is and I love you too much to let you suffer any more. Let's talk about it some more, but not tonight, eh? I've already had a chat to Jonty and I guess the two of you might want to talk to each other. That's okay. Let's all talk about it some more tomorrow."

She gave me a big hug and those lovely gentle fingers stroked my hair. "Oh Mum," I said, "I do love you."

"And I love you too, Hetty, more than anything." And with that, she was gone.

It was a few minutes later when Jonty crept into my bed and cuddled up to me. It was the old Jonty back, at least for tonight. "Does she hate us, Hetty? Is that why she's going?" I tried to explain to him what Mum had said to me. It wasn't that easy and I guess it all came out a bit muddled. But I did try to get Jonty to understand that mums and dads don't always get things right just like Carol had encouraged us to appreciate. He was still quite adamant that he didn't want to go anywhere for holidays, but I sort of hoped he would change his mind; Jonty wasn't one to miss out and he did love Mum really. But, the big but was my dad. My dad could put so much pressure on both of us that he could make it almost impossible to go against him and what he'd decided was best. I couldn't oppose him so and of course Jonty couldn't either. Jonty fell asleep and a bit later on, I crept out of my room to crawl into his bed. Eventually, I fell into a troubled sleep and woke up the next morning feeling tired and bad tempered.

I was relieved that nothing about Mum's plans was mentioned the next day. It was like last night's bombshell had never happened. We went ice-skating in Telford and one of my friends was there so we ended up going to McDonald's for a special treat afterwards. We dashed home and before we knew, it was four o'clock and Dad was outside tooting his horn. Jonty, as usual, couldn't wait to get down the path, barely pausing to say goodbye to Mum. Mum and I clung a bit harder than usual to each other and there were tears in her eyes as we said goodbye. "See you on Wednesday, Mum," I said as brightly as I could manage.

I wasn't sure whether or not to say anything to Dad, but maybe I should have done because later that evening, Jonty blurted it out. "Mum's leaving us, she's going to live in Newcastle and we've got to go there for our holidays, all of them."

"That's not true," I said. I tried to put Mum's plan more accurately to Dad.

"It seems like I'd better have a chat to your mum. It's the first I've heard of it – just like her to attempt to win you over first. Bloody typical – always trouble that woman. If she's doing a runner, then I need to know what it's all about. I wouldn't be surprised if the boyfriend isn't around in this little arrangement. How convenient to say it's work and trust her to blame you two and me. It's obvious really, if there wasn't a boyfriend, she'd have wanted to take you two as well. Didn't think of that now, did you? And you didn't wonder why? Oh, Hetty, so grown up, but so gullible."

I'd never really doubted Mum but now it was happening again as I began to question Mum's 'story', Dad's doubts somehow seemed so plausible and so I somehow didn't challenge Jonty when he told Dad that Mum had blamed Dad for making arrangements she didn't like and then that she'd said that Dad had left her with no choice – that it was all his fault that she had decided to leave and now Jonty was equally unhappy about Mum's plans and wasn't going there in the holidays. I just sat and listened to Dad's angry retort and his promise that 'no one will force either of you'. It didn't give me much hope that Dad was going to listen to Mum. For a fleeting second, I hated them both – why couldn't I have a mum and a dad like Suzie had – a warm, cuddly mum and a quiet, rather boring dad.

Of course Dad spoke to Mum during the week and then on Tuesday evening, he talked to us again. "Mmm, it seems you're right. Your mum is upping sticks and moving to Newcastle, she's got a transfer all arranged. How convenient.

Anyhow, if she thinks that you're going up there to stay for half the holidays, she's got another thing coming. It just doesn't work like that and anyway she hasn't got anywhere near enough annual leave to be able to manage it and she hasn't got any family left up there and she hasn't been in touch with friends for years."

Of course Dad had got Aunty Nicky. She was always around any times when he wasn't during the holidays so there was never any problem covering and anyway he always seemed to be able to take as much time off as he wanted because he was the boss. I knew Mum's holidays were more limited so I guessed he had got a point. Maybe Mum didn't really want us to stay very often and was just saying it when she knew it couldn't happen. All those little doubts and fears, always there, making it impossible for me to make any sense of the horrible mess I was sinking in – like quicksand, a bottomless pit that would slowly drag me under.

"Well, I'll probably arrange for her to have a few days in each of the holidays with you, but she'll have to come down and fetch you and bring you back home and I don't expect that she'll want to do that. It would certainly test her commitment." He laughed that nasty hollow laugh which I'd heard more often recently.

"But Dad, Dad that just wouldn't be fair."

"What wouldn't be fair?" retorted Dad. "It's your mum who has decided to go so it's hardly going to be fair to expect me to drive halfway across the country just to fit in with her arrangements. Come on, Hetty, show a bit of sense." Put like that, Dad's point of view sounded perfectly reasonable. "No, no, no. Your mum will just have to put up with it and if she doesn't want to come down and fetch you, then tough. I guess she won't see you – she'll just have to prove how much she really cares."

"Well, that suits me anyhow," said Jonty, "because we'll have a new puppy by then. I won't really be able to go and leave him."

"I don't even want a puppy," I screeched. I certainly didn't want a puppy if it meant that I couldn't see my mum.

"And anyway, I don't know why you have to be so mean Dad, why can't you meet Mum half way? That's what Katie's mum does 'cos her dad lives a long way away."

"Whatever Katie does isn't anything to do with us," said Dad. "This is for me and your mum to decide and I'm certainly not going to have you telling me what's fair and what isn't, Hetty. So enough, leave this to the grownups."

"But Dad, it's about us…" I tailed off – the look of utter contempt that crossed Dad's face stopped me in my tracks. I felt completely crushed. Dad didn't usually get short with me, but it had happened more recently. If I voiced an alternative opinion to his, he made it very clear that it wasn't that he didn't agree with me but that it wasn't possible for anybody else to even consider another version or interpretation. I felt sick with worry. It seemed like all my worst fears were about to unfold. I was going to lose my mum. I had no one to talk to, nobody understood and if I did try and talk to my dad, all he did was get angry. And if I tried to talk to my mum, all she got was upset. So, I was left with nobody.

Sure enough by the next week, there was a 'to let' notice outside Mum's house. So, she really was going. I had hoped perhaps she wouldn't really go. As usual, Jonty hadn't come on the Wednesday so it was just Mum and me and somehow when Jonty wasn't there, it made it easier to talk to Mum. I didn't like to admit it but I know that it was because I could say things to Mum which I knew wouldn't get back to Dad. Jonty was his ears and his eyes, anything and everything he'd report it back to Dad. It seemed to be his way of scoring brownie points and Dad just lapped it up; I could feel it building a wedge between him and me and I felt so desperate – this was the last thing that I wanted to happen. So when I got the opportunity to chat to Mum, I grabbed it.

She talked some more about her job in Newcastle and how she was considering finding a property on the coast at Whitley Bay and getting the Metro into town each day to save driving and parking. She had fond memories of Whitley Bay and had decided it would be a super place to live. It all seemed so cut and dried, as though Mum had been planning her move for ages, but had kept us in the dark until the last moment. Her new job started on 1 August, in no time at all really. Was she just using the new arrangements as an excuse? Was the real reason that that she wanted to go and have a fresh start without us?

Properties in the Whitley Bay area were apparently a similar price to houses in Shrewsbury, whereas they were much dearer in Newcastle on Tyne itself, so Mum hoped she'd be able to get herself a three bedroomed seaside house. She had looked up old friends who lived in the area and she was going to go up and stay with Sarah and her husband, Tony, for a long weekend. She would probably stay with them for a few weeks when she started her new job until she could sort something out for herself. Working for a bank meant that it would be much easier for her to get a mortgage. I guess it was just making the monthly payments that was the hard bit but as Mum said, this job would be at a higher grade than her current one so money wouldn't be such a struggle for her. I just didn't see how, if she was staying with someone else, she'd be able to fit me and Jonty in. Perhaps she didn't really want to – that niggly little voice again droning in my head.

Mum explained that she and Dad had tried to have a discussion but surprise, surprise, they couldn't agree about how often Jonty and I would come up to stay. Dad was adamant that he wouldn't share the travelling. Sadly, there wasn't time to waste and she would have to go back to court and get an agreement set out in a court order. She attempted to reassure me that she'd never go and leave everything up in the air without any firm plans for Jonty and me being made.

I respected her for that and I realised then that I did trust her, but did I trust my dad? No, if I was really honest – if I dared to be honest, I don't think I did. I'd known for ages that Dad lied when it was convenient or twisted the truth to suit him. There had been that time when he had been in bed with his secretary and he had lied about being at work. If I was really straight with myself, I knew that he had encouraged us to misjudge Mum always making himself seem the 'good guy' and somehow Mum being the one to blame. But when I was with him, I found it impossible to challenge him, the thought of telling him he was lying, I just couldn't. I sort of went to jelly inside, I feared his sarcastic response and him not loving me. He always had an answer ready which left me floundering and tongue tied. Perhaps it was like Mum said it had been for her, when she stopped believing in him and idolising him, he turned against her, it was all or nothing. So with that fear nagging away I had to keep on convincing him by hanging on to every word he said that he was the only one for me otherwise I'd lose him. The hard, cold truth was that it was all or nothing with me and Dad. I knew that. I also knew that was the only reason Mum had decided that she needed to move away. Of course, I wanted her to keep on being there for us, well for me, but I could see now that it would always be the same, it would always be a battle to spend time with her because whatever arrangements were in place Dad would always fight to change them. Dad had to keep in control. Let's face it, he was jealous of everyone else threatening his place in my life and Jonty's. I knew deep down that he had to control me; that wasn't what I wanted but I wasn't strong enough to resist because in spite of all his bad points, and yeah there were lots. I loved him, I loved him so much it sort of hurt and I needed him – he was part of me and I couldn't imagine coping without him. He'd always been my big idol and I didn't think that could ever change but I really, really wanted both Mum and Dad and now it seemed like I was going to lose a huge chunk of Mum. I believed her when she promised we could still spend some super times together in the holidays and being by the seaside would be different and exciting. Very different to Shrewsbury or Welshpool. When I could gather my thoughts rationally, I was reasonably cheerful about the new possibilities, but when other thoughts and doubts slipped in, I just felt wretched and blamed myself. I hated myself; I blamed Jonty; I hated Jonty; I blamed my mum and I hated my mum; I blamed my dad but I couldn't hate him.

I tried talking to Jonty again the next evening. It was difficult, he had dug his heels in and had made his mind up that he didn't like the sound of going to Newcastle at all and of course Dad had encouraged him to believe it was entirely his choice whether to ever go there. He perked up a bit when I said it was most likely going to be Whitley Bay and that was by the sea, but he still moaned about the puppy which we hadn't even got yet and I doubted we ever would. Dad kept saying, "Well, in a few months when everything is settled." But the weeks just flew by and still no puppy. Jonty continued to moan about leaving Dad as well. He had never really had a problem with leaving Dad until recently but just lately, it seemed that he didn't want Dad to be out of his sight. And Dad seemed to pander to it rather than telling Jonty to 'grow up' as he sometimes used to say when Jonty was particularly tiresome.

The summer was progressing; it would be my birthday soon and Jonty's after that. Before we even knew it, it would be the end of term and next year I'd be going to the senior school. I'd had no difficulty passing the exam and at nearly thirteen, I felt quite grown up. I think my mum recognised more than Dad that I was maturing, beginning to form my own independent views and needing to exercise a degree of autonomy. There was something about Dad that made me realise that he wanted, no he needed, to keep me as his little girl. Perhaps Mum moving away would give me a chance to be me when I was there with her. It was that thought that helped me to cope rather than watch myself shatter into a thousand tiny pieces.

Chapter 24

Within a few weeks, Mum had begun packing. It had all happened so quickly, I suppose a bit of me had hoped that it wouldn't run smoothly and so delay progress and she'd have a change of heart and stay. But no, she was really excited and there was every sign that matters would be completed very quickly. Mum had been up to stay with Sarah and Tony for a long weekend and she came back excitedly telling us there were lots of properties on the market in her price range and some were almost on the seafront. She clearly loved Whitley Bay describing it as a lively place which she was sure we would love. Newcastle was a beautiful city, much bigger than Welshpool or Shrewsbury with cinemas and art galleries, shops and a recently developed waterfront with the amazing Sage Centre across the river in Gateshead for concerts and events.

I was sort of pleased for her but at the same time, I felt angry. It sounded like she was really looking forward to going even though that meant leaving us. She didn't seem to be too concerned about how difficult it would be for me and Jonty, she just sort of assumed that we'd share her excitement. I was curious, I wanted to know what it was like but I was also scared, really scared. Dad never mentioned her going and when I brought it up and Jonty started telling him what she'd told us, he just said, "Oh never mind all that now, I'm sure she'll tell us all sooner or later." He made it very clear that as far as he was concerned, she barely existed. I felt as though I'd got to keep Mum and Dad in two separate compartments and juggle them so as not to mix them up. I guess that the bit of me that my mum got was getting squeezed smaller and smaller. Would she eventually just vanish?

It was a couple of weeks later when Mum asked me if I wanted to come up with her to have a look around Whitley Bay. She hoped that Jonty would want to come too and was suggesting a date in mid-June when we had a couple of PD days, so it would not mean missing any activities on the Saturday. It sounded a great idea but then with a sinking feeling, I realised that for a start Jonty wouldn't want to go and then Dad would come up with some reason or other why it wasn't possible for me to go either. In spite of that, I talked enthusiastically to Mum about it, especially when she said that by then she hoped she'd have some houses to view.

Sure enough when I brought it up with Dad, his immediate response was, "Well, I don't think that's a particularly good idea, Hetty. You see your mum's dragging us back to court, she won't see sense, she's totally unrealistic and the idea that dragging you all the way up there before you even know whether you're going to be able to go at all is a really bad idea. In fact, not one that is even worth considering." Cold water poured down my back; well that's what it felt like. What was I going to tell Mum? She'd be so disappointed and yet Dad's arguments seemed, as usual, so reasonable. I knew they were going back to court but surely, it wouldn't be like Dad just said that we wouldn't be allowed to even see Mum in Whitley Bay or Newcastle? Panicky feelings filled my head.

"But Dad, they're not going to stop us going, are they?"

"Well, it's not that, Hetty, you see it's your mum not being reasonable and expecting me to put myself out and drive all the way up there and back and leave you in some place I don't even know. It wouldn't be responsible of me – there are so many ifs and buts and well, we can't trust her, can we? So you see, it just isn't that simple. You don't understand, you're not old enough to appreciate the complications and the risks."

"But Dad, I'm nearly thirteen, of course I understand. It's up to me, surely I can say whether I want to go or not."

"Mmm. You're a bit too big for your boots sometimes you know, Hetty. You and Jonty aren't old enough to make decisions like this for yourselves. I will decide because I know what's best, I am responsible for your safety and wellbeing. You're in my care, not your mum's."

"But I thought –"

"I don't really care what you think, Hetty."

"But, Dad, I thought you had to share…"

"That's only in name, it's not the reality of it. We just had to go along with that to keep your mum sweet. The truth is that you live with me, I'm your main carer, I look after you and I'm the one who's always there for you and your mum just pops up and down when it suits her and now she's planning to move hundreds of miles away. That's not caring about you, I've told you, Hetty, she doesn't really care about you and Jonty at all and she's doing this just to get back at me. It's spite, pure spite. She'd much rather just pack her bags and go and start a new life with her new boyfriend."

"But Dad, I don't think she's got a boyfriend."

"Look, everything that she tells you, you just lap it all up – you believe her cock and bull stories, you take everything on board as the absolute truth. Hetty, one day you'll see the truth, you'll see through her just like I did. I just hope it's not going to be too late. I don't want you wasting your life hoping for something that's never going to happen. She's never going to be there for you, face reality." And with that, he was gone.

I was totally shell shocked. I couldn't believe what he had just said. Surely, Mum cared about me and Jonty. Surely, she did, but if so, why was she going? "Oh come on, Hetty," said that sensible little voice in my head. "You know that your dad's too tricky for her just like he is for you and he isn't ever, ever going to change. You know that and Mum knows that and your mum's doing something about it." I bashed the thoughts out of my head, I didn't want them there, they made it all too difficult.

Dad must have told Mum that he wasn't agreeing to us going up for a visit to Whitley Bay. She spoke to us both about it on the Saturday saying how disappointed she was that it couldn't happen. She seemed annoyed, well annoyed with Dad anyhow. I didn't want to hear it. "Like I said, Hetty, your dad always causes a problem, he always upsets everything."

Whether that was true or not, I didn't want to hear Mum running Dad down, I was scared to hear it.

So I blurted out, "That's not fair Mum, you know Dad's trying to get it right for us and you're the one who's leaving, you're the one who's going miles away, you're the one who's making it all difficult, don't blame Dad."

"Yes, it is your fault, Mum," Jonty piped up. "I don't want to go to Whitley Bay. I don't want to go at all. Dad's right, you're running away from us, you're leaving us, you don't care about us."

The words were said now and we couldn't take them back. Mum looked horrified, like she couldn't believe what she'd heard. She stood shaking her head – had we both turned on her? I could see that she was trying to pull herself together and fighting back the tears. "Let's leave it for now," she whispered.

All three of us were pretty tense that evening. Usually we would play a game of Cleudo together but nobody wanted to tonight, so we watched the TV instead. I was relieved when it was a reasonable time for us to go upstairs to bed. Why oh why was it all so difficult? What had I done to deserve this? Was I such a horrible person? Had I really caused so much trouble? I knew it must be all my fault, let's face it, there wouldn't be any arguments if it wasn't for me. I didn't know how to make things any better, I couldn't put it right. Maybe when I grew up, it might be different – at least what I thought might count for something then. But that was years and years away – how would I survive till then? Jonty crept into my room later on. He wanted to talk but I pretended to be asleep. I didn't want to talk to him, I didn't know how to. I hurt so much there wasn't room for his pain too, I wanted to just go to sleep and for everything to go away, to be happy and carefree again but I knew it wouldn't be any different next morning.

The only bright thing on the horizon was that Carol was coming to talk to us. Dad was clearly annoyed that she was involved again. He had already given us a pep talk about making sure that we really understood that Carol was on

Mum's side. He was emphatic that we needed to be very careful what we said to her. We had to remember that we three stuck together and resisted her attempts to pick us off one by one, because that's what these social workers always did. "By all means, be nice and polite to her but just be very, very careful what you say because rest assured she'll twist your words around and before you know it, she'll be insisting that you said the opposite of what you really said and you won't be able to do anything about it because you won't be in court when she tells the judge her fairy stories. These social workers, they have a lot of power and influence and they cosy up to the judge and hey presto exactly what they want happens." But what did we want? Somehow, I couldn't be sure it was what Dad really wanted. I just knew much as I wanted and needed him I didn't want to lose my mum either.

Chapter 25

It was the first week of June. My birthday was on the tenth and Jonty's was two days later, but Dad seemed preoccupied and didn't even want to talk about how we could celebrate. I knew that he was thinking about the court hearing and sure enough, he broached the subject one night. "Well, you two, we're going to have to have a plan and know exactly what we're doing."

"What do you mean, Dad?" I looked at him questioningly with a rising sense of panic.

"Well, we need to show a united front. Like I said, Carol's going to come and talk to you. I know how she wheedles you around and gets you to change your minds, so we all need to be pretty certain of what we're going to say before she comes." Jonty seemed all for it, but I looked doubtful.

"But Dad, I thought the whole thing was that it would be a chance for me and Jonty to say what we want to Carol."

"Well, within reason, but not when you're put under pressure to say what she wants you to say. I know how these social workers work, believe me. I've got real experience of them and I know what they'll do. I know how she'll get around you and before you know where you are, you'll be agreeing with her and of course, she's on Mum's side, she couldn't care a damn about me." Jonty just lapped it up. He hung on every word that Dad said. I just couldn't say anything and of course Dad took that to mean that I agreed with him.

"Anyway, I've got it all worked out," Dad continued, "so listen on you two and take note so that you've got your stories perfect for when Carol comes. You're going to make it quite clear to her that you really love being here in Welshpool and Shrewsbury and that you're very upset and shocked that

Mum's chosen to move away. It feels like she's deserting you and deep down your fears are that she isn't really bothered about you any more are confirmed. You are quite sure that the best way that you can manage it is to just go and see her for a short while very occasionally. That way we can all be happy. You know I don't even mind if you went up in the summer for a couple of weeks and I would take you one way and Mum can bring you the other way. Then maybe you could go again for a short visit around Christmas time. In between, you can write to each other and ring each other or send emails."

"I don't like sending emails," said Jonty. "So I'm not doing that and I don't like writing letters either, it's boring."

I heard Dad's words but they made no sense. Whatever was he saying? Did he really mean that I would only see my mum twice a year? And did he believe that that would be okay, that I didn't care about her anymore? Words of protest flooded into my head but they jammed in my throat and wouldn't come out of my mouth. Instead, I heard myself agreeing with Dad. "Yeah, yeah, yeah," I muttered. What about all my protests? What about saying 'Dad, Dad what do you mean – that's not what I want? Why are you stopping Mum seeing us? Why are you being so mean? Why are you being so selfish?' But none of that came out. Much as I tried, I couldn't challenge him – 'coward, coward' – screamed my inner voice. Dad gave us both a big hug.

"I know I can rely on you two. We're a team, the three of us, nothing's going to daunt us and of course if you're feeling a bit nervous about Carol, you can always insist that she sees you both together. In fact, I think I'll say that to her that you've both been very uncomfortable about the thought of being split off and I think it would be better if it was here at home, I'll go upstairs out of the way and then you can both talk to her but you'd have that reassurance that I'm on hand."

I couldn't believe what I was hearing. Carol was my only chance. She was the only person in the world that I felt I could talk to and really say how I felt and express the fears I had but Dad had sussed it out. He knew that I trusted her; he knew I wanted to talk to her and he was going to stop me. He was so clever, he always was. He did it in a way which made it seem that it was the right thing to do and I just didn't know what to say in response. Well, perhaps I did but I didn't have the nerve to do it because, yes, the same old story, he wouldn't love me anymore. He wouldn't want me if I wasn't totally loyal to him and if I hadn't got my mum because she was moving away, I needed him even more.

But Dad hadn't finished yet. "Mmm, I don't know if you realise but your mum wants to continue the court order that says you live with her as well as with me. But of course that's not going to be how it really is at all, is it? You're going to live here and see a bit of her sometimes when she can fit you in. So, I think it will make everybody feel much more secure and safe if you both just live with me and have contact with Mum. That's what most parents do, they don't have this thing where they're sharing their kids. It's never been equal anyhow, you've always really lived with me. Yeah, it goes right back to when Mum drove us all out and we had to run away because she was so dangerous and unpredictable and we just didn't have any peace. We didn't have any choice; we had to get out. She seems to have just sailed though and had everything her own way ever since and she's got to face the reality now that life isn't like that and for once in her life, she can't have exactly what she wants. She's very lucky that I'm going to be so agreeable to her having anything to do with you really. If she chooses to live at the other end of the country, that is her choice and she has to put up with the consequence that she's not going to see much of you two. Like I keep telling you, she wants to start a new life, free from you two but she's so clever she's kidding you she wants you – doing it for you! Rubbish, she's doing it to spite me. Face it kids – she's dumped you."

It just didn't seem to enter Dad's head that we both missed Mum and we couldn't imagine not seeing her when she went away. He seemed to think that the relationship was only one sided and that it was just about Mum not wanting us anymore, and that wasn't true anyway. He'd got no idea of how wretched we felt and I guess when I thought about it, I could see that he didn't really see that Mum was of any importance in our lives at all; she just didn't matter to him, so why would she matter to us?

It made me really cross that Jonty didn't seem to have a mind of his own at all. He just lapped up everything that Dad said. But to be fair, maybe a couple of years ago, it would have been like that for me but it wasn't now. Still I wasn't voicing my protests either. I hated this growing up, it was just so difficult, maybe I don't want to grow up, maybe I just want to stay young and carefree. It felt like my whole world was spinning out of control and I couldn't control anything. I couldn't manage anything and I didn't know what to do. I felt so little, so helpless, so lost, so desperate and now the one person who could help had been snatched away by Dad.

Nevertheless, Carol and Dad must have had a discussion because Dad's suggestion of her seeing the two of us together at home with him around didn't happen. I got a note from Carol a few days later saying that she had arranged to pick me up from school the following Thursday. Of course, Dad knew about the appointment but he didn't say anything. Perhaps he realised how much I needed to talk to Carol. But my optimism was crushed on Thursday morning when he said, "Just remember what we said, Hetty, don't let the side down. I need to be confident that I can rely on you. Remember where your loyalties lie. Don't for goodness sake go and spoil everything like you've done in the past. I know how you like to please everybody but Carol's nothing to you, she'll be out of your life soon. I'm the one that matters and our family – that's you, me and Jonty, just us – so make sure you get it right. I tell you, I'm relying on you." The weight of responsibility was crushing me. There was nothing I could do – I wanted Dad to love me and approve of me but I also knew that meant him owning me and controlling me. I'd be his puppet on a string and my mum would fade away 'cos that's what he wanted.

Years before, we'd been to Morecombe Bay and I remember looking across the sands. They had looked so smooth and so inviting and Dad had told us about the dangers lurking underneath the quicksands in the bay and how they would swallow a person up – they would sink in and just disappear without trace. That's how I felt now. I was sinking in this great mire. No matter how much I struggled, I couldn't fight my way to the surface. It was swallowing me up. The weight of responsibility placed on me was unbearable and I just didn't know what I could do. It was a difficult day at school. I couldn't concentrate at all and I got told off a couple of times. Suzie knew I was meeting Carol and gave me a hug. "Look, be brave, Hetty, tell her how you really feel."

"But she'll have to tell my dad and then he'll know what I've said. I'm scared, I can't lose him Suzie, I can't."

"Well, if you say what your dad wants you to say, how's your mum going to feel? And you'll feel responsible about her then. You should be loyal to yourself, Hetty; you can't just please everybody else."

Oh yes, that sounded so sensible, easy for her to say. She didn't have a mum and dad who hated each other. She had a nice easy mum and dad. I'd give anything to have her mum and dad instead of mine. Well, not really, but a mum and dad like them. I stupidly wished my mum and dad didn't hate each other but deep down I knew it would never change. "It's going to be like this for the rest of my life, I know it is. How can I grow up? Not with all this going on."

Carol gave me a big smile when she met me. She was in her car waiting in the layby. I jumped in and immediately burst into tears. "Where do you fancy going, Hetty, to have a chat?"

"I don't know," I blurted, my eyes and my nose running simultaneously. "Could we just go and park up somewhere and talk in the car. I don't really want to go in a café or anywhere. I look such a mess."

"Sure, that's okay. Let's drive to the layby by Attingham Park and park there by the river."

It was a beautiful day, warm and sunny. I should have been happy but I just felt like my insides were tied up in knots. I wanted so much to tell Carol how I felt but I was scared, really, really scared. Carol sensed how it was for me, acknowledging how difficult all this must be and how painful.

How brave I would need to be if I was to say how I felt, what I hoped for when I was stuck in what seemed to be an impossible situation wanting to get it right for my mum and my dad. She understood exactly but even so, it wouldn't make things any easier; it wasn't going to solve anything, it didn't give me the answers. It still felt that I had to choose either Mum or Dad. Carol helped me to appreciate that my mum wasn't running away and that those doubts and fears that I'd had about her love for me were not reality. She encouraged me to convince myself by recalling the good times we'd had together and how Mum had willingly accommodated all the activities Dad arranged for us. "Do you think she's trying to make it easier for you by taking away all the times you have to choose either her or your dad?" Carol posed. I thought about it and realised that Carol may well be right and if so, her moving away may not diminish our relationship with her.

Of course what Carol said made sense and I wanted to believe her, but these doubts crept in. Carol made it sound straightforward but that assumed Dad would be reasonable and of course, he wouldn't be. Not seeing my mum every week just seemed impossible even to think about. Carol encouraged me to consider what the future might look like and how I'd like things to be. What I'd like to happen and perhaps most importantly what I could do to help things work better. As she said, I couldn't change how Mum or Dad behaved or how Jonty reacted. I could only actually be responsible for myself. I didn't have to tell Carol how fearful I was about losing Dad's love. She knew. Without me saying anything. She knew how special he was, how important, how I couldn't voice an alternative view to his, except inside my own head.

Chapter 26

Carol and I met several times. It helped me to begin to make sense of what was about to happen and so I could work out what I hoped the future would hold. I knew I wanted to see Mum during each holiday but knowing how I would survive in between was impossible to visualise. To ease the situation, Carol suggested that maybe Mum could come down midterm for a weekend and stay with a friend so Jonty and I would be able to meet up with her. We talked about using Skype and phone calls and letters. I love writing and I thought that maybe having regular correspondence with Mum might make things easier, but would Dad demand to read those letters and would he expect to censor any letters I got back from Mum? I guessed he would, so that would spoil everything. He didn't want me to have any secrets and he would want to be sure that I wasn't saying anything bad about him, that I wasn't plotting anything behind his back. I had to face it, unless I totally agreed with Dad, he didn't trust me. I knew from lifelong experience that with Dad you either had to be totally for him, or he just assumed you were against him, there wasn't any half way.

Carol explained that it was usual for parents to share travelling and that meeting half way might be better than relying on one parent to fetch or deliver us. Whilst I agreed, a bit of me was really panicked – would Dad find some excuse for it just not to happen? Carol helped me to accept that the feelings of self-doubt that flooded my head were generated by my concerns about Mum and Dad and the unrealistic but very real belief that I was responsible for their happiness; that my lack of confidence and conviction that I was pretty worthless all stemmed from feeling powerless in the face of such huge,

huge difficulties which she insisted weren't my fault. She kept reminding me that none of this was my fault; sadly, I had a mum and dad who weren't able to get it right for Jonty and me. She wasn't criticising them but trying to help me realise that it wasn't my job to get it right for them and that I didn't have to choose one or the other. That I had a right to love both of them and to see my mum as often as it was possible even though she was moving away. Mum and Dad had a responsibility to me and Jonty to make sure that happened. It all sounded so clear, so certain, so fair – so why did I just know there would be problems all along the way? 'Cos of your dad' that little voice of mine insisted – I didn't want those thoughts, I couldn't go there.

Carol had similar conversations with Jonty. He was reluctant to say much to me but what a different story it was when Dad was around. I was seething, he always emphasised to Dad how he'd told Carol in no uncertain terms that he didn't want to go to Whitley Bay and that he couldn't care less whether he ever saw Mum again. I knew this wasn't true, I knew he'd told Carol he was scared he'd lose Mum and that Dad wouldn't let him love her and a bit of me hated him for being so two faced. But even then, I realised that he was just a very, very scared little boy who didn't dare to love Mum because he couldn't bear the thought of his dad not loving him any more than I could. Dad had both of us trapped.

Dad had taken Jonty and me to Alton Towers for our birthday treats and we'd been allowed to take our best friends too. Of course, I took Suzie and Jonty took his friend Bertie. I knew that Bertie's mum and dad didn't live together and that more recently, Jonty had talked to Bertie about how it was for him. I was pleased, I'd always worried he hadn't got anyone to talk to and that had encouraged him to hide the reality of our lives from his friends. We'd had a fantastic time, of course we had, who doesn't love Alton Towers? We'd gone on all the rides and felt sick and dared each other to go on the more scary ones, well Suzie and I did, but Jonty and Bertie were envious because they weren't quite tall enough. We'd all gone on the log flume together and even Dad had enjoyed it, as we all screamed and whooped as water sprayed over us. Just a little bit of me wished that Mum had been there too.

We did have a sort of birthday celebration with her too a few days later. We went for a picnic in the grounds of Powis Castle and she'd been pleased we wanted to take our friends with us but somehow it wasn't quite the same, it wasn't as exciting as usual celebrations because there was this black cloud hanging over us that soon Mum would be gone and we'd never have another chance to enjoy ourselves like this again. We wouldn't even see her on our next birthdays, she'd be up in Whitley Bay and we'd be stuck down in Welshpool waiting to see her during the next holiday; that's if the court let us and if Dad ever took us.

In my darkest moments, and yes, I had lots of them, I just knew he'd wreck it, he didn't want me to see Mum, not ever, not really. He hated her and all the Carols in the world couldn't change that. I tried to reason myself out of those feelings of self-doubt and to get rid of the nagging voice in my head insisting 'Dad might win, Dad might win, you might hardly ever see your mum again. He only wants you to go in the summer and maybe at Christmas and then the weather would be too bad and you probably wouldn't be able to go anyhow. There'd always be some reason why he couldn't take you'. Those black thoughts descended on me and spoiled any time we did have with Mum. I desperately wanted things to be different. She kept asking me why I was so miserable and I just didn't have the words to explain. Sometimes I just snapped at her. "Well, you're leaving us, dumping us. What do you expect?" It sounded so cruel, I couldn't believe I could be so nasty to Mum, but I couldn't help it – the words just poured out. I reckoned if I wasn't miserable, I'd just howl and howl and howl and never stop. The tears would pour down until they drowned me, that's what it felt like, I felt oh so wretched and I don't think Mum and Dad had any idea. Just like Carol said, sadly parents don't realise how difficult it is for their children.

Chapter 27

Carol 1

To be honest, I wasn't surprised to hear that Hetty and Jonty's parents were back in court. It had been one of those cases where I had experienced nagging doubts that the future would be plain sailing. Shared residence was certainly not something which Jeremy had wanted and he had only reluctantly agreed at the eleventh hour to avoid the expense of a final contested hearing. However, I had been surprised when not long afterwards, Hetty and Jonty's solicitor had contacted me to say that Ceri had made an application for a change of arrangements because she would be moving away. She wasn't applying to take the children with her but she wanted clear cut contact arrangements and a secure place in the children's lives well established prior to her move. The court had reappointed me to meet with the family to gain Hetty and Jonty's wishes and feelings and to prepare an addendum report.

What a difference those few months had made. At the time of the previous court hearing, Jonty had shown some reluctance to spend much time with Ceri, refusing to go during the week and insisting he needed to stay with Jeremy. I'd spent several sessions with him encouraging him to chat about home life so I could understand what was triggering his change of heart. It had soon become clear that Jeremy's negativity towards Ceri rather than their own experience of her was no doubt encouraging Jonty and Hetty's anxiety. They had been equally relieved to express their concerns and hopes for the future and then for clear-cut arrangements defined in a court order, rather them having to carry the can and make endless painful choices themselves. Without doubt, that had been a huge relief. Jonty had expressed in no uncertain terms that he wanted to spend the majority of his time with Jeremy, however, he made it very clear that like Hetty, he wanted regular time with Ceri. Hetty, always the peacemaker, wanted it to be equally fair between her parents, but almost certainly didn't want her mother to be the 'loser' as she put it. A 60/40 split of the children's time seemed right and had been reluctantly, as I say, agreed to by both parents.

Now within months, Jeremy had apparently eroded those arrangements with Jonty flatly refusing to spend time with Ceri during the week and then full of excuses and complaints at weekends. Once he was with her, he seemed okay as long as Jeremy wasn't around. Talking to Ceri, she made it clear that her realisation that life would never be any different had reluctantly driven her to make the drastic decision of seeking a work transfer. She was planning to relocate to Whitley Bay, commuting into Newcastle where she had secured a new and better-paid job. She explained that she had spent much of her childhood in the north east when her parents had moved there from Ferndale in the Rhondda valley after the closure of the coal pits in the 1980s. I knew that her father had died of pneumoconiosis during Ceri's teenage years and her mother of a stroke whilst she was at university. Her two sisters had immigrated to Canada but Ceri had no doubt felt a certain sense of kinship with the area of her childhood.

Yes, it was a good promotion with more pay and it would give Ceri a better chance of starting again but at what personal cost? She had sensibly ruled out the possibility of weekend contact with the children, and to be honest, it would have burdened them with the impossible strain of long tedious journeys and I guess Ceri just wouldn't have the means to meet the financial costs she would incur – either funding the children's travel or her own. Instead, she was proposing the children spent 50% of all holidays with each of them and for them to continue to share the residence of Hetty and Jonty. Had she really weighed up how difficult such a change would be for Hetty and Jonty and that their interpretation of her move was highly likely to be that she had abandoned them –

almost certainly that would be the explanation Jeremy would gleefully promote. Ceri insisted she wanted to get it right for the children and for them to understand that her only wish was to make life easier for them; she considered it imperative that Hetty and Jonty each had a chance to talk to me and hopefully to feel able to tell me how they really felt about what she saw as Jeremy breathing down their necks and controlling everything they did. I wondered – was that an accurate depiction of life with Jeremy? I realised that much as I may surmise that this was the case, that unless the children opened up to me it remained pure conjecture which would be hotly denied by Jeremy and any court. I wondered – did Ceri really appreciate that her proposal was likely to create as many new obstacles to the children's relationships with her as it solved?

My discussion with Jeremy left me in no doubt that if Ceri relocated, a continuation of shared residence was going to be a major sticking point. Jeremy considered that the children's sole residence with him was perfectly justified. Ceri was moving away, it was her choice, she could have contact, but no he certainly wasn't going to agree to sharing residence and as to a 50/50 arrangement in each holiday, that just wasn't feasible – Ceri didn't have sufficient annual leave and he wasn't going to agree to anything which meant that the children were inadequately cared for or farmed out with child minders. "Over my dead body and a waste of time going back to court – there's no argument, she just needs to get real and appreciate how accommodating I am," were his final words on the subject. There was no suggestion of what the children's views might be. From past discussions with him, I knew that in Jeremy's eyes, the children would 'of course' mirror his views exactly.

All cases are unique and present different challenges but somehow this family were particularly tricky. Jeremy certainly held the trump card, Ceri without doubt underestimated that she was facing an uphill struggle. I mulled over the facts. Ceri must have hit rock bottom and felt really desperate to have decided on such a drastic move. I guess she'd reached the end of her tether and it was all too painful to carry on battling for Hetty and Jonty to spend quality time with her. To give her her due, she knew that the pain she was suffering was mirrored by the children. She had reluctantly accepted that it wasn't going to get any easier for Jonty or for Hetty realising from her own bitter experience Jeremy was never going to change and never going to give in.

I had spent considerable time with both parents encouraging them to appreciate Hetty and Jonty's need and permission to love them both. I had read their statements and considered their proposals and now I needed to arrange to see Hetty and Jonty together and then separately. I needed to carefully consider all the possibilities. How was I going to go about eliciting the information and detail I needed from two children who had learned to be guarded and cautious when discussing their parents? Without doubt, Jeremy will have painted me as someone the children should be wary of and I was well aware that his amicable jolly demeanour thinly disguised his belief that I was the fly in the ointment, someone to guard the children from.

Chapter 28

Carol 2

My task is invariably to figure out how best to engage with a particular family. I need to consider what encourages particular parental behaviour and thought patterns and to avoid falling in to the trap of labelling individuals. Experience has convinced me that to do so fails to illuminate the nuances and complex dynamics of each family. What seems to be happening with the Taylors is a gradual, subtle but very definite erosion of the children's relationship with Ceri, and seemingly for no apparent good reason. So where does the blame lie? Is it with Jeremy or is there some hidden deep-seated problem with Ceri just as Jeremy so readily insists?

In my experience, there can be a whole raft of reasons why children become estranged from one parent or the other. Almost always the rejected parent is the one who is non-resident, that is, in the child's mind the one who 'left them', 'deserted them' and of course the one who ceases to be the main influence in that child's life.

On occasions, there is justifiably good reasons for a parent to be rejected. The parent who has been abusive towards a child during the family relationship is quite rightly rejected by that child when the separation occurs. They usually need little encouragement from the resident parent although the ex will inevitably be blamed by the absent parent. In my experience, parents are notoriously bad at accepting responsibility themselves where relationships with their children are at stake. Sadly, in some families, the relationship between the child and the non-resident parent was so tenuous before separation that rebuilding a new and strong relationship in the absence of a firm foundation is almost impossible however much support the resident parent gives. Once again, it is likely that the resident parent will be blamed for turning the child against their absent mother or father.

Invariably, whatever the cause, the child's reluctance to engage is usually loud and clear to the resident parent. Of course, that parent will listen and take notice when their child becomes angry and critical of the absent parent. Some of the child's heightened emotions may be coping strategies as they struggle with the massive upheaval of the breakup of their family impacts upon them. The child of a broken family has to manage a whole raft of emotions; they hurt and are often bewildered and scared. However, with the right level of reassurance and encouragement, usually those negative feelings gradually dissipate and the certainty of a continuing good relationship with both parents helps enormously. However, in the absence of genuine support from the resident parent, loving both parents becomes increasingly challenging even for the most resilient child. Screaming that you hate the absent parent may at least make the parent you live with happy but at what personal cost?

Children who have rejected a parent in the absence of abuse or any other legitimate reason may well harbour a secret wish for someone to call their bluff, compelling them to reconnect with the parent that they claim to hate. At least then, they don't have to choose one or the other. This means that it is imperative that whilst the children's stated wishes regarding parental contact have to be listened to and considered, they can never be determinative in contact arrangements. To do so may mean that the confused, frightened child ends up with the absent parent missing from their lives. What if the child insists that they hate one parent? Hatred is not an emotion which comes naturally to any child. On occasions, it is a parent's own hatred of their ex that can intentionally or subconsciously encourage a child to hate or fear the other parent for no justifiable reason. On those occasions, the mental and emotional health of that child is endangered, not just in the present but ongoing often extending into adolescence and adulthood and affecting every aspect of their lives.

I know full well that so often children will identify with the resident parent in order to maintain their relationship with them even if that means stating their dislike of the other parent. They simply cannot risk stepping away from the party line because that would risk rejection from the person that they depend upon. Identifying with the resident parent avoids more pain and so becomes a necessary survival strategy.

Many may argue that a child who rejects a parent must have a valid reason that somehow the hated parent must be responsible for the child's dislike of them. Yes, in some cases, I am sure that is the case, but somehow in this family, I can't find anything amiss in Ceri's relationship with either child. There just don't seem to be any legitimate reasons for the children seemingly to push her away. Both Hetty and Jonty describe a close and loving relationship with Ceri; which I observed very quickly got back on track after the pain and upset of their parents' unplanned separation, in spite of there being quite a long gap with no contact at all and seemingly no active encouragement from Jeremy.

It is easy to misinterpret the family dynamics in families such as this. How simple it would be to blame the targeted parent, Ceri, for contributing to the children's rejection of her. 'Poor Ceri couldn't cope with the children's love for Jeremy and so began to find fault with them and when they objected her behaviour became more extreme and more negative'. How easy it would be to absolve Jeremy, to give him the benefit of the doubt. Life with Ceri must have become unbearable for him and the children, why else would he leave the luxury and comfort of the family home? On the surface, he seems to have a very healthy, loving and normal relationship with both children but I know from experience that if I dig down a bit more under the surface, there is likely to be a clinging enmeshed parent-child relationship, one which may well suppress the children's natural feelings of their need and love from Ceri. They will be unable to resist his manipulative behaviour designed to maintain their solidarity with him. They will be in no doubt of the risk of rejection by him; it is something they will fear if their loyalty to him is misplaced. Without doubt, this will quell any resistance or objection on their part and encourage their apparent negativity towards Ceri, at least when Jeremy is around.

Of course, it is highly likely that as the children became more distant, more detached that Ceri will have begun to exhibit symptoms of anxiety, depression and fear, symptoms which so easily generate a tendency to irrational behaviour and angry outbursts; not major character flaws but signs of frustration, powerlessness and extreme sadness. How easy it is, especially in the heated atmosphere of a courtroom then to label Ceri as being the 'guilty party'. True those flaws which she displays may well on occasion contribute to the children feeling somewhat unsure and so expressing that as their dislike of her. However, the reality would be that on occasions, she seems different to the calm and stable Ceri they know and have experienced throughout their lives and it doesn't make sense to them if suddenly her behaviour becomes unpredictable. Jeremy is unlikely to attempt to reassure them but instead he will seize the opportunity to fuel their fears and suddenly they are thrown into confusion and turmoil and so they back away even more. As a result, poor Ceri is driven to utter despair by Jeremy's demeaning and controlling behaviour. She watches powerlessly as her relationship, the close and loving relationship that she had with both her children, is eroded, perpetuating the cycle of instability, her anxiety and anger and unpredictable behaviour in turn reinforces Jeremy's power over the children.

So what can I do to a) make sense of what is going on in this family and b) attempt to encourage a resolution which is best for both children? To start with, it is critical to consider the family history. What was the parents' relationship really like in the past? Were there hidden difficulties? Was it as Ceri says that once she no longer worshipped Jeremy he engineered change, gradually chipping away her self-confidence and manipulating arguments so that she always carried the blame and gradually lost the children's respect?

As always, my aim is to establish a shared parenting arrangement. 50/50 is invariably impractical in most families – work commitments, parenting skills and preferences need to be taken into account but when there is an agreement in which both parents accept that they are equally responsible for their children, the risk of them encouraging the children to turn against one or the other of them reduces considerably. They can see that it actually becomes much easier for the children to maintain a normal relationship with them both and of course, children are less susceptible to the toxic influence of alienation. Neither parent fears that they will lose their children completely. In many cases, I have dealt with in the past parental conflict reduces and a level of co-operation is established albeit pretty shaky at the beginning.

Why isn't that pattern apparent in this family? Does Jeremy's behaviour suggest that something more sinister is going on? Does his persistent undermining of arrangements, his apparent need for control hint at narcissistic tendencies? If so, I have a difficult task on hand. I cannot change a parent's inbuilt character; I have to work out if his behaviour is a consequence of the separation or is the true Jeremy actually depicted by that behaviour? Only when I have worked out what is really happening can I begin to look at ways to make an impact and bring about change.

However, from experience, I know that if there is a character flaw and Jeremy's behaviour is not driven by heightened emotions surrounding his separation from Ceri but his inbuilt personality – that in fact he has narcissistic tendencies – that means that reducing his power of manipulation is likely to prove to be impossible. I know full well that there are cases where to continue fighting for some sort of shared parenting can cause such extreme emotional pain for the child that it perpetuates the emotional abuse. In those few cases, the only solution may be to wait until the child's eyes are opened and as an adult, they make judgements about their parents and then chose the parent who gives the unconditional love rather than the parent where love comes at an impossibly high price.

So if that is the case in this family, what is the best that I can hope to achieve? Well, without doubt, what I will aim to do is to encourage an arrangement which at least leaves the doors wide open. This is not defeatist but is about facing reality. I know full well that changing residence and forcing the children to in effect choose Ceri would mean that they lose Jeremy, something which I suspect neither child has the emotional capacity to manage at this stage of their lives. But equally the pain and hurt, if they in effect lose Ceri, will be equally unmanageable for them. The compromise may be that they spend considerably less time with Ceri but that time is of prime quality – quality rather than quantity may be the only child centred option.

Chapter 29

Carol 3 – analysis before court hearing

I'd had meetings with both parents and several with Hetty and Jonty. I could see that Ceri's decision to move away was at least in part motivated by her wish to make it easier for the children. It tore her in two to see how tortured they were, as they continuously tried to get it right for both her and Jeremy. She reacted angrily when I suggested that her pull to return to the area where she spent her childhood was nevertheless partly fuelled by her desperation to start a new life, to rid herself of the man who had disempowered her for so long. I could understand her argument that it was entirely for the children and that Jeremy's ongoing influence on every aspect of her life was clearly preventing her from moving on, but there was no doubt that encouraged her tunnel vision and inability to see the situation through the children's eyes or experience their pain and confusion that losing her would generate. She no doubt wanted to believe that like her, they would find life so much easier if there was a distance between the parents and clearly defined holiday arrangements. Could she honestly say that she couldn't imagine just how painful it would be, in particular for Hetty? How the children would, in their bewilderment, take little convincing from Jeremy that she had deserted them. She was providing him with the perfect ammunition and from my dealings with him, he would leap at the golden opportunity to further alienate the children.

To be honest, Jeremy wasn't particularly easy to engage with on a meaningful level. Frustratingly, he seemed incapable of empathy and either couldn't or wouldn't perceive that the children could possibly have a view that differed from his own. He assumed their automatic compliance and used that to exploit the children disregarding their need and right to have an unfettered relationship with Ceri.

At ten and thirteen, Jonty and Hetty's differing stages of development meant they managed their struggles to maintain divided loyalties differently. Struggles that were triggered by constantly having to choose either mum or dad. Jonty's emerging alliance with Jeremy was his coping mechanism. Initially, this had been pretty mild and somewhat hidden, just an occasional reluctance to go and see Ceri and then he had started complaining about her. His stories were often fanciful, but nevertheless, they were lapped up by Jeremy. However, in spite of that, he had continued to also say how much he cared about his mum and that was borne out by their relaxed and easy relationship for much of the time when he was with her. More recently, it had become increasingly obvious that juggling his emotions was becoming too difficult and in desperation, he had attempted to distance himself from mum as his way of managing his impossible dilemma. His alliance with his dad had become stronger and was clearly encouraged by Jeremy. From experience, I knew that allegiance was likely to become more pronounced and extreme. It wouldn't be long before Jonty was refusing to visit or to have any involvement with Ceri. It was a foregone conclusion that he would follow this pattern unless Jeremy discouraged it. Of course Jeremy wasn't going to do that, on the contrary I was pretty sure that he'd rub his hands in glee if at least one child turned their back on the woman he detested. Hetty, that bit more mature, was struggling but at least at this stage was still able to maintain a good relationship with both parents. Her strategy was to keep them separate and was a precarious position for her to maintain.

Consciously and subconsciously, both children would be balancing their own experience of their time with mum with overt and covert contradictory messages from dad such as the unsubstantiated hints that Ceri had a boyfriend waiting in the wings and that was her real reason for leaving. The hints that she was dumping them, the suggestion that she couldn't wait to start a new life and that she didn't really care but just wanted to get her own back on him. In their desperate attempt to maintain stability in their lives, the only ostensible solution to manage their distress would be for them to decide that one is the 'good' parent and the other is 'bad'. The reality of good and bad in both would just not be a feasible option.

My concern is that Jonty is on the tip of rejecting Ceri and experience shows that once entrenched in that mind-set it is particularly difficult to remedy. Children become stuck and continue to make a desperate attempt to prove their allegiance to one parent, the parent that they feel they depend upon and who often unhealthily depends on them. They have no choice but to become hostile and rejecting of the other parent. Sadly, one day Jonty may have to come to terms with his childhood belief that forced him to exclude a decent, loving mum and without doubt, that will cause irreversible damage in his relationship with his dad.

Whether Hetty will have the resilience to continue to juggle a relationship with both mum and dad remains to be seen. Sadly, the odds are stacked against her too. Both children have such an enmeshed relationship with their dad, one which he needs, which he feeds upon. He encourages and expects to be adored, raised to lofty heights by his children just as he had demanded from his wife. It would seem that Hetty would find it increasingly difficult to reconcile the positive experience she has with Mum with implicit contradictory information from the dad she loves, adores and so desperately needs and fears losing.

It is encouraging that currently Ceri at least recognises the children's need for a positive and meaningful relationship with her and Jeremy and seems to be making an effort to avoid negative remarks or criticisms about Dad. This is in stark contrast to Dad's frequently stated belief that Mum is important when in reality his sarcastic remarks: "You are so gullible, Hetty – taken in by her – too nice. She doesn't care about you and she's dumped you for a new life etc., etc." Seeds of doubt designed to undermine the children's confidence in Mum so that they are no longer sure of her love for them. That ploy of Jeremy's encourages my view that as far as he is concerned, her value in the children's lives is negligible.

It is predictable that as time progresses in the face of his opposition, Ceri will struggle to continue to consider that the children need both parents. This change of heart is likely to be fuelled by the contradictory changes she will witness in the children's behaviour. More than likely when Hetty is with her and away from Dad, she will experience a relaxed, comfortable and affectionate Hetty and it will make no sense to her that Jeremy insists that Hetty is really indifferent about spending time with her. Whilst with him, Hetty will have little choice but to join her brother in toeing the party line and reinforcing Dad's views that of course the so-called experts got it wrong. Jonty and Hetty will have to at least appear to share his view that Mum plays no valuable part in their lives. It is likely that when Hetty is with her dad or in proximity to him, her behaviour towards her mum will as a consequence become cool and distant. What a terrible, terrible muddle this poor child will experience, perhaps because of her more advanced stage of development, it will be even more painful than her brother's. She will have the cognitive ability to have a more objective view of what has happened with the means to be judgmental and critical of both her parents, but that will be in secret. The reality is that in order to maintain her relationship with her dad, she will have to openly blame her mum, an untruth which Hetty will find increasingly difficult to live with.

I have concerns that both children's self-esteem will be damaged by the parental conflict. The signs of them both feeling a sense of worthlessness are already visible, believing that they are the cause of their parents' problems. In the future, the spinoff will be that it is likely their own ability to maintain relationships will be adversely affected. Having to keep secrets from one parent or the other will encourage them that being deceitful or sneaky is an acceptable way, and perhaps the only way, to manage difficult situations.

As both children become older, they will sadly lack the benefit of witnessing their parents managing disagreements in a healthy constructive way and without such a positive role model, they will be ill equipped to deal with conflict themselves. Research suggests that may well trigger aggressive or bullying behaviour in either child and without doubt, it will damage their belief in themselves and in what they can achieve. They will be burdened by unresolved anger; anger which will make no sense but which may well spill over and affect every aspect of their lives and as a result misuse of food, alcohol or illegal drugs, or other forms of self-harm may be a welcome solace from unbearable pain and give them a false sense of being in control.

Whilst a robust court order clearly defining arrangements for both children may well assist, and at least initially encourage contact, it seems almost inevitable that gradually the children's contact with Ceri will dwindle. Ceri lacks the financial resources and I fear the resilience to keep fighting through the courts and the likely scenario is that the day of reckoning will be postponed until they are mature enough to stand up to Jeremy and to recognise him for what he really is. Sadly, whilst a two-day court battle may well solve the immediate future, at the same time it will antagonise the situation and deepen the antipathy between the parents. The likelihood of parental co-operation will evaporate.

Mum's solicitor, Katrina Barker, and the children's solicitor, Michaela Brookes, are both experienced advocates determined to seek the best outcome possible for the children; neither will mince their words, they will encourage parental dialogue be it in person or through them. But sadly, Jeremy's solicitor, Simone Fletcher, is known to be adversarial and she is more likely to ramp up the hostilities and increase the tension between the parents rather than encourage resolution. We have an excellent judge in Henrietta Haines. She is known for her wisdom, her ability to grasp the situation and to deal with it in a fair and child centred way.

I have listened carefully to the children and they have made it very clear to me that they want a relationship with both parents, although Jonty struggles with the notion of one with Ceri in the face of his father's lack of support and constant criticism of her. In spite of spoken protests, neither child really wants to be put in the position of actually having to make choices or decisions about contact and they would much prefer arrangements to be clearly decided, ideally by both parents, but Hetty at least understands that any level of agreement is unlikely.

Ceri's proposal of 50% of all holidays is sadly unrealistic; even she can see that her enthusiasm for that arrangement has given Jeremy more ammunition to fuel his insistence that she makes empty promises which have no substance. The children are both at private school and Ceri's holidays cannot possibly cover seven or eight weeks each year. However, in spite of Jeremy's protests, keeping a pattern of regular contact is important, and they should spend quality time during each holiday with their mother. Jeremy's own proposal of only two visits a year, more than anything, is a stark demonstration of his lack of commitment to the children maintaining a relationship with Ceri.

I have discussed with Ceri the possibility of her making occasional trips down to Welshpool or Shrewsbury and staying with friends and seeing the children from there. Subject to successfully juggling her finances, she favours the idea but until she knows whether Jeremy will pursue his right to force a contribution from her through the CSA. Her available cash remains unknown. Ceri knows full well that Jeremy is entitled to claim once children are no longer living with both of them and anticipates he will pursue any means to make life more difficult for her. She insists she has every intention of supporting the children in every way that she can but her limited financial resources means that she will struggle to fund extras once she has a mortgage and associated household expenses plus a contribution towards the children to find each month.

In common with other children of eleven and thirteen, Hetty and Jonty seek a sense of fairness between their parents and a meeting place half way between Welshpool and Whitley

Bay was greeted favourably by them both, though of course it was discounted by Jeremy, unless trips are limited to his suggestion of twice a year. I put forward the suggestion that handovers at the Hartshead Moor Services on the M62 would be equidistant for both parents.

Ceri had agreed with my suggestion but Jeremy had made the counter proposal of handovers at Birch Services – an arrangement which reduces his travelling time and I guess he would strongly object to handovers at Hartshead Moor if the hearing didn't go his way.

I inevitably go to court in the hope that there will be some agreement without a contested hearing, but in this case, Jeremy's resistance and reluctance to consider anything other than his own point of view makes that an unlikely outcome. A robust court order may be best for Hetty and Jonty.

Chapter 30

Court Hearing Wrexham County Court 18 July, Case No WP39651

Cross examination of Carol Maitland (ISW) by Simone Fletcher, Solicitor for Jeremy Taylor

SF	"Now come on Ms Maitland, surely you can see that we've got a desperate father here who just cannot keep up with his impetuous ex-wife who really can only put herself first and just fails to see how important the children's needs are?"
CM	"No, I don't agree. I think Ceri's move to Whitley Bay was a desperate attempt to try and make things less difficult for the children."
SF	"Less difficult! She walked out on them, how could that make it easier for the children?"
CM	"She knew how difficult it was for them just as it was for her. How their father would undermine and chop and change arrangements and continuously put them in the position of having to choose between him or her. She realised just how hard it was for them and so by putting a distance between them, it may take away that pressure or at least minimise it."
SF	"Well, superficially that may well be correct, but surely you can see how

	devastated the children were when their mother just decided to up and go? I see at paragraph 36 you say that she 'thought carefully through her actions'. Remind the court Ms Maitland, of how the children and indeed their father heard about mother's move. You hesitate, well let me remind you, isn't it correct that she told the children during a weekly visit without having the decency to talk to their father first. She let them do her dirty work. They were the ones who had to work out how to tell him. Of course, he was devastated knowing how it would just turn their world upside down. Surely, you can see that he has spent all his time since the separation trying to normalise things for the children and trying to help them come to terms with their mother's unpredictable and inappropriate behaviour."
CM	"Forgive me, but is that a question or is it a statement? I need to remind the court of the facts. There has been no evidence that Ceri's behaviour has been inappropriate in any way at any time. We've got a mother and father here who have very different versions of their relationship but it is clearly documented from my visits that I've witnessed two children with an increasingly good relationship with their mother which over time –"
SF	"Yes indeed, I know what you've written but I didn't ask you that."
Judge HH	"But Miss Fletcher, I'd like Ms Maitland to finish what she was about to say. Carry on, Ms Maitland please."

CM	"After a gap without contact, the children very quickly reinstated their relationship with their mother. As time has gone on, there is clear evidence that it has become increasingly difficult for them to juggle their relationships with Mum and Dad. They have been put under immense pressure and evidence suggests that pressure has been instigated by their father, rather than their mother. She is the one who has backed down and in her own way tried to make it easier for the children. Yes of course, they've had to deal with their separation from her and that's been incredibly difficult and painful for them. No doubt, she has underestimated the impact upon the children and how easy it is for children to misunderstand and misinterpret, but she was not motivated by any intention to escape from them. Sadly, that's the message that they've been given by their father. Those mixed messages have increased the children's confusion, mistrust and immense sadness."
SF	"Well, I think their father would deny that."
CM	"It's what the children have clearly said."
SF	"Yes, but surely you can see that the children say whatever you want them to say, they know you're on mother's side. They will give you the 'right' version, not necessarily the truth."
CM	"With respect, I'm not on anybody's side, I just want what is best for the children and here we have a mother and a father who demonstrate that they cannot live close to each other and

	facilitate the children moving between their two homes. A distance between them necessitates clear cut arrangements for when the children will be with each of them."
SF	"Let's turn to Mrs Taylor's recommendation, her proposal of what should happen in the school holidays. She suggests a 50/50 split of time. Is that reasonable?"
CM	"It would be the ideal as I've said in my report, but as I explained, no I don't consider that it is feasible because she just hasn't got sufficient annual leave to be able to cover that amount of time. The children attend private school and there is parental agreement that they will remain there in which case they have 14 to 16 weeks holiday a year. I know that Ceri hasn't got 8 weeks annual leave, so I would suggest that the children spend a substantial amount of time in each of the main holidays and 50% of all the half term holidays with her and the rest of the time with their father in Welshpool."
SF	"Mrs Taylor is suggesting that they should meet half way. Is that what you're proposing? That this mother who has randomly chosen to move to the other end of the country now expects her ex-husband, the children's father, to drive up and down the country to suit her?"
CM	"Let me correct you. Newcastle is where Mrs Taylor spent much of her childhood and of course we all know that the normal arrangement is that parents share the travelling."

SF	"But she doesn't have to live in Whitley Bay, does she? She's chosen to start a new life there and it's hardly surprising that Mr Taylor wonders whether it is so that she can start a new relationship and gradually push total responsibility for the children on to his shoulders. Just having them to stay when it suits her absolves her of day-to-day responsibility. Surely, you can see that's what springs to his mind?"
CM	"That is mere speculation, there is no evidence that mother has embarked on a new relationship. She has in fact totally denied father's frequent suggestions to the children that they are to be marginalised by a new boyfriend."
SF	"Of course he mentions it to his children simply because he's trying to help them to understand something which must be beyond their comprehension. Their mother's walked out on them. She hasn't put forward any logical reason he's trying to help his children to make sense of the awfulness of it."
CM	"The children's mother has spent a lot of time explaining to them in an age appropriate way why she feels it best for her to move away and how she can ensure that she continues to have a good relationship with them. But – and this is immensely sad for Hetty and Jonty – that is made more difficult if she has first to convince them that what their father has told them is untrue. Of course it's a tricky situation, particularly for Jonty, because he's too young to understand that sometimes parents are not entirely fair."

SF	"Meaning who?"
CM	"Meaning that I think Jeremy deliberately misconstrues Ceri's motives so convincingly that it looks as though she's abandoning the children and this only fuels the children's confusion."
SF	"You really don't like Mr Taylor, do you?"
CM	"I don't like or dislike anybody that I work with. I aim to have a good working relationship with both parents to be fair and to remain neutral so that I can encourage the best outcome for the children and ideally an outcome which is agreed and arranged by them, not imposed on them by the court. Of course I don't always agree with Ceri or with Jeremy but if they choose to construe that as me not liking them, then that's unfortunate and it's even more unfortunate if their mistrust and dislike of me as a consequence is then fed to the children so that they too develop a sense of mistrust."
SF	"Are you inferring that's what Mr Taylor is doing?"
CM	"From what the children have told me, I know that is on occasions what he is doing."
SF	"And you choose to believe what the children tell you?"
CM	"I think that having worked with children for as long as I have, I get a pretty good idea of when they are telling me what they think I want to hear and when they are just recounting what has actually happened and how things are at home. Yes, at times they are critical of their

> mother and of their father and that is normal and healthy. I don't sit questioning them, I encourage them to believe that they really can have a good relationship with both parents however impossible that might seem at times.
>
> Hetty and Jonty love both their parents – that is abundantly clear – and both parents have so much to offer. It is the children's right to have an unfettered relationship with them both."

I knew it would be a challenging court case. Ceri's solicitor had done a superb job encouraging her to paint a very positive picture of her motives for her move to Whitley Bay and her proposals for arrangements for the children. Of course, that had been challenged by Jeremy's solicitor and the children's solicitor had been able to encourage Ceri to speak passionately and very sincerely about her relationship with the children and how painful her decisions were for them. I knew that Jeremy's solicitor would be on the attack but underestimated how easily she unnerved Ceri who struggled to respond to her accusations and assumptions and as a consequence, her arguments and reasoning sounded weak and ill-thought through. It is inevitable that in cases where there is little or no common ground, one or the other of the solicitors will be on the attack as they cross examine me. I remained convinced that Ceri's desperation to ease the children's pain and her own clearly had motivated her to make the decision to relocate but it was her own desperation which encouraged her to underestimate just how much the pain of separation would affect the children. She failed to appreciate how Hetty, in particular, would feel bereft when she left Welshpool. I knew that that would be seized upon by Jeremy's solicitor and I had spent time pointing out to Ceri that whilst her actions were well intentioned, it was inevitable that there would be unfortunate repercussions too. Repercussions which I believe she could now appreciate and was determined to manage as best she could.

Jeremy had been confident and very sure of himself when he was led through his evidence by his solicitor. He was a charismatic man, well used to public speaking and he knew how to capture attention. But I doubt he had bargained for the wisdom and experience of either the judge, Ceri's solicitor or Hetty and Jonty's solicitor. They challenged his negativity towards Ceri, the messages that he was giving to the children and those actions which on the surface were for the children but which undermined Ceri's arrangements and curtailed the children's time with her always on the pretext that it was what they wanted.

As Judge Haines said in her summing up, "Whilst there are many positive qualities displayed by both parents, the pain that their separation had caused the children was long lasting and both needed to take responsibility for that." But she was particularly critical of Jeremy's apparent attempts to discredit Ceri, to railroad any opportunities the children had to spend additional time with her and to tightly control the time that they did have so that he was complying with the order but in such a way that there was no wriggle room, nothing extra, it was as though he believed it was a concession for her to have a relationship with Hetty and Jonty and she was quite sure Jeremy did little to discourage Jonty's reluctance to have contact with mother. Indeed on occasion, it was clear that on the contrary, he would seize those opportunities to present Jonty with impossible choices. In her view, the evidence presented made it highly likely that both children had a fear of displeasing their father.

She recognised that the move meant that the main carer would be Jeremy, there was no alternative, the court order had to reflect the reality of the living situation and the amount of free time that Ceri had meant that her time with the children would be 'contact with' rather than 'live with'. She knew that this would be disappointing to her and she wanted to ensure that when the order was drafted that it included an expectation that Ceri would be included in all important decisions about the children. She reminded Jeremy that as the children's mother, she continued to have parental responsibility and would always have that position in their lives. She considered that meeting at a half way point on each occasion the children were to stay with Ceri would diminish any fear the children may have of one or the other not turning up and she hoped that although it was a very clearly defined order, in the future a degree of flexibility would be possible. She considered that at this juncture, this would not be advisable. She did, however, expect that minor changes would be managed by the parents and would not necessitate a return to court an experience which was emotionally damaging for Hetty and Jonty.

Chapter 31

The court hearing was early in July and I knew that it was going to be for two days. I wondered what on earth they would all talk about for so long, surely they could just listen to what Carol said was best for us? But then, I guessed that if Dad didn't agree, he'd try and argue it his way and Mum would try and argue it her way, but even then, how could they make that last for two days? I just wanted it to be all right. I didn't want a load of adults to fight about me and Jonty – 'it's all your fault' came this persistent voice in my head. 'Just go along with Dad and it will be all right, all this nonsense will stop'. It wouldn't though, even I knew that.

The court hearing was a Monday and a Tuesday so we weren't seeing Mum and on Monday after school, I tried to get a sense of how Dad was feeling. He seemed preoccupied and just simply shrugged it off saying, "Oh well, let's see what happens tomorrow," but said nothing more and I was left guessing what he was really thinking. Jonty and I talked a bit but I found it really difficult to hear Jonty putting on such a different side when he was talking to me and then to change tack when he was talking to Dad. I tried to make him see that he was being disloyal to Mum but he wouldn't have any of it, I know now that it was just too hard for him and I feel guilty because I guess I increased his pain rather than making it easier. I wasn't always the good sister that I liked to believe that I was.

I was surprised when during my last lesson on Tuesday, I had a message from the school office to say that Carol was waiting to see Jonty and me and that she was coming into school to have a chat to us both. We were nervous, really nervous, what was she going to come and tell us? Why was she at school? I wasn't expecting this. Jonty's hand crept towards mine, I held it tight, he needed some reassurance from his big sister and I needed him too.

Carol came in with a big smile on her face. "Hello, you two. Let's go somewhere quieter, shall we?" We went upstairs to one of the smaller offices where there were some comfy chairs. It looked out across the playing fields. Carol explained that the court hearing had finished and that the judge had asked her to come and explain to both of us what had happened rather than for us to have to rely on either Mum or Dad telling us. She didn't explain why but I guess that a bit of me realised that sometimes mums' and dads' interpretations of the truth was a bit off the mark and ours were the worst offenders. Carol explained that the judge had made it very clear that we were to see as much of Mum and Dad as was possible and that she wanted arrangements to be fair. But she had to take into account the fact that there was a long distance between here and Whitley Bay and so obviously, visits could only be in school holidays. She went on to explain that we'd be seeing Mum during each of the main holidays and each half term holiday with Mum and Dad meeting half way to take us and to bring us back. In between times, if it was possible, Mum would come down to see us in Welshpool but that would depend on whether she would be able to make arrangements with her friend and as Carol said, if she could afford the cost of the journey. Visits to see Mum wouldn't be for half the holidays because it was important that she had enough time off from work to be able to take care of us. However, there would be at least two weeks in the summer and a week at other times in the main holidays and half of each half term.

Carol went on to explain that if Mum and Dad decided in the future that one of them wanted all the October half term and the other wanted all the February half term, then that would be okay but it would be up to them to decide amicably between them, the court wouldn't expect them to come back to court to make any adjustments. Likewise, if Mum planned to drive all the way to Welshpool so that she could see her friends rather than meet halfway, then maybe Dad would drive to Whitley Bay to fetch us back. It was expected that there would be flexibility and parental give and take which would work around us.

It all sounded so easy, but that was what it was meant to be like; I guessed the reality was going to be very different. Even at thirteen, I could see that. Jonty immediately said, "What if I don't want to go? What if I don't like it? What if I don't want to leave Dad?" His questions spilled out, a bit of a jumble but nevertheless giving a very clear picture of his confusion and his fear of upsetting Dad.

"Of course it won't be that easy for you Jonty, nor for you Hetty," Carol said reassuringly. "The judge stressed that there's an expectation on your mum and dad to try to get things right for you and that you've both suffered enough and that's not fair." Carol made it clear that the judge had heard through her what we were saying and listened to the concerns we'd voiced and had also heard directly from Mum and Dad and what they believed we wanted. Carol explained that parents so often just couldn't see the situation through their children's eyes and really believed they knew what we wanted mirrored their own wishes. That had become clear during the two days and helped the judge to understand how painful it was for us.

The judge's final decision was based on her analysis of all that she had heard and she had stressed that there was an expectation that everyone would make the new arrangements work. It wasn't for Jonty and me to have to decide every time we were due to see Mum whether or not we would go. Dad knew what the arrangements were and it was up to him to help us to make sure that it happened. As Carol talked, I felt a sense of relief. Jonty looked okay too. I just hoped with every bit of me that Dad would be reasonable, was that really too much to ask? I couldn't bear it when he got angry – that's when to stop the risk of him not loving me I either agreed with him or fell silent – the words I so wanted to say remaining jammed in my throat choking me. Of course, it meant he just went on believing I shared his negative views of Mum. In spite of that, I felt so much better talking to Carol. She was so calm, so reasonable and she knew how both Jonty and I were struggling. She was our life buoy, the one person who would keep us afloat in this raging sea of emotions.

Carol drove us both home. Dad obviously knew that she was meeting us and that she was explaining the future plans to us. His car was parked on the drive, I was scared, really scared. What was he going to say? Would he be angry? I couldn't bear that. Would he rant and rave and say nasty things about Mum? "Go on," said Carol, "go on, in you go." And with a quick wave, she'd gone. Dad greeted us with a big smile on his face.

"Come on kids, I've done bangers and mash for tea. Beans okay for you both?" He didn't mention Mum, nor the court case, nor seeing Carol, and so we didn't either. It just sort of like, melted into the background. I can see now that that's what he intended, it was just his clever way of gradually erasing Mum, but I didn't see it at the time, I just felt an enormous sense of relief that he wasn't angry.

And that's how it went on for the next few weeks. He just never mentioned her and so neither did we, it just seemed easier that way. But of course it wasn't, not really. True, on one level it caused less hassle but all my fears whirred around in my head.

The date when Mum was moving came nearer and nearer. Jonty was seeing Mum again but he never mentioned her going and he no longer talked to her in the way that he used to. There seemed a sort of distance between them. Oh yes, he chatted all right but it was all superficial about the stuff he'd been doing at school and at karate and swimming and his best mate. Oh and of course what he'd been doing with Dad and how wonderful Dad was. I used to watch Mum and I saw this sadness in her eyes when she looked at Jonty like she knew she'd already lost him. Could I have done more – was it my fault? At thirteen, I lacked the insight to really understand how it was for Jonty and so I heaped blame upon myself and as I did, my confidence and self-assurance slipped even further away.

Mum and I did talk. We made the most of Wednesdays when Jonty wasn't there. She didn't say much about the court hearing other than she was relieved that the judge seemed to understand why she was moving and had seen how important it was that there was regular contact and for the arrangements to be defined, as otherwise it would be difficult to make them happen. She'd been disappointed that there really had been no choice but for the order to say we lived with Dad. She'd explained, just as Carol had, that we were spending most of our time there so that's what the reality was, but when Mum told us, I knew that she was bitterly disappointed. She assured us that it was written in the court order that she should play an important part in any decisions about us like schools we attended but the way she said it, I just got the impression she thought she was fighting a losing battle. Like me, she knew Dad was a winner, he never lost and he never backed down.

20 July is a date that will always remain imprinted in my head – the date that my mum moved away. It softened the blow slightly knowing that we were going to spend the first week of August in Whitley Bay with her although I still had this nagging doubt that Dad would somehow find a reason for it not to happen. I'd said goodbye the night before and so had Jonty, we'd clung to Mum with tears streaming down our faces. I'd wanted to go and wave her off the next day but Dad arranged for us to set off early to visit our uncle for a few days so we weren't even going to be there. So Mum left Shrewsbury without us. I cannot describe the feeling that I had knowing that my mum was no longer around the corner from school and only half an hour from Welshpool, that empty, empty hollow feeling which Dad was oblivious to. He just seemed really bright and cheerful as though he'd shaken her off, she was an irritating fly and she was gone. He didn't have to think about her any more, he didn't even mention her going, he just asked me why I was so miserable. Did he really not know? I couldn't tell him, that was for sure. What was the point? He'd have laughed at me. I couldn't bear that. Of course, he must have known, I realise that now – it was part

of his plan to quietly erase Mum and to win – just like he always did.

Chapter 32

We had a good time at my uncle's, we always did. It was great being with our cousins but I wanted to get back home. I couldn't wait to see if there was a letter from Mum, surely there would be. I tried not to let Dad know that I was so keen but I couldn't stop myself rushing in and rifling through the pile of post on the mat. "Hey, whoa, steady on there," Dad said, as he snatched the pile from my hands.

"But I wanted to see –"

"Haa, remember what we said, Hetty? I need to read any letter that comes from your mum and then of course I'll let you have it. But we need to make sure she isn't writing stuff that will upset you – you know how she plays the victim – 'poor little me'. I have to protect you from getting hurt."

I guessed that the green envelope with Mum's distinctive spidery writing on it was the one I so desperately wanted. I craned my neck to see if it was a Newcastle or Whitley Bay postmark but Dad covered it with his hand. "Don't worry, I'll pass any letter on to you after I've checked it over."

"But, but –"

"No but, young lady, it's what's best – you know that. I have to make sure you are safe. We can't trust that mum of yours; you know that as well as anyone."

I didn't dare argue with him, I couldn't risk making him angry but I couldn't get it out of my head. I fell out with Jonty a couple of times that evening, I wanted my letter. It wasn't fair, but then of course Dad was just protecting me – or was he? Conflicting thoughts tormented me. It was just before bedtime when Dad finally handed Mum's letter to me. "Oh well, she seems to be settling herself in. But don't forget, I want to read what you write back. I don't want you writing a load of rubbish to her. Remember I've got your best interests at heart, young lady, and I know you sometimes get a bit carried away. Don't be too soft on her, she's the one who's left you; you know that and now she's gadding around up there and having a good time. I doubt she has much time to think of us down here."

I ran upstairs with my letter. The tears ran down my face as I read it, it was like Mum was in the room with me. I could hear her voice and feel her arms around me. I shut my eyes and there she was right there with me. In her letter, she told me all about her new job, describing people she worked with and what she was doing and how lovely it was at Whitley Bay. She was sure Jonty and I would enjoy beachcombing for shells and even fossils and at low tide, we could walk across the causeway to St Mary's lighthouse. Her descriptions were so vivid that I could picture it all even though I'd never been. 'Only a couple more weeks and then I'll be seeing you both and we'll have a whole week together to relax and have fun'. She was counting off the days.

I tried to share her excitement but I had this nagging, nagging doubt, would our holiday in Whitley Bay even happen? Dad never mentioned Mum and Jonty only mentioned her to me when we were alone, never when Dad was around. It was like she was fading away. Maybe Dad would forget all about our planned holiday or knowing how much he hated Mum, he might refuse to take us. I wanted to share all my worries and fears with Mum but there wasn't much point if Dad was going to censor my letter so what I did write was pretty sterile and stilted. I gave it to Dad and his comment: "Mmm, seems like you're getting the message, Hetty, it's good to see you're not being quite as kind to your mum as you usually are, you're usually all soft and sentimental and so easily won over by her whining and playing the victim. Perhaps at last you're seeing through her and realise the games she plays." I was horrified, of course I wasn't feeling any different about Mum, but I couldn't find the words to protest and I guess my silence reinforced his belief that I shared his twisted, hateful view of Mum.

The night before the planned visit, I was so excited but scared, oh so scared. Jonty had been umming and ahhing all the week saying he wasn't going and then he was. He had very begrudgingly packed his case. Dad had left it up to us to sort our stuff. He didn't buy us any new clothes and he didn't even check that everything we needed was washed. So I sorted it out as best as I could for me and for Jonty. I guessed if we ran short, Mum would get us some new things. I longed for Dad to say something, anything about our week with Mum but I waited in vain he said nothing other than to tell us he'd miss us and to make sure we really wanted to go. No words of encouragement, nothing to reassure Jonty.

Dad had begrudgingly agreed to drive to the Hartshead Moor Services car park that Carole had suggested even though he reminded us twice the night before the holiday that he was actually driving further than Mum which demonstrated how kind and considerate he was even though Mum had chosen to desert us. He had been quite emphatic that although he'd do it this time, he and Mum would have to reconsider arrangements next time. I'd looked up how long the journey would take. I was pretty convinced it would be nearly three hours but Dad insisted that we'd do it in far less time. There wasn't any point arguing with him. I couldn't win.

The next day, I was up bright and early and unusually, Dad was late coming downstairs and then Jonty was in a really grumpy mood and nothing would make him hurry. I wanted to scream 'please, please I want to see my mum' but of course I kept silent willing them both to be ready to leave on time. Just as we were about to get in the car, Jonty decided he needed the loo again and that was another ten minutes' delay, I was fuming. And then, blow me if Dad didn't decide that he needed to make an urgent phone call. By then, I was seething inside but I was also so scared, what if Mum got there and we weren't there? She might just go, she might not wait. 'Of course she'd wait' my little voice told me. 'Don't be ridiculous, Hetty'. Dad normally drove fast but this time he stuck rigidly to the speed limit. In response to my 'Dad aren't you driving slowly?' he tapped the speedometer and said, "It's a 70 mile an hour limit, Hetty. I'm not going to break the law, am I?"

"But you –"

"But I what?"

"Aaaa…" I never finished what I was going to say. There was no point – Dad put some music on so there was no need to talk. Jonty was engrossed in his Game Boy.

We got to the car park almost twenty minutes late. "There she is, there she is." I was really excited and all my fears vanished and my heart was thumping wildly with excitement.

"Yes, I can see her rubbish old car," Dad remarked. Mum had parked on the far side of the car park and although the car park was nearly empty, Dad still chose a spot on the opposite side.

"But… Dad…"

"If she wants you to come and stay, she'll have to come over and fetch you, won't she?" he smiled.

Jonty slid down in the seat. "Come on, Jonty," I said, "get your stuff, let's go."

"Aha, whoa there you two. I'm not having you running around a busy car park, that wouldn't be safe. Your mum can come over here when she's ready and then –"

"I'm not going!" shouted Jonty, immersed in his Game Boy, "I don't want to."

Dad's response scared me. "It's entirely up to you and Hetty whether you go or not. I'm not stopping you but equally I'm not forcing either of you." Carol's promises that the judge had made it clear Dad had to make it work were a joke, as usual he'd do what he wanted. He unfolded his newspaper and began reading it, leaving us sitting there in the back of the car. There was no sign of Mum.

"Please, please Mum, come over please," I silently begged her, wiping the tears from my cheek. Then I saw her – she'd been to the loo and was running across the car park. She must have guessed that Dad would choose a spot miles away to park but his silver BMW was pretty distinctive.

Dad had pressed the child locks so I couldn't even open the door. "Dad, Dad, let me get out, please, please," I begged.

Reluctantly, he pressed the button. I leapt out. Mum had got a big smile on her face and she held her arms out and I ran into them. I smelt that lovely mum smell as her arms closed around me. It was magic, absolute magic. But then, I pushed away. Panic over came me, I was scared, Dad was watching me. I couldn't let him see how much I cared about Mum, he'd be angry and then, and then... I pushed those thoughts out of my head. I turned back to the car. "Come on, Jonty," I said, "come on."

"I don't want to go," he mouthed through the window and dropped his head. But then, he looked up and saw Mum, his stony face quivered – there were tears in his eyes.

"Why don't we all go and get a cup of tea," said Mum brightly.

"Only if my dad can come," said Jonty. "I can't leave my dad, I want my dad."

"Please Dad, please, please. Let's all go to the café and have a drink," I implored. It was worth a try – anything to get Jonty on side.

"Oomph," Dad sighed. "I suppose I've got no choice. Is that okay, Jonty? It's up to you, mate. There's no pressure on you." Of course Dad wasn't going to encourage Jonty, I knew that but I wanted it to be different.

It took ages for Dad to get out of the car and for Jonty to follow him. Mum and I walked ahead. She had her arm through mine and I felt a strange mix of delight and discomfort, conscious that Dad was behind us. We got to the café and I watched Dad and Jonty go to a table over by the window whilst I went with Mum to the counter. I knew what they'd want, diet coke for Jonty and a cappuccino for Dad. We took the drinks over and Mum tried her best to make bright conversation. Dad barely spoke and although Jonty didn't exactly ignore her, he wasn't particularly forthcoming. It felt so awkward. I just willed Dad to go so that both of us could go off with Mum but of course, our bags were still in the car. Mum chatted about Whitley Bay and was clearly trying to capture Jonty's attention. He looked half-interested but there was no way he was going to let Dad believe he was really bothered about seeing Mum. I was angry with him but at the same time, I felt desperately sorry; it was hard for me and I realised it must be a million times harder for him.

Eventually, we went back to the car, Mum made several attempts to talk directly to Jonty. First he said yes, he'd come but only for two days, he wanted Dad to come up and fetch him and of course Dad refused. So then he said he'd come next time but he didn't want to come this time. I wanted Mum to try and persuade him, I wanted her to shout at Dad and tell him that it wasn't fair, but she didn't. She just shrugged her shoulders and said, "Okay then, well if that's what you want. You know how much I love you, Jonty; I just want us all to be happy." She just seemed to roll over and give in. I hated it, I hated her, I hated what was going on but said nothing. I just grabbed my bag and gave Dad an enormous hug and then ruffled Jonty's hair. "I'll see you next Saturday, okay then?"

Dad's parting shot was, "Well, you know where I am, Hetty, if you need to come home earlier, make sure you tell your mum and ring me and I'll meet you. Don't forget. I know how hard this will be for you and how brave you are."

Brave! Hard! What did he know about it? He didn't understand at all. But I loved him and needed him and saying goodbye was much harder than I thought it would be. As we walked back to Mum's car, Dad swooped by. There was no sign of Jonty, he must have been hiding in the back engrossed in his Game Boy again. I guessed he'd be really sad and just as confused as I was. But at least I could relax and just be me with my mum. I knew we'd have a fantastic time, I just knew. But I also knew that when I went back to Dad, I'd make out that it was difficult being with Mum and I hadn't really enjoyed it. Is that what it was always going to be like from now on? Is that how we'd be for the next few years until I was old enough to make my own mind up about when I went and saw either of them? Is this what they'd done to me?

Chapter 33

Although Mum's house was small, in the middle of a terrace it was just off the sea front. It was absolutely fantastic being two minutes from the promenade, then down the steps and on the beach, the soft sand, the rock pools and the waves rolling and breaking. Mum and I spent ages searching amongst the rock pools beachcombing, picnicking and walking along the shore to the north side and St Mary's Island. When the tide was out, we walked across the causeway to the lighthouse. It was magical and Mum knew so much about the area, including the best fish and chip shop and who sold the biggest ice creams. We walked into the town centre trying out cafés and browsing around the shops. It was a bustling little place. I guess in winter it would be a bit dead but with the summer visitors, I loved it. We explored further afield too driving up the coast to Bamford with its castle and sand dunes and we had a great day out at the castle and walkways at Alnwick. We went into Newcastle on the Metro and I loved it all – I was so happy for my mum – she seemed so different – relaxed and more confident like the old mum I remembered from a long time ago.

There wasn't time to talk about Jonty or Dad, or even much about Welshpool or Shrewsbury until the last night. Mum was sitting on the bed as I was reluctantly packing my things ready to go the next morning when suddenly she burst out with, "I've been looking at the grammar schools around here, they're really good, Hetty, why don't you think about coming and living here?"

I looked at her aghast. "But Mum, Dad wouldn't want to, he wouldn't want to move again."

"I don't mean all of you, I mean just you. Why don't you come and live here with me?"

"But, but Mum," I panicked. A bit of me wanted to say yes, yes, of course I will, but then the image of Dad flashed before my eyes, a furiously angry Dad who'd no longer love me. "But Mum, that's not fair, you shouldn't ask me that. It's not fair, it's not fair. I hate you, I hate you." The words just spilled out, the anger, the frustration, the fear. Mum tried to put it right, but somehow the spell was broken. I pushed her away rejecting her hugs and kisses and with a sinking feeling, I knew then that it was never going to be the same between Mum and me. Life would always be a see-saw with Mum or Dad fighting to be up on top and watching the other one crashing down to the ground and of course I knew that it would always be Mum thudding to the ground because Dad couldn't lose, he always made sure he was the winner.

The next day, we arrived at the service station before Dad. We sat in an awkward silence, I could see that Mum was fighting back the tears and wasn't surprised when suddenly she blurted out, "I'm going to try and come down in September for a weekend and then hopefully I'll be able to see you. It's such a long time 'til the October half term and I don't think I can wait that long, Hetty."

"That'd be great Mum, that'd be great." I really meant it. I missed her so much but it was just Dad – he got in the way. I was relieved she didn't mention anything more about me living at Whitley Bay. I flung my arms around her and we hugged. "Oh Mum, I miss you so much. I wish you'd never moved away. I know it was hard but it's so hard you not being in Welshpool or Shrewsbury anymore."

"I know, my pet, there just wasn't a perfect answer, but come on, we've had a great time and I can't tell you how sorry I am asked you about coming to live here. I know that you can't, whatever you really want doesn't count, your dad just wouldn't let you go, it just wouldn't work. I'm sorry I made it even harder for you."

She hugged me close and then we saw Dad's car swooping into the car park. "Quick, quick." I broke free and fumbled for the door latch. We walked across the tarmac and Dad made a big show and fuss of me flinging his arms around me and sweeping me off the ground. It was embarrassing really and I could see Mum standing awkwardly alongside. Jonty was pleased to see me again, but he seemed tongue tied around Mum, I guess he felt guilty because he hadn't been to stay and no doubt he'd missed her just as much as I did – he just couldn't let on. "Come on, we can't hang around," said Dad, "we need to be off. It's a long drive." Mum went to hug me but I resisted, instead giving her a small peck on the cheek and then we were gone.

Dad didn't even mention my trip he was too busy describing in detail exciting activities he and Jonty had enjoyed. I guessed he wanted me to be jealous and to think I'd missed out. What really hurt was how he kept making such a big fuss of Jonty. A bit of me panicked, convinced that Dad didn't love me as much because I'd been to Mum's and he was punishing me 'cos I'd been disloyal to him. I knew it wasn't fair but I didn't want to let myself blame him, I didn't want to think badly of him, I didn't want to get angry. Why? Because it was too dangerous 'cos I feared losing him.

We knew that for the rest of the holidays, Dad was taking time off work or else working at home so he could always be around for us. But we never expected what came next. I'd only been back a couple of days when he suddenly announced that Amy was coming to stay. "Amy? Who's Amy?" we both chorused.

"Well, she's a friend of mine and she's coming to stay for a few days, she's really nice, you'll love her."

"Who is she, Dad? We've never heard of her?" Jonty and I were intrigued.

"Well, you'll soon see. She's arriving later."

"What? Today?"

"Yes, she's driving up from Cardiff, that's where she lives. She's got a lovely house right down by the sea."

"Oh, you mean like –"

"No, I don't mean like your mum's little shack. Amy lives in Cardiff and she's got a luxury flat overlooking the harbour."

"Cor, Dad – that sounds fantastic," said Jonty. "You mean she goes sailing and surfing and all the stuff like that?"

"Well, I'm sure she does and she'll probably invite you all to stay."

"Cor, that'd be great," said Jonty.

A bit of me was aghast. So, Jonty would happily go and visit this Amy, whoever she was, but he wouldn't come and stay at Mum's. I knew I shouldn't be bitter and angry but I was.

Amy arrived later that day. She was nothing like I expected. Although she was old, she was loads younger than Dad with long, glossy, brown hair and she wore really tight jeans and heels and her long nails were painted a gorgeous shade of green. She'd got the sort of makeup which looks professional with really big eyes and her silvery top made her look sort of glamorous. Nothing like Mum; she was always in jeans and a tee shirt or sweater with trainers and just looked comfy and casual and mum-like. Dad had described Amy as just a friend, but when she arrived, he gave her a big hug and a few minutes later when I went in the kitchen, there they were in this embrace and Dad's hand was running up and down her back and they were kissing – proper kissing like on films. It was sort of uuurrggh horrible. I ran upstairs, I didn't know what to make of it but I knew that Amy wasn't just a friend; I wasn't stupid of course Amy was Dad's girlfriend. Amy was Mum's replacement. Amy was the person who Dad wanted to be with and I was supposed to like her. Well I didn't, I hated her. Dad did a barbeque that evening and if I'm honest, I'd have to admit that Amy tried her best to chat to me and Jonty. It sort of worked with Jonty; after all it was pretty easy to win him over when she talked about surfing and jumping the crashing waves on the beach, he was really impressed. I knew I was being rude when I hardly mumbled a word in response to her questions and sat there glaring, refusing to join in. I could see that Dad was annoyed with me but I couldn't help it. I hated her.

That night after Jonty and I had come up to bed, Dad came into my room. He stood there with his arms folded across this chest. "I'm really disappointed in you, Hetty. I thought you were a bit more grown up than that. I've got every right to move on in my life, you know that. My wife's ditched me for someone else and Amy's someone special. She understands me and it's not a constant struggle to keep her happy like it was with your mum. She's fun and she enjoys life."

"But I didn't even know she existed, Dad," I said in my defence, "it seems like she's moved in and taken over."

"Don't be ridiculous, of course she hasn't taken over. But yes, Amy and I want to spend a lot of time together so you're just going to have to get used to her and stop being such a selfish little girl." His words stung just as they were meant to. It was always the same with Dad, if you didn't agree with him, he made you feel so uncomfortable and so unwanted so you just caved in.

"But Dad, I was just scared of losing you."

"Don't be ridiculous and so dramatic, Hetty, of course you won't lose me." Briefly, his smile returned and he ran his fingers through my hair. "I know how much you love me. I know how hard it was going away last week and staying with your mum, you were really brave to do that but don't worry you're not going to have to go that often, you did it for her. I know all this silliness is because you feel so insecure having gone to your mum's and no doubt you've been bombarded all week with her moans and groans. But don't worry, I want to make it up to you. We're going to have a really good time and Amy's such good fun you'll adore her and she loves doing all the sorts of exciting activities you like doing so come on, let's dry those eyes." I let Dad hug me and stroke my hair. I wanted to feel reassured, I wanted to feel loved, but I knew that Dad just didn't have a clue about how I felt about Mum. He'd dismissed her, she was his ex and he expected me to do the same. Like he said, he'd moved on and that's what he expected Jonty and me to do. I guess he felt he'd almost succeeded with Jonty and that it wouldn't be long before I followed suit. After all, I was his puppet on a string.

Amy stayed for several days and I tried hard to hate her, it felt disloyal to Mum unless I did. But, you know, I couldn't help but like her. She was such good fun, a good laugh and Dad seemed so much more relaxed and happier when she was about. I tried to keep thoughts of Mum pushed out of my mind; it was easier that way – in fact, the only way.

A letter from Mum arrived on the Friday. I saw it on the mat and went to pick it up but Dad got there first. "Whoa, my young lady, you know the rules." And he snatched it up before I could. He hadn't given it to me by that afternoon but instead broached the subject whilst Amy was there. "I'm concerned about the letter your mum has sent, Hetty. I think it might be a bit confusing for you and Jonty."

"What do you mean? What do you mean, Dad? Confusing? I want my letter. I want to know what Mum's writing to me, please."

"Well, it seemed to have slipped your mind to tell me that she's been asking you to go and live with her in Whitley Bay. That's just not on, it's totally out of order and I'm not having it. He banged his fist onto the table, the letter clutched between his fingers. No wonder you arrived back here in a state, all that pressure she'd heaped on you. Selfish bitch, as usual it's all about her. No, I need to deal with this officially and nip it in the bud before she gets any other ideas."

"But Dad –"

"No, no, no buts, I know how difficult she's made it for you. You're so brave, Hetty, but sadly not always very tough when your mum is playing victim. I'm going to make sure it doesn't happen again. I'm not having you going up there if she's going to put pressure on you like that. Trust her to do it when Jonty isn't around. She knew Jonty would say something to me straightaway, but you're always the softie, aren't you?" Amy put her hand out to catch hold of mine; I pulled it away, I didn't want her giving me a cuddle.

"My Mum and Dad split up when I was about your age," she persisted. "I know how hard it is but your dad's right, it's not fair if your mum's putting a lot of pressure on you to go and stay there when it's already been decided that you're living here. Let your dad sort it out, Hetty." I hated her – how dare she interfere? But of course, I said nothing in Mum's defence. 'Coward' muttered my little voice. 'You're weak, a coward – as bad as your dad'. I tried to push the thoughts away, but I was scared.

I didn't quite know what Dad meant by 'sort it out officially' but I soon found out. The next evening, Dad told us he'd been to his solicitor who had immediately sent a letter to Mum reminding her in no uncertain terms of the details of the final court order and warning her not to pressure Jonty or me to make changes or there would be serious consequences. I guessed Mum would be so upset but worse was to come. Dad insisted that Jonty and I had to sit down and write a letter to Mum saying that we were very happy living in Forden and under no circumstances did we want to live in Whitley Bay. "But Dad –"

"There's no buts, Hetty, we need to nip this in the bud and stop it before it gets hold. As I say, I don't want your mum upsetting you." And so like the good little girl I wanted him to believe I was, I wrote the letter. I hated myself, I felt I'd let Mum down and myself. I just hoped that Mum would know that I didn't hate her. Jonty's letter was abrupt, just simply 'I want to live with Dad, I want to live in Welshpool. Jonty'. Of course I wanted my letter to be much more gentle and I didn't care that Jonty got the Brownie points. "Well done, old man, straight to the point, good for you. Come on, Hetty, just get on with it." What choice did I have? I convinced myself none – but the nagging voice 'coward, traitor' drummed into my head, as I wrote telling Mum that I needed to stay in Welshpool 'cos of school and my friends. I felt awful, but I did it.

I guess that was the turning point, things were never going to be the same again and I think Mum probably realised that she was fighting a losing battle, she would always have an uphill struggle, everything she said or did would be deliberately misconstrued by Dad and used against her. I didn't realise that at the time but I can see now that it wasn't a case of her not being strong enough, it was that Dad was a bully who expected and demanded to be worshipped by everyone and if you pushed him off his perch, he'd simply crush you. That's what he'd done to Mum and he'd do it to me too. Except that I needed him, I couldn't survive without him, so I did as I was told. A bit of me admired Mum – she'd broken free; I couldn't even bear to think about doing it myself.

Chapter 34

We spent the last week of the holiday down in Cardiff staying in Amy's flat. I'd imagined it to be just a little bedsit, but it wasn't, it was huge. She owned a nail studio in the city. It was clear that she and Dad were smitten with each other and they wanted to spend every weekend together. Of course, it meant that Amy planned to come up to stay with us because of our horse riding and Tae Kwon Do but she didn't seem to mind, other people ran the studio when she wasn't there. I would just have to get used to her always being there – a wedge between Dad and me and of course I resented her.

Dad and Mum must have had words because Mum's letters from then on just seemed flat and impersonal, full of news about places she'd been to but nothing about her or our relationship or future plans. She didn't mention coming down again in September like she'd promised me. I was disappointed and it was hard writing back to her, it felt like she was slipping away, but oh I missed her so much. I'd sit looking at the photos of us together at Whitley Bay which she had sent to me reminding me of the fun times we'd had. That holiday had meant so much; little did I know then that there would never be another holiday like that.

I had expected that we'd have half of the October half term holiday with Mum and I was really shocked when Dad said, "Do you remember when the judge made the court order, she said that one of us could have all of the October holiday and the other the February holiday? Well, your mum and I have agreed to swap so you're spending all the October holiday with me so we can go to Cardiff again for a week."

"Great!" said Jonty. "That'll be fantastic!"

"But what about Mum?!" I screamed.

"Oh come on, Hetty, don't tell me you'd rather spend a freezing cold October in Whitley Bay rather than having a fantastic time in Cardiff again? Come on – there's no contest!"

"But I was looking forward to seeing Mum," I mumbled.

"Oh come on or you're going to spoil it for all of us," was Dad's crushing remark.

I knew I wasn't going to get any sympathy from Dad. Why had Mum just agreed to swap like that? Little did I know that she hadn't had any choice, Dad had simply told her that was going to happen and if she didn't like it, she'd have to go back to court and of course she couldn't do that, she couldn't afford to. He had her over a barrel – absolutely stitched up.

Yes, I'm almost ashamed to say that we did have an exciting time down in Cardiff. The weather was quite good and with wetsuits on, the sea still felt warm enough. We had learned a bit about surfing the first time we'd been down, so were much more confident this time and yes, it was good fun. But I had to keep pushing thoughts of Mum out of my mind, I had to stop myself daydreaming about her because if I did, I just felt so incredibly sad and then so desperately guilty. I didn't dare mention her to Dad because it put him in such a bad mood if I did. Even Jonty didn't want to talk about her, it was like she was gradually evaporating, disappearing and soon I feared she'd be gone.

At the end of the week, Dad and Amy said that they'd got something really important to talk to us about and we were going to go out for a special meal and then they'd tell us. I think a bit of me guessed what they were going to say so it wasn't really any great surprise when they told us that they loved each other and that they were going to move in together. But because Amy had got her studio, Dad was going to relocate, with us, down to Cardiff. "But, but…" I didn't finish. One huge thought leapt into my mind – *Mum*. "But what about Mum? What does she say?" I blurted out to Dad. He immediately misunderstood my hesitation.

"It's okay, I've had an offer for my business and with my experience, I'll be head hunted in no time. There are plenty of really good schools so you and Jonty can transfer without a problem, there's so many more sporting opportunities; it'll be great living by the sea. We'll have a fantastic life together. After all you've been through, you deserve as much as I do to be happy and settled."

I looked at an atlas later on to see how far it was from Whitley Bay to Cardiff, it was 325 miles – however was I going to see my mum? How was I going to live without Suzie and the school that I depended on? Everything I'd always known was in Welshpool and Shrewsbury and now I was going to lose that as well as losing my mum. It felt like my whole world was disintegrating beneath my feet. A huge weight was crushing me, squashing me. I felt suffocated, I couldn't breathe. I wanted to be a little girl again, a little girl without any worries, without any troubles, with a mum and dad who loved me and I could love them, both of them. I didn't want all this bad stuff, all these difficult decisions I had to make. Except the reality was that they were always made for me by Dad so I never got a say, not really.

My life just felt out of control, I was on a merry go round and whirring faster and faster and faster. I wanted to get off, I wanted to stop but I was rooted to the spot and couldn't move.

I never made a conscious decision to stop eating but I missed a couple of meals and the hunger pangs gave me this sense of freedom, a light headed, floaty sort of feeling and somehow I felt that I was in control of me. I guess looking back, I can see that was the start of a downward spiral which all too quickly took over control. I couldn't stop it. All those feelings of power soon became a hopeless powerlessness. Depriving myself of food, feeling that deep gnawing hunger which I couldn't allow myself to quell became all consuming, but at least it blotted out the pain of losing my mum and everything I'd ever known.

Chapter 35

We went home the next day and Mum's letter was on the mat. Of course I was pleased that it had arrived but at the same time I was angry; angry with Dad for disrupting my life but angry with Mum too. Did she know that Dad was going to take us to Cardiff to live? If so, why hadn't she done anything about it? I knew it wasn't fair to blame her, but it was easier to direct my anger towards her rather than Dad. I wanted her, I needed her but I needed Dad more. I knew Dad would vet the letter and was panicking a bit when Sunday afternoon arrived before Dad gave it to me. "Well, it seems like she's making an effort and coming down. Fancy that. She must have a free weekend, perhaps her boyfriend is busy. But let's wait and see; she's full of empty promises."

I grabbed the letter quickly and sure enough, Mum was coming to Welshpool next weekend. She was driving down early on Saturday and she had Monday off. She planned to pick us up after our Saturday activities and spend all of Sunday with us. She said she'd get Dad to agree for us to go out for a meal and come back later on Sunday evening. Did she really believe it would happen just like that? Or was it like Dad said just 'empty promises' designed to make us like her?

My hunch proved right and Dad soon scotched any idea of co-operating. "Huh, let's be clear about this, she fits around us. And that doesn't mean expecting Jonty to go if he doesn't want to. I'm not having him put under any pressure by her and of course there's no question you'll be back by five o'clock at the latest on Sunday, you've got school the next day. You need to be fresh for that and you need to get your homework finished off. You know what a rush Sunday evenings are."

I knew it was a lame excuse but I didn't know what to say. The best I could muster was, "But Dad, I'm not a baby, surely coming back for half past eight is okay. Just once!"

"Huh, no Hetty, not on your life it would set a precedent. Give that mother of yours an inch and she'll take a mile. That's her, that's how she operates. It's always about her and what she wants and needs, she just expects us to drop everything to fit around her. Well for once, I'm standing firm and not being taken for a mug."

I knew how unfair Dad was being but I'm ashamed to say that I couldn't even argue with him. A bit of me realised that was exactly how it had been for Mum and still was. She'd just got nothing left to fight with and that, she had no alternative but to accept whatever he said. And now, I was doing the same. I hated myself, I was rubbish, I was horrible – a really horrible person – I didn't deserve to be happy, I'd caused so much misery.

I guess missing meals just became part of my life because all that pain and sadness about Mum and Dad sort of melted away when instead I felt a gnawing empty ache in my stomach, a dizzy light headedness which somehow gave me a tiny glimpse of being in control. That's what beating my hunger did for me. I curled up in bed holding my rumbling stomach and was overwhelmed by flashes of crispy fish and sizzling chips, of chocolate éclairs oozing with cream; food I'd always loved but now I denied myself. I felt a sense of power, of being in control and my pain melted away.

A bit of me knew how dangerous the path I was treading was. I was losing weight fast but I just couldn't stop depriving myself of food because that would let my demons loose and give them space to torment me until my head exploded. Of course, my weight loss didn't go unnoticed. Meal times had always been haphazard since Mum left and more so since we moved back to Welshpool. In fact, we didn't always sit down together to eat so it was very easy to miss a meal and then lie to Dad. But he soon commented, "You've lost weight, Hetty."

I brushed it off. "Yes. It must have been puppy fat; I guess it just goes naturally at my age."

"You look a bit pale," Dad carried on. "Maybe you need a boost, I tell you what, I'll get Amy to suggest something suitable." Bloody Amy! What does he have to ask her for? I wanted to hate her, it just made it so much easier even though a bit of me really liked being with her and I actually liked the dad that I had when they were together. But that was being disloyal to Mum and... Oh, help please help, I can't go on like this, my life it just seems such a mess and it's all my fault.

The following Saturday was bright and sunny, quite surprising for a November day. When I finished my riding lesson, I looked up and there was Mum standing by the office. I ran to her and flung my arms around her. "Oh Het, I've missed you so much," she whispered. I saw her looking quizzically at me. "Gosh you've lost weight, Hetty."

I tried to brush her comments away. "Well, maybe a pound or two, it's just natural for me to lose weight at my age."

She smiled and said, "Anyhow, let's make the most of our time together. I thought we could go to Montgomery Castle. I made some of that soup you love and I thought we call and get some chips to go with it."

"Oh, I've gone off chips Mum, but the soup, that'd be fine and maybe we can have some fruit or something." I didn't look at her because I knew that Mum could read me like a book, her mind would be whirring around thinking, 'What's going on here?' But she didn't say anything.

It was great climbing up to Montgomery Castle – we could see for miles around and it was somewhere that I'd always loved going to. We had our soup and a good tramp around. I challenged her about Dad's move demanding to know what she'd done to resist. She looked so hurt and so sad. "Yes, he told me, Hetty, he didn't ask me – it was all decided before he told me and believe me there's nothing I can do about it."

"But Mum, can't you go back to court? Can you fight him?" I knew it was futile but I just wanted her to. I don't know what I wanted her to do. I guess I just didn't want it to be so easy for Dad.

"Het, I can't fight any more, I really can't. I just don't have any strength left. Whatever I do, your dad just finds another way to undermine my relationship with you and with Jonty."

"But that's not fair, Mum, that really isn't fair. You're the one who moved away, Dad's only doing the same thing." I knew how hurtful my remarks were and hang on a minute, why was I defending him? I just seemed to bat from one to the other, that's why I was so screwed up and unhappy. It was futile to talk about it anymore and I guess both Mum and I realised that and we just wanted the rest of the time we had together to be good but I know we both kept our conversation superficial skirting around the issues that really mattered.

I was worried when we drove back to meet Jonty but Mum seemed quite buoyant and confident that he'd be fine. I didn't know what to expect. If Dad turned up, I was pretty sure that Jonty wouldn't even come with us. Mercifully, Dad wasn't around and Jonty came bouncing over to us and gave Mum a hug. The next few hours were just like old times. Jonty took a little while to relax but he was soon laughing and joking like the old Jonty. Before Mum dropped us off, she made arrangements to collect us from home the next day and I saw a look of panic cross Jonty's face. Although he didn't say anything, I just knew that it wouldn't be straightforward and I was even more certain that Dad wouldn't help.

I tried to chat with Jonty later but he just kept shaking his head and saying, "It's difficult, it's difficult with Dad you don't know how hard it is."

"I do know, but Jonty Mum loves you, you can't just give up on her. That's so mean and selfish."

"I can't just give up on Dad either. You're being horrible to him," said Jonty. "Now go away and leave me alone." And with that, he slammed his bedroom door shut. I guess he was just as screwed up as I was, but he showed it differently.

Dad was annoyed because I didn't want any breakfast the next day. "Don't be ridiculous, Hetty, you need to eat and if this is what it means when you go out with your mum, then I won't allow any more visits."

I grabbed an apple from the side. "Jonty, aren't you ready yet?!" I screamed outside his door.

"I've got tummy ache, I'm not sure I can come."

"Oh but Jonty, Mum will be so disappointed," I pleaded with him, I was frantic.

"It's not about Mum, it's about me. You know what Dad said, I haven't got to be put under any pressure. It's up to me to choose." He sounded just like Dad, not the Jonty I knew. I hated him then I felt an overwhelming anger – not with Jonty, but with Dad.

"But Jonty, we had such a good time yesterday. Look it's five to ten, Mum's outside, she's waiting to collect us. Please, please come!" The door remained firmly shut.

Dad stomped up the stairs. "I told you, Hetty, I'm not having Jonty put under any pressure, it's up to him to decide. Now Jonty, do you want to go or not?" Put like that what could he say? Well, it was obvious really.

"No, I don't want to, I don't want to go, Dad. I'm scared." I could hear Jonty sobbing and of course, Dad assumed it was because Jonty thought he was being forced against his will to see Mum. It never entered Dad's head that Jonty was as hurt and confused as I was.

"Right now, Hetty, no arguing, you heard what he's saying loud and clear. Off you go and tell your mum he doesn't want to come." So, that was it – just as I knew, Dad wasn't going to even attempt to encourage Jonty.

"But –"

"No buts, young lady. If you want to see your mum, that's up to you but Jonty's told you quite clearly he doesn't want to come. Off you go. And be back by half past five at the latest."

I could see Mum's disappointment. "Why don't you say something to Dad?" I asked her.

"Hetty, it's no good. I can't." I looked at her in amazement.

"You mean you're just going to give up on him?"

"It's not like that. You don't understand, you're a child."

"I'm not a child, I'm nearly fourteen, I know what I'm doing and I know what Dad's doing to you and it's not fair.

But why can't you do something? You're meant to be the grown up."

"Look, I know all this is too difficult for Jonty. I realise that and much as it hurts me not to even see him, I'm not going to make it worse for him by rowing with your dad. He knows I love him and that I always will and if it means that at the moment we can't see much of each other, then that's how it will be. I don't want him to hate me and believe me, Hetty, if I force him, then he will. I really don't want that, Hetty, believe me, there isn't any other way." Tears streamed down her face and she made no attempt to brush them away.

I looked at her in horror. A bit of me knew that what she said was right, but I had this overwhelming anger welling up inside me. I was angry with Dad, I knew that but I couldn't admit it; that was too dangerous so my anger spilled over onto Mum and I screamed at her, "That's so unfair, Mum! You're just blaming Dad for everything. You're the one who left, you're the one who ran away, you're the one who made Jonty feel like he didn't matter anymore." I knew it wasn't true and I knew that I was hurting her, but I didn't know how to stop the flow of words released from that burning anger threatening to destroy me.

In spite of that, we enjoyed our day together although if I'm honest, it was like a big black cloud hanging over us and I knew that sitting up on top of that big black cloud was Dad. We were all his puppets. He pulled the strings and we danced, we danced to his tune, there was no choice.

It was so hard saying goodbye to Mum at half past five. I didn't know when I'd see her again. Hopefully, sometime in the Christmas holidays, but there was no certainty in spite of the court order. According to Dad, that's when we were moving to Cardiff. I remember watching Mum drive off down the road, my heart gave a lurch. "I've already had my tea," I insisted, as soon as I got in. I hadn't but I needed to feel that hunger, I needed that to ease my pain.

"Well surprise, surprise, at least she got you here on time," said Dad barely giving me a second glance. But he didn't say anything else. He didn't ask me a thing about our day or how Mum was, it was like she just didn't exist.

Chapter 36

The autumn term went fast. I tried to blank out the realisation that we were going to move. I couldn't bear to consider how I was going to cope. I loved Suzie, she was the one person I would always rely on, she was always there for me, she knew me inside out so it didn't make sense that I kept falling out with her. One day she confronted me. "Hetty, I really don't know what's got into you. I know you're moving away, I know it's hard 'cos it is for me too. I know what's happened about your mum but why do you have to be so horrible to me? I thought we were friends, I thought we trusted each other. It just seems like you've closed up and don't want to talk and I'm really worried about you, Hetty, you've lost so much weight, you just seem, well, different somehow." I burst into tears.

"I just don't know how to go on, Suzie, I really don't. I don't know what to do. I don't know whether my dad's right and that my mum really doesn't want me, or whether it's like my head's telling me that's just not true, that it's my dad who doesn't want my mum to have me because he can't have her. It's all or nothing with Dad it always has been, but I just need him. I don't know how to even exist without him and I know it's like Jonty said ages ago if I have my mum, I can't have my dad and oh, Suzie, what shall I do?" It all just flooded out along with huge sobs, as I clung to her with my tears splashing onto her shirt collar.

Talking to Suzie of course didn't magic all my problems away but it made me feel a bit better about Mum and Dad. At least she understood how awful it was but my denial of food was a different story – a secret I kept locked away deep inside – my way of surviving – denying food and then not giving in to my hunger was a compulsion, an obsession. I needed that gnawing hunger and the power of refusing to satisfy it because then I felt like I wasn't losing control completely. It seems crazy now that I used refusing food, albeit subconsciously to help me cope with the pain of having to choose between my mum and dad and then losing everything that mattered to me.

There were hugs and tears and promises to keep in touch that last day of term. I shall never forget it. Suzie and I clung to each other. "I'll come and see you often," I promised, "and you must come and see me. Please, please Suzie, do come!"

"Of course, I will. I'm not going to forget my best friend, am I? But you'll make new friends at your new school, you're bound to and that will make it easier. She sounded so confident – so sure of herself – I was full of fears and self-doubt. And I'm sure your mum is going to make as many opportunities as she can to see you. At least there's a court order so your dad's got to honour the holidays."

She didn't know my dad. "I don't think he will, I don't think he could care less," I protested. "He knows that Mum can't go back to court, she can't afford it so what can she do about it?" I know I sounded defeatist but I'd lost faith in mum.

The move and settling in to Amy's flat went by in a daze. It was just before Christmas. What a stupid time to move. I just wanted to see my mum but Dad brushed the idea aside every time I even mentioned it. I hadn't had a letter for the last couple of weeks 'cos of our post being redirected, but maybe one had come and Dad hadn't let me have it. I just didn't know any more, I didn't trust either of them. I rang Mum a couple of times and on the second occasion, she told me that she and Dad had arranged for her to see me in Shrewsbury for a few days after Christmas, no going back to Whitley Bay. We'd be staying at Aunty Nicky's and going out with Mum on a couple of days. Dad had to tie up some business ends in Welshpool so he wasn't really doing Mum a favour as he insisted. Jonty and I went with him as planned and we all stayed at my aunty's. It was good to see her and Uncle Colin. Mum came down on the train because the weather was so unpredictable and I spent the day with her. I didn't even dare to mention to Dad that it was meant to be two days, he just got so angry. "I'm trying to settle us in our new home and get used to a new job, Hetty, how on earth do you think I have time or space to arrange for you to see your mum for more than one day? It's just not on, don't be ridiculous, you're lucky to even see her on one day. Can't you even be grateful? You're so selfish." His words stung, I hated it when he criticised me because when I wasn't what he wanted then I knew he didn't love me anymore. The looks he gave me were like the looks he used to give my mum. It felt like cold water pouring down my back and I was scared, really scared. Of course, Jonty came with us to Shrewsbury and he enjoyed seeing Aunty Nicky and Uncle Colin again but of course, he wanted to spend as much time as possible with his best friend in Welshpool. He begrudgingly agreed to see Mum with me so we could have lunch together in his favourite restaurant and wasn't at all bothered that the planned two-day visit was now just one day. He was excited about living in Cardiff and the prospect of going to a new school and being by the seaside, they were all just too tempting for him. They'd won him over.

Well, on the surface they had, but I can see now that he was hurting just as much as me, he just showed it differently. He immersed himself in all the new stuff so he could block out all the pain and hurt. That was his way of coping and of course, it secured his position with Dad. We were both going to a nearby private school so of course we had long school holidays and it was the second week of January when term began. The girls were all friendly and made me really welcome and it seemed like it was going to be okay but little did I realise that their initial enthusiasm would soon dissipate as they went back to their cliques and established friendship groups and I was left a hanger on, friends but on the outside of every group. I didn't have anybody special and I sank back into myself even more. I think the other girls probably thought I was a bit odd, the girl who never seemed to eat anything, a bit of a party pooper. I looked really thin by now but Dad was so wrapped up in his new relationship with Amy and settling

216

in to his new job that he hardly noticed. He just seemed to let me fend for myself much of the time. So not eating was easy and slowly, I became a slave to my obsession.

I'd always been clever and a high achiever and I was determined to do well academically, at least that would please Dad and he'd be so proud of me. I got good grades and was near the top of my form so it was something of a shock when at Parents' Evening, several members of staff expressed their concerns that they were worried that although I was academic I was so lacking in confidence, so introverted, so distant and so unwilling to put myself forward yet they were sure that I'd got hidden capabilities. They queried with Dad whether there were issues at home and of course that made him really angry; he hated people prying into what he called our personal life, it was private and always had been. I could sense his tension and saw the flush to his face as he brushed the suggestion aside, "No, no everything's fine but there are a few problems with her mother. She's gone off and abandoned her." I opened my mouth to try and speak but no words came out. I didn't even have the guts to defend my mum, I hated myself. Of course, the teachers thought that she was the problem and pitied me because I no longer had a mum who was either interested in or cared about me. Was that perhaps the best way of thinking about her? Would it make it less painful if I convinced myself that she really didn't care? It would please my dad. So yes, it would make life easier. I hated myself but I knew that that's what I was going to do. It was the only choice I had, so I grabbed it with both hands.

Chapter 37

Dad came to my room that evening after I'd gone to bed. He must have heard me sobbing. He sat beside me and put his hand on my head and stroked my hair. "What's up, my love?" It was just like having my old dad back, I could feel my heart thumping, I wanted to please him so the words just poured out.

"Oh Dad, I'm in just such a muddle and you know I've been thinking you're right, you've been right all along – I just didn't see it – I didn't want to but I know now. Mum clearly doesn't love us anymore, that's why she went away. I know you've always said that but I didn't want to believe it and I guess that's been upsetting me." I knew what I was saying was lies but I saw this look of pleasure – there wasn't really any other way of describing it – cross my dad's face. He put his arms around me and hugged me close to him.

"Oh Het, I'm so pleased we've got to the bottom of what's worrying you. I've been really bothered about you. I knew there was something that was stopping you eating and meaning that you weren't settling in your new school and now I know it's because you've been trying to make out that your mum is a different person to the one she really is. Now you've faced the truth about her it'll be a million times better."

"Traitor, traitor, traitor!" the parrot on my shoulder screamed in my ear. "You miserable, little worthless creature, you've sold your mum down the line!" I batted those thoughts away. I'd got my dad back.

If anything, controlling the food I ate, or rather didn't eat got even worse after that. By publicly denouncing Mum and saying that I didn't really care about her any more meant that the pain I felt at losing her was even greater but I had to keep it hidden. The reality was that I'd made a difficult situation even more complicated because now Dad could use what I'd said to him as a reason for batting Mum off even further.

I knew that we were meant to go to Whitley Bay in February half term when Mum wrote to say that she was looking forward to us staying there for the week. But Dad immediately piped up with, "Gosh, I've got that much work on with this new job I really don't have time to be driving up half way and then again at the end of the week. If your mum wants you, she's going to have to come down and fetch you and then bring you back. I don't suppose you're really bothered now, are you kids? Now we've all learnt the truth about her." My heart started thumping, my mouth felt dry, I bit my lip, fighting back the tears. I knew that Mum couldn't drive to and from Cardiff and then back again.

"But Dad…" I started.

"Come on Het, I'm trying to make it easier for you. Look, you've been much better the last few weeks. You've been much brighter and you haven't endlessly been going on about her, so why don't we just take the opportunity to push her into the background a bit more? Then everybody will be happier. Don't worry, I'll explain to her that you need time to settle here. There's nothing for you to explain or feel guilty about. Remember she's the one in the wrong, not you and Jonty."

"I don't even want to go up to Whitley Bay in February," said Jonty. "I've got my friends down here and I want to see them in the holidays. Mum's not that important to me. Like Dad says, she's the one who's been horrible to us and left us." It seemed he just wanted to be doubly sure of Dad's approval and of course, he won a big hug from Dad.

"Of course you need time with your friends – I just wish your sister had settled in as easily as you have."

I reckon Dad must have spoken to mum 'cos surprisingly a couple of days later, he announced, "I've arranged for you to go and stay at Suzie's for a few days at half term. If your mum wants to come down and see you whilst you're there, then that's fair enough."

"But Dad, the court order –"

"Court orders are fine as long as everybody agrees about them. What's your mum going to do about it? She's already demonstrated that she's not that bothered or she'd have been back at court in a flash."

"But Dad she –"

"Don't start making excuses for her, Hetty, otherwise we're going to get back to where we were and I thought we were moving on. Remember that chat we had when you realised how cruel your mum's been? The trouble is, you are far too kind to her – you've got to be tougher, she doesn't deserve everyone being nice and making excuses for her."

That night, I heard Dad and Amy arguing. I craned my head to hear what they were saying. Amy was really annoyed that Dad was prepared to take both Jonty and me back to Welshpool to stay with our friends at half term and was arranging with Mum for her to come down and see us there. "Just let go of her, can't you?" I heard Amy say. "She doesn't bother about the kids so why put yourself out making it easy for her? I wanted us all to spend some time together and really get to know each other as a family and now you're going to be charging off to Welshpool and staying with your sister in Shrewsbury again. That's ridiculous, what's the point of us being together? I've told you I can't keep leaving my business – my life is here and I thought you wanted to share it." She sounded angry and frustrated and I heard Dad snap back at her but he didn't sound as confident as he usually did. Amy was a feisty young woman and I didn't think she'd stand any nonsense, especially from Dad. She made it very clear what she thought and what she wanted and demanded.

The pull of staying with his best mate was enough to win over Jonty, although his only reference to Mum was to check with Dad that he didn't have to see her if he didn't want to. I was a strange mix of cross and sad when Dad assured him that it was his choice and there was no pressure.

It was great seeing Suzie again but staying there didn't work out all that well. Suzie's mum was at her wits end trying to find something to give me to eat. I think she got fed up with me saying that I wasn't really hungry, but then I'd sit poring over recipe books or looking at menus in shop windows. I guess it didn't make sense to her and it was crazy to me too. I was tired, desperately tired and I know it was because I wasn't eating properly. Suzie was annoyed with me because everything she suggested was met with an 'okay' but without the enthusiasm I'd always shown in the past. She seemed relieved that the plan was that Mum was coming down to meet up with Jonty and me for the day. But Jonty then left a message with Suzie's mum to say that his friend's mum had made arrangements for a special day out for him and his mate that day and so he couldn't see Mum. I was wound up about it but there was nothing I could do and it seemed no one was going to put any pressure on Jonty, especially Dad. When I spoke to him, his response was clear. "Jonty's moved on, Het, it's what you need to do too. I'm so disappointed if you've fallen under her spell again. I really thought you'd realised the truth about your mum." His words stung and left me silently sobbing myself to sleep.

Mum came to Suzie's house. She'd travelled down in the early hours of the morning so that she could get there by 11. Of course, Suzie's mum and Suzie made a big fuss of her, they'd known my mum for years and loved her to bits. We had a good day although Mum was surprised that yet again I didn't want any lunch. "Hetty, I'm really worried about you, you just seem never to eat anything and I'm –"

"Of course I eat, Mum, I eat loads," I just snapped back fiercely defensive, "it's just that I had a really big breakfast and I just don't want any lunch. Maybe tonight I'll have something before I go back."

"Okay, shall we go to the pizza place?"

"Well, I'm not really keen on pizza."

"Since when?" said Mum.

"Well, I'll have some chicken or something. Chicken and salad or something like that." Mum shook her head in despair, I think a bit of her knew what was happening, but she couldn't work out why or what she could do about it. She was scared of frightening me away and I guess she was desperately sad when all she could see was the daughter she loved disappearing, literally fading away.

The day was over far too quick. My intentions to be somewhat cool and distant with Mum hadn't worked at all. Of course not. Not wanting her was a sham for Dad's benefit, the reality was so different. I'd clung to her and sobbed my eyes out, telling her that I was so unhappy. I loved her so much and missed her dreadfully. "Hetty, let me ask you something, do you pretend to your dad that it's different? I'd rather you told me, I'm not blaming you, I'm not cross with you but you see your dad reckons that neither you nor Jonty want to see much of me anymore and it just doesn't make sense 'cos when we're together…" her voice trailed off. I felt awful.

I put my head down and mumbled. "Well, it's really difficult when Dad asks me, and I think that sometimes I say things that aren't quite true because that makes things that little bit easier. I don't know what I believe any more, Mum, I just want it all to stop. It's all so wildly out of control and I'm scared."

"Oh, Hetty! What have we done to you? I'm so, so sorry my darling."

Chapter 38

Amy tried her best with us, both with me and with Jonty. It was clear that Jonty was her favourite – it had been so easy for her to win him over, he was just so enthusiastic, lapping up every new suggestion she made. She was young and good fun and although I didn't really want to like her, I couldn't help myself, she was so bright and attractive and confident – full of life – one of those irresistible people which I envied. Now I so often wonder what on earth made her hook up with my dad. After that half term holiday when I'd got so upset, I was determined that whilst I'd pretend to Dad that I wasn't that bothered about Mum, I wasn't going to make any effort with Amy. At least I could do that for my mum.

I came in from school one afternoon, Amy was there. That was unusual, generally she and Dad weren't home till almost 6 pm and Jonty and I fended for ourselves after school and clubs. "Oh Het, how lovely to see you," Amy beamed. "Let me make you a hot chocolate with swirls of cream on top and a chocolate flake."

"No, thank you," I mumbled.

"Oh come on, Het, you never seem to have anything special – come on, it's my treat."

"My name's Hetty," snapped crossly. "I don't like being called Het except by my friends"

"Oh, oh, sorry, sorry." Quick as a flash, the smile disappeared and a glimmer of annoyance crossed her face before the smile returned. I guess she wasn't used to people brushing her aside. I didn't trust her and I certainly wasn't going to make life easier for her. I guessed she hated me as much as I hated her.

The next minute, she turned around with a big smile beaming across her face as she banged two mugs of hot chocolate with lashings of cream on top down on the counter in front of me. I looked at her in amazement. "Come on," she taunted, "I know you really want one. Go on, go on, have it, have it. I know what you're up to and how much you want to guzzle it down." And all the time, there was that stupid smile across her face. She was goading me, daring me to break my resolve. I'm pretty certain she knew just how much will power it cost me to resist the things I loved to eat, denying the cravings was agony and she knew it, but I had to do it to stay in control, I was scared to let go. Suddenly, with a whoosh, all the anger I'd been denying so long welled up inside me, I felt as if I was going to explode into a million pieces. And then, wham, the hot chocolate flew across the room, it hit the wall, the mug broke and the brown stains of chocolate spiked with blobs of cream cascaded all over the carpet. Amy's reaction was instant. I hardly saw her move but I felt the crack as she slapped me across the face. "You little bitch!" she screamed. "You ungrateful little bitch, you're jealous, that's what's up with you! You're trying to split your dad and me up. I know your game. Get out of my sight before I –" she didn't finish her outpouring. Her face was almost touching mine as she yelled at me, her eyes blazing – her spit spraying my cheek.

I ran upstairs in a daze, my cheek was smarting. I looked in the mirror and saw the red mark. The horrible, horrible woman. What did my dad want to be with her for? I lay on my bed and sobbed and sobbed. Was I crying because of what Amy had done or was it because I'd lost my mum and I thought I was losing my dad and all my friends were in Welshpool and Shrewsbury? I'd got nobody here and I hated it and I hated myself and I hated everything and it was all my fault.

Dad came up the stairs soon after he came in from work. I leapt off the bed and ran to him expecting him to take me in his arms, but to my horror, he pushed me aside. "What's got into you, Het? How dare you behave like that?"

I looked at him askance. "But she –"

"Of course Amy reacted to how you behaved. She had to stop your crazy outburst; goodness only knows what you would have done next. It was the only way she could stop you. A perfectly normal and a very sensible reaction. She was trying to calm you down, you idiot, you were obviously going berserk."

"But –"

"Don't 'but' me, you're the one who's in the wrong, not Amy. Amy's tried her damndest to get it right for you two and you are such an ungrateful little b –" He didn't finish the word and I guess he was going to say something derogatory but he held back. Nevertheless, he went on and on and on telling me how appalling my behaviour was, how ungrateful and spiteful I'd become. His outburst seemed to me to be out of all proportion and it just left me a quivering wreck. He insisted that not only did I clean the mess up but I had to apologise to Amy and if it my cleaning wasn't to her satisfaction, I'd have to pay to have a professional cleaner in and that would mean I'd have no pocket money for months. His final stinging remark as he left was, "You've let me down, Hetty, you've really disappointed me, you're just like your mum and if you're going to behave like that, there's no place for you here." I looked at him in utter disbelief – my world fell apart, I couldn't believe what I was hearing. So all my fears were true, he really didn't want me and he preferred Amy to me. I hated her even more, she'd annoyed me before but now I really, really hated her but I couldn't let my dad know that because he'd just get rid of me like he'd got rid of Mum and I'd already told him that I didn't want my mum anymore, so I'd have nobody because Jonty wasn't the brother I'd always been close too, he'd been won over and firmly belonged to Dad and Amy. Life couldn't have been worse.

Of course for the next few days, I did everything I could to win Dad over again. But it was hard. Amy was cool and distant. She listened to my apology but her words of acceptance had no warmth – she just went through the motions like she had no choice. She was distant and clearly disinterested in me although she went out of her way to make a real fuss of Jonty and of course, he just lapped the attention up.

I guess that was when I started to do little spiteful things that would upset and annoy her but which she wouldn't be able to pin on me. I know it seems petty and it did to me even then but I didn't know what else to do, but I just had to do something or I'd go mad. I'd hide her car keys or drop her shopping list in the bin or switch off the plug to her phone when she was charging it. Or I'd spit in her cup of tea or coffee or hide one of her shoes in the junk cupboard. Stupid little things really, things that would annoy her no end but she couldn't prove I'd been responsible for although I guess she had a pretty good idea what was going on. On the surface, there was a sort of uneasy truce between us but deep down I think we both loathed each other even more than we had done before the hot chocolate incident. She didn't trust me and no doubt realised I was jealous of the relationship she had with my dad. I was madly jealous because I knew he cared more about her than he cared about me. In fact, he didn't really care about me at all and that was unbearable. I had to win him back, I just had to.

Dad made the suggestion that I started horse riding again. It was an activity I had loved whilst I was in Welshpool but somehow I'd lost any enthusiasm to do anything and so I told him I was too busy with my school work. He just accepted that 'cos of course it was essential that I achieved A grades. Jonty had loads of friends and went to his Tae Kwon Do lessons and was in the junior club team. He was looking forward to surfing in the spring and summer whereas all I did was to go to school and work really hard. I didn't have any true friends, I didn't bother going out. I just sort of faded into the background, the odd girl who didn't eat much, a bit of a party pooper, on the periphery of friendship groups so of course I never got asked to anything, nobody bothered with me – my self-esteem and confidence ebbed away even further.

I wrote regularly to Suzie, I had to try and sneak a stamp so that Dad wouldn't ask to see my letters. However, he'd stopped bothering to insist he read Mum's letters, I think he was totally convinced that I shared his view and was no longer really bothered about her. With Dad, you agreed or you were just dismissed – there was no alternative view. Mum wrote most weeks but her letters had become brief, just news about places she'd been to or films she'd seen and books she'd read. It seemed she'd accepted that Jonty and I had a new life now and that no matter how hard she tried, it was going to be really difficult to maintain the sort of relationship that we'd had. It was quite clear that the court order had been chucked out of the window as far as Dad was concerned and the only way that Mum would get to see us was if we went to Shrewsbury and stayed with Aunty Nicky and she came down there. I guess even I accepted that it was too much to expect her to drive all the way down to Shropshire and then all the way back up to Whitley Bay and then do the journey again when it was time to come back. So from then on, visits to Whitley Bay only happened in the summer holidays and sadly, Jonty never bothered to come. At the time, I thought that it was cruel and selfish that Mum didn't fight for Jonty and I asked myself over and over why did she give up so easily? It was only as I got older that I realised it was like she'd told me that day in Shrewsbury before we moved. She appreciated that Jonty and I were suffering the pain of separation but we were managing it in a different way and she had accepted that putting pressure on Jonty and expecting him to tell Dad that he wanted to see his mum was too much for him. It would make his pain unbearable. I begged Dad to let me travel on my own on the through train from Cardiff to Manchester and then change on to the Newcastle train but he'd have none of it. "Six hours alone on a train – that would be so irresponsible of me, Het – no, I'm not exposing you to a risk like that. Remember, I'm the parent in charge of keeping you safe." How ridiculous, but I knew better than to argue with him.

It was just before I took my GCSEs that Dad told Jonty and me that he was buying a house. I immediately thought that he meant a house for him and Amy, but no, he explained that although he and Amy were staying good friends, that it was better if each had their own properties and more especially that we had our own place. I started to panic if things weren't working out between him and Amy, had he sussed how mean I was to her? Did he blame me? I don't know, he didn't say. A bit of me hoped that he would move back to Welshpool but no such luck. His new job was working out well and he'd already seen a house in Cardiff that he liked and so that was that there was no discussion. It was a ten-minute walk to Amy's but at least I didn't have her breathing down my neck. It seemed from what Jonty told me that Amy didn't want the two of us around. She wanted it to be just the two of them and separate homes seemed to do the trick.

As was predicted, I did extremely well in my GCSEs but my teachers' unanimous view was that I'd got insufficient outside interests and if I genuinely wanted to pursue a medical career, I'd need to show that there was more about me than just achieving academically. It had always been Dad's dream that I'd be a medical student, he'd told me years before that had been his ambition. His own father had been a doctor, but I'd never met him, he died before Jonty and I were born. Dad hadn't really talked about him, but Mum had explained that my dad had always felt he'd been a disappointment to his dad because he never made it to medical school and his ambition was to relive his own dream through me.

I don't know whether I actually ever considered whether I wanted to be a doctor, somehow I'd gone along with the idea – because it was Dad's I just accepted it and didn't really consider any alternatives. I knew I'd got the brains to do it and I reckoned it would guarantee that Dad would love me. How naïve and stupid was I to think that I could win and then hold onto my dad's love? It wasn't real love, unconditional, dependable love but then as a teenager, I had thought that it was all I really wanted or needed. I remember telling Mum in a letter that I intended to realise my long-held ambition and pursue a medical career. Her response surprised me. Whilst she was delighted if I could truthfully say that was what I wanted to do, but she asked me to consider carefully and to be sure it was really what I wanted and I wasn't just trying to please my dad. I'd responded angrily to her suggesting she was having a go at Dad but I realise now she knew me, she knew my game that I believed that I could win him over, I could please him so he'd love me after all she'd done the same for years. 'If it is for your dad' she had written, 'then, Het, you need to think carefully. It's a big commitment. You'll never be truly happy and eventually you may resent your dad'. Why was she trying to crush my ambition – how mean was that? But I couldn't completely ignore that irritating little voice – 'it's true, Hetty – you're trying to buy your dad. Being a doctor isn't what you really, truly want, you're kidding yourself'. I batted the thoughts away and refused to listen. I was going to be a doctor.

At the end of the first year of sixth form, Dad relented and allowed me to catch the train myself from Shrewsbury up to Newcastle via Manchester. Mum met me at the station and I was surprised to see how fit and well she looked as she waved madly from the platform. We ran and hugged each other and I felt a warmth spreading through my whole body. "Oh, Mum."

"Oh, Het." We chorused together. We sat and talked for much of those few days and I remember sitting by the sea, looking across to St Mary's Island.

"Het, I'm worried about you," she told me. "I've always been worried about you, but you're going to do yourself long term damage if you carry on depriving yourself of food. You're so thin and pale and you just haven't got the life and vitality that you should have. Where's your zest for life, your curiosity, your excitement? You seem so sad and never seem to do anything exciting like other girls of your age. It's not just about work you know, just follow your dreams and do what you want to do. Don't trap yourself in something that you're not really going to be happy in." Surprisingly, I wasn't angry with Mum but nevertheless, I had to bat off those niggly thoughts which insisted that she was right and what I was planning wasn't for me. I didn't really want to be a doctor but I was going to do it because I wanted my dad to be proud of me and to love me, just like I'd always wanted, even when I'd been a little girl. I'd always done everything to be liked, wanted and loved by him and that meant I'd always denied any real ambitions that I might have. In spite of that, I hadn't got the guts to argue with her so I reassured her that it really was what I wanted and the conversation moved on to what else besides good A level grades I needed to do to get into medical school. Mum suggested community work of some sort, that maybe working with the elderly or people with learning disabilities would stand me in good stead. I promised I'd think about it and convinced her – well, I'd like to think I did – that I'd eat sensibly. I knew I wouldn't – couldn't – and that I needed that denial of food just like a junkie needs heroin.

However, when I went back to Cardiff, I summoned up enough enthusiasm to go along to the local riding school and offer to help with the well-established Riding for the Disabled group which rode each week. They were delighted to have me especially when they realised I could ride and knew about horses. It wasn't too taxing, or too exhausting and it meant that I'd got a genuine reason, an excuse really, for not doing all the exciting things that the girls at school were enjoying. I didn't want to go out drinking and clubbing on Friday and Saturday nights. I was scared to drink alcohol. I was terrified of losing control. The bit of control that I did have in my life was solely derived from denying myself food and I clung on to that. I couldn't afford to lose control in any other areas of my life. I knew the girls at school considered me to be a bit of a goody two shoes as my mum would have said. But I did have one vice – I took up smoking unbeknown to my dad; well, I assumed he didn't know, he never said anything but maybe that was easier for him seeing as he smoked. I found it helped to depress my appetite, so black coffee and cigarettes became my staples, they kept me awake during the long nights as I wrote essays, solved scientific problems and studied hard, always ensuring my grades were top.

I was taking biology, maths and chemistry A levels and each subject was demanding. Any spare weekend time was spent at the riding stables, I loved it there – the children from three years to fifteen had a variety of challenging physical and emotional difficulties. Watching them master riding techniques was so rewarding with their squeals of delight and their ability to bond with the ponies they rode. It was the one part of my life that I loved. Dad didn't really bother about me at all, he rarely commented about my appearance and just seemed to accept that I would be at home or at the stables. Occasionally, he remarked, "It's good that you don't go gadding around the town like so many of the girls of your age do. I'm glad you're sensible, Het." And I was delighted to have his approval. Being sensible was easy I couldn't allow myself to be anything else, I really had no choice.

And so, my childhood and my adolescence slowly slipped away without me even noticing. Looking back, I can see I never got a chance to have fun and freedom or to discover myself. I was crushed and squeezed into the mould my dad created for me. I was his possession, his prisoner and the consequences of escape were too awful to consider.

Chapter 39

The following autumn, I joined the hundreds of other would be hopeful medical students as I did the usual around of possible universities. I don't know what made me pick Leeds, but I set my heart on going to the medical school there. I got a conditional place after a fairly challenging interview. Surprisingly, Dad had been quite happy to drive me to Leeds; he didn't seem to mind about the distance or the prospect of me being so far away. He was basking in the glory of his daughter being on the road to becoming a doctor.

I worked incredibly hard determined that I would get the three A*s demanded by Leeds and predicted by my tutors. And I did. As I stood with the other girls on that results day, I knew before I ripped open the envelope that I'd get what I'd wanted. After all, study had dominated my life and if I'm honest, I'd been totally driven by the prospect of pleasing my dad and gosh, was he over the moon! He insisted that he took Jonty and me out for a slap-up meal and of course, Amy came too, although her mumbled congratulations were through gritted teeth. I wasn't really sure about their relationship, I very rarely saw her and Jonty reckoned that she was probably seeing other fellas but that Dad didn't mind. I don't know, maybe he was seeing other women too. Managing my persistent denial of food and the exhaustion I constantly experienced meant there was very little time for me to think about anything. I even managed to blot out Mum for much of the time. Yes, her letters came most weeks and I saw her occasionally in Shrewsbury or Welshpool and each summer in Whitley Bay but often Suzie would come down and stay with us in Cardiff, so I didn't get to Shropshire as often as I had.

That last year, I had gone up during the summer holidays but somehow Mum and I had seemed distant from each other. She didn't mention my weight or how skinny I was but I saw her looking at me sometimes, a sort of wistful look. We kept conversation impersonal, about books and films and politics and religion but not about real emotional stuff which mattered and never about my dad. I think both of us realised that it was all just too painful so best to ignore it and superficially have a good time together. But it was there and it got in the way of us being really honest with each other and to tell the truth, it felt like I was putting on a bit of an act when I was with Mum. It was sad because we'd always been so close.

I was lucky I could stay in halls that first year so there wasn't the added pressure of finding somewhere to live. I remember travelling up at the end of September. Dad hired a small van so he could take all my stuff and Jonty came too, I'd been surprised he wanted to. He'd done pretty well in his GCSEs and was going into the sixth form, but we weren't as close as we'd been in the past. He had his own friends and his own interests and he wasn't really around a lot of the time. He rarely bothered about Mum and she left him to it.

It is etched in my memory how ecstatically happy Dad looked that day when we unlocked my room in Leeds. Of course, I realise now it was never really about me, but he was reliving his own unfulfilled dreams. "You work hard, Het. I know I can depend on you. I'm so, so proud of you," he beamed. "And you'll meet all these fantastic people, people like you, you never know you might meet a nice fella, just think – two doctors in the family. Think of the money you'll have." That was the trouble with my dad, it was always all about money, status, power and material possessions. Things which, as I'd got older, I'd realised weren't a priority for me. I just wanted to make a mark on life but in an ordinary way and to sink into the background, not to be in the limelight. I cringed at the thought of being showy like him.

I felt completely out of my depth during Fresher's Week. It just seemed to be one mad party after the other and copious drinking and staying out till the small hours. However, I made friends with another student who seemed to be more like me. Parveen wasn't keen on socialising and drinking night after night. It was easier for us to opt out together. True, we joined a few societies and really had no choice but to go to the Freshers' do, but I'd felt like a fish out of water. Everybody seemed so sophisticated and so much more worldly than I was. I was relieved when Parveen and I could slip off back to the sanctuary of our rooms. She didn't pressurise me about food nor about my family but I guess she gleaned Mum and Dad weren't together and how tricky that was.

I longed for lectures to start so I could immerse myself in study but then I was somewhat daunted by the amount of work we would be expected to get through. The years of studying for exams spread before me endlessly and although I batted the thoughts away, there were several times when I wondered, *Gosh, Hetty, is this really what you want?* Of course it was, I convinced myself. And so, I got down to it and worked incredibly hard. Parveen was equally committed and ambitious; we went out occasionally to a film or debate but I didn't have the mad experience that seemed to be an essential part of most student's lives.

I hadn't really had any experience of boys, prior to now I'd avoided them. To be truthful, I'd been wrapped up in school work and helping at the riding school, so it had been easy to convince myself that that was all I wanted. I can see now I'd been scared, scared of relationships, scared of anyone seeing my scrawny body and desperately scared of rejection. We'd been at uni a couple of weeks when Tony, a second-year medical student, sauntered over to Parveen and me as we sat outside one unseasonably warm lunch time, my initial panic surprisingly soon abated as he straddled across the chair opposite us, looking relaxed with his warm, engaging smile. Conversation just flowed, he was so charming and easy to talk to and he seemed genuinely interested in us. Before I knew it, we were exchanging mobile numbers and as he wandered off, Parveen laughingly told me that he fancied me. I shrugged her off, "No, of course not, it's you he fancies." But secretly, I wondered, hoped. Did a bloke really want me? Sure enough, a text later on that day suggesting a drink that evening convinced me that he did. I wasn't used to drinking alcohol, I was too scared of losing control but with a bit of gentle persuasion from Parveen, I plucked up the courage and met Tony in the crowded students' bar. Panic set in immediately. *Oh gosh, why have I come?* I felt hopelessly out of my depth. But then, Tony welcomed me with a smile just for me and then he made it so easy, his arm casually around my shoulders and a pint in his free hand, laughing and joking with the group surrounding him. He was a popular bloke. Gorgeous too. I sipped my half pint of lager knowing I wouldn't drink it, and hoping nobody would notice if I pushed it amongst the pile of empty glasses on the table, I could hardly believe that it was me he wanted and a warm glow spread throughout my body. Later on in the Ladies, a couple of girls from my course smiled and then Fiona casually remarked, "Be careful, Hetty, Tony's got a reputation, just watch your back, don't get hurt." I could feel myself colouring up.

"I'm fine," I retorted, "don't worry about me, but thanks." I batted her words away – of course, he wants me.

It was late when Tony and I left the bar; he followed me up to my door. Did I really think he'd say goodnight and just go? How could I do anything other than invite him in? He sort of expected it. My mind's a blur but afterwards when Tony had crept out, I lay there in the dark hating myself. I'd never intended the first time to be like that, rough and wham, wham, all over. I'd fantasised a beautiful romance, but that wasn't for me, I wasn't worth that and now, well I was just a cheap slag, free for anyone to use or abuse. He hadn't forced me, but desperate for someone to care about me, I hadn't said no even though that little voice had screamed in my head 'stop it, Hetty, stop it!' Oh yes, I wanted him. 'No' my little voice hammered 'all you want is to be wanted'. Sleep eventually overcame me but I woke that next morning feeling wretched and scared.

Of course, I wasn't really surprised later when Tony did no more than give me a cursory nod as he sauntered across to a different group of girls. I watched as he embraced a tall,

235

leggy blonde; my heart was lurching and pounding in my chest, I could feel every pulse in my body and a wave of nausea washing over me, a griping pain in my guts and sweat trickling down my spine. I knew I had to get out before I screamed, I felt overwhelmed by this terrible, terrible sense of loss, an unbearable, indescribable aching pain which racked my whole body and left me trembling and shaking.

Later, Parveen discovered me sobbing on my bed, my eyes red and puffy and my pillow soaked with tears. My reaction to Tony's rejection had been so unexpected to me, so disproportionate. I couldn't make sense of it. At first I pushed Parveen away. "No, no, I'm fine." But she insisted.

"Hetty, listen my love. Your pain isn't just about Tony, it's so much deeper; he's the catalyst, he's released the pain lurking deep within you, but it's for you to work out what it's really about. But my guess is that your dad is at the bottom of this." I knew she was right but I couldn't face the truth. I couldn't live without my dad, I needed my dad, I was utterly dependent upon him. Oh yes, I knew that he controlled me, managed me 'cos he'd done that all my life, but I adored him. It was then that the realisation came that in return I was forfeiting my freedom, my free will. I had to face the truth that my grief wasn't because I'd lost Tony or my virginity but I was mourning my lost childhood, the family that I thought was mine, my damaged relationship with my mum and perhaps even more the loss of my right to be me, to blossom and grow into what I wanted in life. I knew that my dad had stolen so much, but still I didn't know how to break free, I was like a tiny fly trapped in a spider's web and as fast as I struggled to break free, another sticky thread pulled me back, holding me fast and squeezing the life out of me.

How I managed to keep going those next few weeks I shall never know, I felt so utterly wretched but I was on autopilot and I just put my head down and filled the days and nights with work. I continued to achieve the high grades that I demanded of myself but my mood plummeted and I sank into a pit of desperate sadness and despair. Even Parveen struggled to relate to me. Somehow, in my weekly phone calls to Dad, I managed to sound upbeat and cheerful and of course he went on and on about how proud he was and how wonderful it was that I was achieving what I'd always wanted to do. Ha-ha! What he'd always wanted me to do. He didn't want to know how I felt because as far as he was concerned, my feelings were merely projections of his own – it would never have crossed his mind that I was an emotional wreck or anything other than the budding doctor he dreamt of.

I was cruising on autopilot and then, I don't know how or when exactly but the crunch came and my world suddenly crashed down upon me. I knew I couldn't go on – I couldn't think, I couldn't function. Frightened and desperate, I confided in Parveen and sobbed and shook as I told her a bit about how it really was with Dad and with Mum; how Dad just assumed, no demanded, I did what he wanted in return for his love. Parveen listened, sensing how hard it was for me, she hugged me tight and said, "Well Het, maybe your mum was right, you're never going to be happy if you're doing something you haven't really got your heart totally committed to. Maybe being a doctor isn't right for you. Be brave enough to be honest, Het, don't let your dad wreck your life."

"I don't know what I want," I whispered. "I just feel a complete failure. I can't get anything right."

"Of course you're not a failure," she said, "of course you're not. You've got so much to offer, you're one of the brainiest people I know but there's so much more to you it's just that somehow that's all hidden, Hetty. I think you have the strength to break free but it will take guts, real guts and if you don't, then you'll regret it for the rest of your life."

I mulled over what she'd said long after she'd gone off to her next lecture and agonised over my relationships with Dad, Mum and Jonty. I don't know how I got there but as dawn broke, I knew that Parveen was right. My mum had been right. I really didn't want to be a doctor. I was shaking with emotion but then a surge of energy shot through me and before I could change my mind, I texted my tutor to arrange to meet him. He must have sensed my panic and agreed to a 9.30 am meeting that day. I was scared but somehow I was able to talk frankly to him. I anticipated resistance, but no, he had a level of understanding previously unknown to me. Maybe he had sussed the truth about me. Of course he didn't want me to leave, I was probably their most able student. But surprisingly to me, he didn't try to convince me to stay and his wise words clarified my thinking. "Being a doctor isn't just about being clever enough to do it; it's about having the right mind set of really wanting to commit yourself. It's a way of life, Het, and if that's not what you want, your mum's right, you're never going to be happy and neither will you make a good doctor. So it's up to you if you want to walk out and leave, then do so and hold your head up high."

That was easier said than done. My euphoric moment vanished as quickly as it came replaced by a sense of foreboding and panic. I shall never forget my phone call to Dad that grey November morning two weeks before the end of that first term. "Dad, Dad." I attempted to start the conversation several times but I couldn't get the words out and of course phone calls were always dominated by Dad. And then, it all came out in a rush. "I'm so sorry but I'm leaving."

There was silence and then, "Leaving where? Don't you like halls? Have you got a flat share?"

"No, it's the course, Dad. I can't be a doctor, Dad." His response was mind-blowing.

He screamed down the phone, "What the hell are you saying, Hetty?! What do you mean? You're leaving – of course you aren't leaving, you fool. What are you talking about? Have you had a breakdown? Are you pregnant? I'll get the little sod if you are." He ranted and raved and I could visualise his red angry face – spitting and spluttering as he paced the room.

Eventually, I blurted out, "I'm so sorry, Dad, but it's not what I want to do."

The penny dropped that I was serious. Then the silence was broken as Dad hissed, "You ungrateful little bitch. After all I've done for you and that's how you repay me. You chuck it all back in my face. You're quite happy to bring shame upon your family. It's all about you and what you want, you're selfish just like your mum. Has she had a hand in this? Just like that scheming bitch. How on earth can I walk into my club and tell them that my daughter has failed? That she's walked out of medical school because she can't hack it. You miserable little wretch. Well, don't come back here. I wipe my hands off you if you do this to me it's the end so think very carefully, my dear Het." His sarcastic tone cut to my core, as he slammed the phone down.

I shook and quivered, chain-smoked and drank endless cups of strong black coffee and of course, I didn't sleep at all that night. I looked a complete wreck by the next morning and I realised I hadn't eaten anything since early the previous day. Weak and shaking, I could barely stand. Parveen's knock on my door was such a relief. She hugged me, held me tight and I could feel myself relax just a little. "Come on, Hetty, this is probably the biggest step you've ever taken in your life. It's not just deciding not to be a doctor, but you're breaking free from a tyrannical father 'cos that's what you need to do 'cos you can't lead your own life unless you do." So wise, so strong. For a second, I envied Parveen and her loving, normal family.

"What am I going to do?" I pleaded desperately to her. "Where shall I go? Dad's chucked me out. He hates me, he's disowned me."

"Oh come on, Het, pull yourself together, you can get yourself a job, and why don't you ring your mum?"

"Mum? Well, she'll just turn around and say 'I told you so, Het'."

"Really? From what you've told me, the love that your mum's got for you is unconditional not with a million strings attached like it is with your dad. She'll be there for you when you need her – like right now – go on – ring her. Trust me Het, just do it."

It was still only half past eight in the morning but I rang Mum's mobile. I could hardly speak and I blurted out, "Mum, Mum, it's Het. I'm leaving."

"Leaving? Leaving what?" She sounded perplexed, anxious.

"I'm leaving Leeds, I can't do the course. I can't be a doctor." It all came out in a jumbled muddle, but Mum got the crux of what I was saying straight away and she seemed to sense that I just couldn't make any more decisions or plans. I needed someone else to take over. "Sort out a few things, get around to the station and get on the train and I'll meet you in Newcastle. Send me a message to say which train you're on and what time it will get in."

"See, I told you," said Parveen. "Trust her, she's there for you, Het."

Parveen came with me to the station. Of course she did, even though we hadn't known each other for long she was a true friend just like Suzie, somebody I could count on. I never thought I deserved it but she was there for me. She helped me to pack a small overnight bag suggesting I come back to clear my room and finish things off properly before the end of term. She thrust an apple in my hand and a bottle of water. I'd calmed down a bit but I knew I just needed time – time to work out how to be myself. That was a daunting prospect, so scary but remarkably freeing, and I sensed a glimmer of hope in the mistiness of my thoughts.

Mum must have arranged the day off straightaway because she was there at the station waiting for me as I slowly clambered down from the train. I was in a sort of daze. I felt terribly tearful and I was like that for the next couple of days. Mum didn't try to encourage me to talk, she didn't put any pressure on me at all, she was just around but in the background. She didn't present me with meals, but simply told me she had stocked the fridge and cupboards with stuff I might like and said I could help myself to what I wanted. She'd be going to work but I could ring any time. Wise Mum, she knew how to begin to ease my pain and confusion.

Suzie was at university in Manchester doing a law degree. I always knew that she'd make a good solicitor, her ambition was to go into family work. She'd seen enough wrecked families and no doubt ours was the prime example and that had convinced her that was where her future lay. We had a long chat on the phone on my second night at Mum's, although it was mainly her talking to me and me sobbing. My tears were endless as I sobbed, "I've lost my dad, Suzie, I feel so lost, I feel like a little boat bobbing around on the ocean with no anchor and no compass – I'm just – well – I'm abandoned – a wreck."

"Ah but you're going to sail to far off places and have a wonderful life!" she retorted. "Come on, Het, I think we all knew that sooner or later, you'd have to break free from your dad. He couldn't have you trapped forever any more than he could your mum. She got out, but it cost her, Het – he made her pay."

"But Suzie, he doesn't want anything to do with me," I sobbed.

"If that's how he feels, you're better off without him." Better off without him? How could that be? 'You know it's true, Hetty, you just haven't the guts to admit it' taunted my little voice.

"But what about Jonty? He'll turn Jonty against me and Jonty will hate me too."

Suzie was down to earth and realistic as always. She insisted, "You and Jonty have a solid relationship – you care about each other – he's not going to let you go, Het. But I think it's best not to think about all that at the moment, simply get in touch with Jonty and then talk to him and when you feel up to it let him hear your side of the story. He's sixteen Het, he's not just going to lap everything up that your dad says."

"Well, I did. For years. I've only just stopped doing it and I'm eighteen."

"Yes, you're eighteen with the whole of your life ahead of you and it's time you had some fun and had some time for yourself. You need to celebrate, Het. Your dad's not going to pull your strings anymore and yes, you're going to have to get used to that. It'll be hard at times, you won't believe you can do it, but you will, I've got faith in you, Het."

"Well, I haven't got much faith in myself," I retorted.

241

"Look, why don't we spend some time together? We've got the Christmas holidays coming up, either come to Welshpool and stay or if that's too difficult, maybe I could come to Whitley Bay and stay with you and your mum there."

It seemed such a tempting idea, I needed Suzie, I'd always needed her just like I'd always needed my mum and now I was overwhelmed to realise that they'd both silently been sitting in the background waiting for when I called. Maybe I wasn't a complete worthless failure. I had to tell myself that, I knew deep down that I could rebuild my life but getting used to not having my dad was unimaginable, it burnt a hole in my heart. But I knew if there was one thing I'd got, then that was will power. I'd denied myself the things I'd really liked to eat for years and that hadn't been anything other than agonisingly painful it had taken an iron will to sustain, so I knew that I really could succeed in rebuilding my life. Mum was going to be there behind me and Suzie and Parveen would never let me down. Maybe life wasn't quite as bleak as it had seemed even two days ago, but God was I tired. I was so, so exhausted. I just wanted to sleep, to sleep without being tormented with nightmares of me frantically spinning and falling into the gnashing blood red jaws of my monstrous dad, waking up sweating and shaking, wild eyed and scared. I longed for a deep and dreamless sleep.

Chapter 40

Mum reminded me later in the week that I needed to go back to uni and finalise matters and clear my room. "Come on, Hetty, it's almost the end of term, you can't put it off forever." I knew it was something I'd been avoiding and I felt bad because I'd ignored a couple of calls from Parveen. She'd been so good to me and now well, somehow it was easier just pretending that part of my life no longer existed. But Mum was right and so when she suggested that her friend Simon, who owned a builder's yard, had offered to drive a van over to Leeds with us to collect my belongings and to clear my room, I could hardly say no.

Almost as an afterthought, Mum added, "And you perhaps ought to try and speak to your dad." Panic, panic.

"I can't, I can't, Mum, I really can't. He's disowned me, he went berserk when I tried to explain. It isn't about me it's all about him and he doesn't want me anymore. It's so unfair, Mum, I just miss him so much." I was scared that if I rang, he'd continue to reject my calls, reinforcing that he really didn't want me and that I no longer mattered or in fact even existed in his life. I'd even avoided speaking to Jonty, scared that he too wouldn't want me. It was this rejection thing, I couldn't handle it, I really couldn't. Sensing my panic, Mum offered to speak to Dad for me. "No, no I can't expect you do that," I retorted. I'd realised that would make the situation even worse. He already believed that Mum had put me up to leaving uni so if she started to ring now. Oh, my mind boggled at the thought of how he'd react. He'd be incandescent with rage, so I chickened out hoping, just hoping that one day he'd forgive me and want me again.

Simon struck me as a decent sort of bloke and it was good to see Mum happy and relaxed in his company. It had been such a long time since I'd seen her laughing. We set off at the crack of dawn and of course as usual, I'd skipped breakfast mumbling some inaudible excuse as to why I hadn't eaten anything. En route Si suggested that we stopped at a service station and got a bite to eat. My heart flipped. God what was I going to do if he presented me with some enormous plate of food that I couldn't eat. I sort of mumbled, "Actually I don't travel very well, I think I'll just have a black coffee." An exasperated look fleetingly crossed my mum's face as she turned away. She just didn't know how to handle my refusal to eat. I'd always had such a hearty appetite and now I just picked at bits and pieces. Mum and Si tucked into a hearty full English breakfast. I was starving, the smell of the bacon made my mouth water, I shut my eyes. I'd have given anything to take a bite but I couldn't, I couldn't let myself. I couldn't bear the thought of everything spinning out of control. I had to hold on, hold on tight.

Parveen met us at uni and she helped pack my stuff into the boxes we'd brought with us. I didn't have that much, and loading it into Si's van was soon done. We all went to the coffee bar down the road. Once again, I heard myself saying I didn't really fancy anything to eat. I saw the look that was exchanged between my mum and Parveen. They knew, they both knew what was happening. We left with me promising to keep in touch with Parveen. It had been hard saying cheerio to the few people that I had got to know and in particular a couple of the tutors I'd really liked. It sort of finalised things. I realised with a degree of sadness that this slammed the door shut. This was it. I definitely wasn't going to be a doctor.

Later that evening, I plucked up the courage to ring my dad's number and although I was bitterly disappointed, I suppose I wasn't surprised when it instantly went to voicemail. "Leave your number and I'll get back to you…" Unless of course that number was mine, I thought bitterly. I tried again a bit later on and the same thing happened. I rang Jonty. He didn't answer either. I plunged into a desperate bottomless pit of despair. Wasn't anybody ever going to speak to me again? Did it mean that Jonty and Dad were united in their belief that I'd let them down, I'd let myself down, I'd failed myself and failed them. But then, surprise, surprise Jonty rang me. He was full of apologies explaining that he'd been busy when I'd rung before. It was only later when he elaborated pointing out that it had been tricky, Dad had been around and he didn't dare to speak to me whilst he was there. He was reluctant to say anything about Dad other than that he'd been absolutely furious about me ditching uni and now refused point blank to allow my name to be even mentioned. Jonty was keeping his head down, he needed Dad, well financially at any rate. He wanted to get good grades and go to uni and his plan was that he too could be free of Dad then. But in the meantime, he'd play along because that made things easier for him. "It doesn't mean that I'm not going to have a relationship with you, Het. I will but I have to keep it secret. I can't let Dad know." I wanted to scream 'traitor, traitor why are you cheating me?!' But who could blame him? He couldn't afford to lose Dad and Dad's love was conditional – follow my rules or you get nothing. Jonty had seen me ousted and of course, he wasn't going to risk the same fate. As long as he was still there for me, then did it really matter? I reassured him that I understood but deep down I felt a piercing stab of envy. I was madly jealous of the relationship he had with my dad, the dad I'd loved and adored and idolised and who I still needed and still wanted and who Jonty didn't really even care about. But I wasn't prepared to sell my own soul for him like he wanted. There was no going back and a bit of me knew there would be no reconciliation – I'd had my chance and blown it.

That awful realisation was reinforced when there was a knock at Mum's door a few days later. "Courier service for Miss Taylor, sign here please." He thrust the mobile handset towards me for my electronic signature and then hauled a large container through the doorway. My heart sank as the door closed and I saw the sender's name and address in block capitals. Mr Jeremy Taylor followed by our Cardiff address.

I knew instantly as I cut the box open that it contained all my belongings – all my life heaped together in one big muddle. Mum returned from work with a cheery 'hi there' to find me with a tear stained face pouring over a heap of books, clothes, toys and jewellery. "Oh Het, my love," she whispered, as she hugged me tight.

"I just can't do it, Mum. I can't sort it out, I don't know where to start. It's my whole life just…" I didn't finish, I couldn't. I felt so wretched, so unwanted.

"Never mind, my love. I'll sort it all out and then you can go through it when the time's right for you." Good old Mum – always there for me. We hugged again and I instantly felt that bit better and so thankful for having a mum who cared.

It was much later when Jonty explained that Dad had wanted to clear my room by taking everything to the tip and he'd persuaded Dad to courier my stuff to me. Dad had relented but he had insisted that it all went the next day so Jonty hadn't time to do more than to bundle everything he knew mattered to me in the box Dad gave him. "I'm so sorry Het, it was the best I could do." I knew it was but I struggled with my conflicting emotions, grateful to Jonty but immensely sad at Dad's callousness.

Not surprisingly, Mum and I rubbed along okay; we'd always got on well and she was out at work each weekday and was cautiously building herself a more active social life. She'd joined a local drama group and at weekends, often went walking with Si and a group of like-minded enthusiasts. It suited me that she wasn't around a lot. I needed time to think and I guess to recover but when Mum and I were together, we enjoyed each other's company and it was great to gradually get to know her again.

She didn't put any pressure on me but as Christmas crept nearer, she dropped a few hints that perhaps I ought to take up Suzie's offer and invite her to come up before the Christmas holidays were over. And then perhaps almost as an afterthought, she asked if I had any plans for the future. I looked at her panic-stricken, I just had no idea. I knew I didn't want to be a doctor but I'd never even considered any other ambition. Throughout my adolescence, I never had an opportunity to be me and to even think about other possibilities. Dad had always assumed – no, demanded – that I'd fulfil his dreams. Having to consider the future for myself, although it was liberating was also terrifying and so, so difficult. I took Mum's advice and invited Suzie to come and stay. Suzie understood that me visiting her was too scary to contemplate because of the outside chance of bumping into Dad if he happened to be visiting my aunty and Uncle and we made plans for her to travel up by train.

Christmas loomed close and I knew that somehow I had to get through the festivities when most of the time I felt in the pit of despair. Mum casually remarked she had been invited to Si's for Christmas. Of course, it had crossed my mind whether this was more than just a friendship but Mum assured me that it was early days and she wasn't committing herself to anything. She looked sad as she stressed that wasn't ready for that and how it would take her a long time to trust a relationship again. If I wanted to come too and join the party, everyone would be delighted. She explained that Si was a widower and he didn't have any children. But his brother and his brother's wife were driving up from Birmingham so there'd be quite a merry household.

It sounded fun but I didn't feel in the party mood and what would I eat? How would I cope with a massive Christmas lunch and then the endless food and drink throughout the day? I felt a familiar rising panic and as my stress levels rocketed, I felt completely out of my depth. I knew I really couldn't just keep opting out of everything when Mum was trying her best. So feeling cornered, I reluctantly agreed I'd go. I'd solve the food thing nearer the time. Mum could sense my dilemma so she suggested that I offered to make the pudding one that I could eat and take it along as an alternative to the Christmas pudding that was sure to be on offer too. At least I could eat some turkey and vegetables and just push everything else around my plate – no one would notice. So phew, it should just about be okay.

My mind invariably turned to Dad and this aching void, this endless emptiness. How could I miss him and need him so much? I'd never had a Christmas without him. My mind raced back to relive all the Christmases we'd had together. I blotted out the bad stuff remembering only the fun we'd had and in particular those that last few Christmases when we'd been with our cousins and Uncle and Aunty. Was all that gone forever? No one had contacted me since I'd been at Mum's. Didn't any of them care about me anymore? Had the relationships we'd had all been superficial and controlled by Dad? Was everyone so loyal to Dad that they couldn't break ranks with him and maintain a relationship with me? On reflection, I realised the reality of that sobering thought. Dad dominated our family and everybody knew that unless they kowtowed to him, they would be discarded just as it had been for Mum and now for me.

Chapter 41

The next few weeks were something of a blur. I sort of limped through Christmas and tried hard to join in the festivities and not to be too miserable. I perked up a bit because Suzie came to stay for a few days just after New Year but all the time, I wrestled with see-sawing emotions, one moment elation and enormous relief that I was no longer trapped on the wrong career path and then the awful realisation of what that had cost me. The wretched, desperate, desperate longing, ache for my dad. How could I have just vanished from his life? Had he really erased all memories of me? In my occasional conversations with Jonty, he was guarded and made it clear he couldn't afford to get involved in my issues. He inferred that he and Dad were okay and seemed to want to reassure me that they weren't close but that I was just never mentioned. That hurt. A deep aching hurt. The realisation that I had lost everybody else in my family too, just like Mum had. Although I had never appreciated her isolation before I suffered the same punishment. The only card that had come from any extended family had been from Aunty Nicky and Uncle Colin enclosing a brief note hoping that Mum and I were well. It seemed so tragic that my previous life, my childhood, everything had just gone. I was left with these impossible, unfathomable emotions.

Mum understandably was exasperated by my refusal to eat. Controlling food dominated my life but I knew that I wasn't really in control – my obsession and my need to deny myself was an unrelenting addiction. Whatever Mum cooked, I would pick and play with, eating the minimum amount. One day she just snapped, "For God's sake, Hetty, I can't just watch you shrivel up and die. I thought it would all be so much better once you'd given up uni and come back –" she started to say come back home. But she didn't finish her sentence. The look she gave me was one of desperation and fear. I burst into tears; I was overwhelmed but flounced out of the room more like a stroppy teenager I suppose because I didn't know how to change anything. I couldn't eat even if I wanted to. I was just obsessed with the need to keep control of that tiny bit of my life because, let's face it, I couldn't control any other part of my life. What a sad mess I was.

It was towards the end of January when Mum casually remarked that Si's receptionist was going on maternity leave and the person booked to replace her had dropped out. He was desperately looking for a replacement and had realised how difficult it was to fill a temporary vacancy. She looked quizzically at me. "I don't like to mention it, Hetty, but is it something that perhaps you could think of doing?"

I looked at her in amazement and then found myself saying, "Well, yes. Why not? I can't just sit around here doing nothing for the rest of my life. I don't know what job I want to do, I don't know what career I want, but yes, it'd be something." And so, I met with Si and it was all set up. The following week, I was there at the builder's yard doing a handover with his current, very efficient, receptionist and thinking, *Oh my God, I can never fulfil the role as well as she does.*

But then, there was another stroke of luck. I had enjoyed occasional rides at the riding stables just outside Whitley Bay. Suzie and I had been up a couple of times and got to know the owner. We had exchanged phone numbers and she half-jokingly had said she'd ring me if she needed any help. Then out of the blue she rang suggesting that maybe I'd like to come and help with some of the young riders. It would be purely voluntary but who knows? And so, I started going there on Saturdays and before long it included Sundays as well. I loved it. I experienced a sense of freedom and at last, I could be myself.

With such dramatic changes in my life, I did begin to feel a bit less despondent. Having some money in my pocket and being able to contribute towards my upkeep and help Mum out gave me a sense of independence. But still food, or rather the lack of it, dominated my existence. I didn't take too kindly to Mum's suggestion that maybe I should seek counselling. I didn't want to talk to anybody, especially about food. Truth be told, I was scared of opening up a can of worms and so I sort of muddled on knowing full well that my tiredness, pale complexion, lack lustre hair were by products of my scanty diet.

In spite of that, I began to experience a happier, more settled life, even building a new friendship group. Although they were older than me, the two secretaries at the builder's yard were really nice and great to chat to about mundane matters. They didn't probe and dig into my past and I felt relaxed and comfortable with them. The staff at the riding school were a great bunch and we seemed to have so much in common. We had a good laugh and again, they didn't want to know about my past life. I just wished I didn't feel so exhausted all the time. I had to face it – not eating controlled my life. I'd replaced Dad's control with an equally powerful control which jeopardised me ever reclaiming my own destiny. In those dark months, I was too scared to even contemplate making any changes.

Charlotte, the owner of the riding stables, and I became firm friends. She was in her early thirties and it was her suggestion that maybe I could consider becoming a qualified riding instructor. She surprised me by saying I showed such natural ability that if I was really committed, she would help me to achieve the necessary qualifications and practical experience saying, "And then who knows? Once you've qualified, I may be able to employ you." I looked at her in amazement. I'd never really thought of horses being my career, but yes, I'd always had an affinity with them and it was something that I knew that I actually did want to do and could do well. Her next suggestion took me by surprise. "Look, I know you're working part time at the builder's yard but that's only, what three days a week? How do you fancy coming here for three days and I'll pay you to help out with the horses, mucking out, grooming feeding and general stable work. You'd have to do everything, but yes, you could get some practice helping with the beginners classes too. And if you fancy it, there's a bedsit over the stables. It hasn't been used for ages and it probably wants a bit of a clean and tidy up but it's warm and cosy and you're welcome to stay there for the days that you're working here if that suits you." I was over the moon. Of course, I'd loved being with Mum and in the early days I'd needed her, but now I wanted my independence and autonomy. After all, I had been denied it for so long – I had a lot of time to make up for. And, well, Mum, she'd got her own life, Si seemed to feature quite a lot in it and I wanted to give them space and time to develop any relationship that might be in the offing. So staying for part of the week in a bedsit at the stables just seemed, well, absolutely perfect. I had a moment's panic when Charlotte suggested that I could have meals with her. Oh my God, how was I going to cope with that? She'd already sussed that I had an eating problem. She was a bit like Mum, she didn't lecture me about it but equally, I could see that she struggled to make sense of how I managed eating so little food.

As winter gave way to spring and then to summer, my days were full and I felt happier than I had done for years, probably forever, I can see that now. I was beginning to be myself, except I still had this awful cloud hanging over me; the rejection by my dad was still incredibly raw. He never got in touch; he continued to block my calls. Jonty remained reluctant to disclose anything about him. I resented that at the time but I can see now that Jonty just wanted to ensure that his relationship with Dad wasn't jeopardised whilst he was financially dependent on him.

Jonty had shared his plan to go to uni and how he was looking at various options and that Durham was one of his favourites. He hadn't seen Mum for a long time but they remained in touch by text and had occasional chats on the phone. Like he said, "I just have to keep my head down, Hetty. It's just best if I don't get involved and then I can get where I want to go. I'm different than you. Dad doesn't control me in the same way." Of course, he controlled Jonty – Dad controlled any relationship he had, but Jonty was more resilient than I had been and not so emotionally enmeshed.

It was towards the end of summer, almost a year since I'd first gone to uni. What a lot had happened in that year. I had at last plucked up courage to stay with Suzie in Welshpool as I was pretty certain that Dad no longer visited the area. We were wandering through the town together planning to go for a coffee after we had done some shopping when who should I bump into but Carol? She'd just been to a hearing at the Welshpool court. She smiled and for an instant, I feared she wasn't going to stop, but when I said 'Carol', she did. I remembered then that she'd always said that whilst she would always acknowledge me, that she would not initiate a conversation once she no longer worked with the family. Carol and I agreed to go for a coffee together and Suzie tactfully went off to do some shopping telling us that she would come back later. We were around the corner from the Royal Oak pub by the traffic lights and so drifted in and found a corner table. I filled her in with what had happened. I struggled to hold back the tears but of course Carol listened intently like she'd always done and was genuinely pleased when I described curtailing training to be a doctor because I'd realised I was fulfilling Dad's dreams not mine.

She didn't seem surprised that my relationship with Dad had broken down when I'd left uni and she was clearly delighted but not at all surprised that Mum had been there for me and that I was beginning to rebuild my life in an entirely different direction. But of course, she couldn't help but notice how thin I had become. She suggested that we had something to eat and I made some lame excuse. She looked at me quizzically remarking, "I think eating's always been a bit of a problem for you, Hetty, hasn't it?" I burst into tears and she listened as I told her how not eating was something that I'd got no control over. I was a prisoner of it just as I'd been Dad's prisoner and I couldn't see any way of escape. I was better than I'd been but I was still rigid about what I allowed myself to eat and what was taboo. It frightened me sometimes how much of my life it dominated. Carol sat thinking for a while and then said. "Oh Hetty, from what you've told me, you feel as though your relationship with your dad is over, but I wonder if you've actually resolved all that happened during your childhood? Whether there's still unfinished business and that that's playing a part in you not eating? Think about it." Of course, I didn't want to think about it, it was just too painful to even contemplate. I still had this deep longing that Dad would one day want me again. That it was really me he wanted, the real me. I clung to that pipe dream, that fantasy and that meant I couldn't bear to face up to the damage he had caused me. Carol knew that but she was encouraging me to find my own way forward and I just wasn't ready. I couldn't go there yet.

In spite of that, it was absolutely delightful catching up with Carol and I told her how much her involvement had meant to me and how she had helped me to make some sense of what had been going on. She agreed to my suggestion that we should stay in touch and I hugged her goodbye knowing that she'd been the catalyst for me to find the strength I needed to begin to be me.

I met up with Jonty that holiday too – he was staying in Welshpool for a few days. I hadn't seen him since I'd gone to uni and a bit of me was nervous. Had he changed? Would he still care about me? Of course he looked taller, broader and more mature but it was such a relief to realise that the natural easy-going relationship we had was still there. We hugged each other warmly when we met. Later over coffee, he told me that he and Dad had been talking about the future and Dad had been enthusiastic when he'd said he wanted to do an MPharm honours degree on his way to becoming a pharmacist. He was doing chemistry, maths and biology at A level and Dad had just naturally assumed he'd go to Cardiff. According to Dad, it had the best MPharm degree course. But Jonty knew that he needed to break free and go further afield. Durham University was his firm favourite. He planned to apply and to come up and visit in the autumn and he would catch the train on to Newcastle to meet me and Mum. "But won't Dad be coming with you?" I queried.

"Nope," said Jonty. "I'm doing this on my own. If I don't go to Cardiff, I'm not sure Dad will even fund me. He hasn't refused but Hetty, you know how angry he gets when life doesn't go his way." I pondered, so just as I knew in spite of Jonty's denial, Dad had indeed got a hold over him and so far Jonty was sticking to his guns. But would he cave in or was he stronger than me and not so emotionally entangled with Dad as I was? "I'll do it somehow, don't worry. I've got my whole life in front of me. I can pay off any debts I accrue," Jonty insisted.

Jonty made it clear that he knew just how much I longed to still have a relationship with Dad. "But Hetty, he's just not worth it. He's so shallow. It's all about appearances and about worshipping him. Can't you see that? It can't ever be for you. You have to be an extension of Dad that's how his relationships are." He went on, "I can see that now, Hetty, and I'm sure you can, but I think you're scared, you don't want to admit it, do you?" I shook my head in denial but deep down that little voice persisted 'yeah Jonty's right, he's got it right, he's got the guts to get it and you haven't, Hetty, and that's why you can't beat your obsession with denying food'.

It was late autumn when Jonty came up to Durham and Mum and I met him at Zizzi's in Newcastle city centre. My eyes were glued on Mum as Jonty strode towards our table. Her eyes were full of tears which spilled down her cheeks as she and Jonty hugged each other. I guess for a moment her memory was of her little boy that had struggled so hard with her break up from Dad. But in spite of that, he had developed into a fine, young man and was fiercely independent. I'd chosen Zizzi's knowing they did a salad of prawns and crayfish which I would eat so nobody noticed that I didn't tuck into those mouth-watering pizzas.

How delightful just the three of us being together. The years melted away, we were happy and carefree for that brief time. Nobody mentioned Dad or Cardiff or Amy although Mum did ask how various aunts and uncles were and Jonty gave us the news on them and our cousins. Jonty was clearly delighted to hear that I'd embarked on training to be a riding instructor and how living in the bedsit at the stables was working out really well for me. Mum told him about Si, although she still insisted that it was early days. Jonty and I exchanged smiles, both wishing more than anything that Mum would find the happiness she deserved.

As Jonty hugged us both at the station before boarding his train, I felt this gnawing, aching emptiness. After all this time, I still craved for my dad's arms around me. *How ridiculous,* I told myself; *that love he had for you it wasn't real, you know that, why do you still keep hankering after him?* I didn't want to face up to the bad bits of my childhood, glossing over them was a way of managing and of coping and still idolising Dad. But of course it meant there was so much unfinished business and that meant I remained a prisoner to my anorexia. Carol had sussed it – she was right, but I knew I wasn't ready yet.

Chapter 42

As we sped northward that early spring evening and I watched the dark silhouettes of the countryside in the fading light, I finally summoned the courage to relive my childhood and adolescence. To analyse with adult eyes those events which had generated a whole raft of conflicting emotions. As I sat there, a sense of relief washed over me but it was short lived and I experienced an overwhelming sense of sadness and loss. I focussed my mind on more recent times. Here I was edging towards 21 and only just beginning to make headway towards being a qualified riding instructor. Yes, it was no longer a pipe dream but reality and a path I wanted to travel. But what a struggle it had been to get there and, if I was honest, my life was still hampered by my anorexia. It controlled me. It scared me by its power. I knew I had to resolve the deep-seated reality of my childhood if I was ever to be free. Just like Carol had hinted. But did I have the courage and the strength to do that now that he was dead? Dad's fatal heart attack had been an unexpected and dramatic end, but had it changed anything?

My thoughts went back to my childhood experience of him. He'd always been such a charming, successful, loving dad, always there for me. I'd adored him, he'd been my hero, my protector, charismatic, popular, the life and soul of any party. Oh yes, I'd grown up watching him relishing being the centre of attention and realising early on that was what he demanded. He was an amazing storyteller and kept adults and children alike enthralled but one thing I learned very early on was that you couldn't disagree with Dad. Well, only about non-threatening stuff, nothing personal or deep. If you dared to, then he flipped into an unbelievable rage, a real, scary anger. His emotions would become disproportionate just like his hatred of Mum had been. That hatred had become unreal, so intense and had fuelled his path of revenge. And I knew that he had encouraged, no Hetty be honest, he had demanded, that Jonty and I shared that intense burning hatred of Mum and then it was as if all of us were totally justified in making life difficult for her because she'd deserved it. I wondered now if he had been jealous and threatened by our relationship with our mum? Did that drive his possessiveness of us? His insistence that we loved only him? Was he scared we wouldn't love him too? He'd shown no empathy with me or with Jonty, no understanding of how we wanted and needed both of them and couldn't bear the thought of losing either of them. He just couldn't, or wouldn't, operate on our wavelength. He denied our own expectations of having two parents and refused to accept that our experience of our mum could possibly be any different from what he wanted it to be. The more I thought about it, the more I realised that my purpose in life had been solely to fulfil Dad's needs. He'd failed to fulfil his ambition to follow a medical career and so selfishly he'd set his heart on me making his dreams come true. It was nothing about me or what I wanted and of course his hold over me meant that I just rolled over and did his bidding contributing to my vulnerability and perpetuating the endless cycle of him living through me. I'd grown up always expecting relationships to fail so avoidance had been a lifesaving tactic protecting me from the hurt of rejection. Now it was so plain to see Dad had been threatened by my early bids for independence and autonomy. He'd denied my budding development and so I couldn't be me, I remained his puppet just so he could satisfy his own unmet emotional demands. I wasn't a separate person. I was an extension of him. He'd sung my praises if I mirrored his views about my career as a doctor and about Mum and so of course I developed a false sense of myself, knowing that the only way that I could retain my dad's love was by denying myself and denying my own needs. The cost of that was a perpetual cycle of self-hate and slowly I became a victim, utterly and completely dependent on my dad just as he wanted. As I had struggled to cope, my denial of food gave welcome relief at first empowering me in a world where I was powerless but then it conquered me and took over my life.

That last phone call from uni when somehow I had stumbled over the words as I told Dad that I was leaving the course and no longer going to be a doctor had been the last time he had ever spoken to me. But although physically he'd severed all links between us, we'd remained united by bonds too convoluted to disentangle. I'd struggled to free myself but I'd remained his prisoner, a little fly in the spider's web. As I pondered my plight, a wave of new emotions bubbled and surged to the surface. They came from deep within me. An anger, a white hot anger, blazing in all its fury fought its way out. I shuddered and closed my eyes as I struggled to manage its magnitude and with the sudden realisation that until today I'd never allowed myself to be angry with the man who had manipulated and dominated my life, who had robbed me of so much and then simply discarded me. Of course, I had a right to be angry.

Back before their separation as his hold over Mum had weakened, he retaliated by slowly eroding her children's need for her. I could see now the manipulative games he had played gradually and oh so subtly winning our affection and loyalty. After the ending of the family life, I had always known he'd wasted no time in demolishing any happy memories Jonty and I had of Mum – filling us instead with suspicion and doubt. I cringed to remember how delighted Jonty and I had been when Dad had arranged Tae Kwon Do and horse-riding slots in Mum's precious time. How he had forced her from our home, wrecked contact arrangements and eventually driven her to make the decision to move in order to retain her sanity and in so doing, sacrificing her relationship with us. He'd dragged us off to Cardiff, away from our home, our school and our friends chasing his empty dreams of love and happiness with no regard for us and all the time convincing Jonty and me that his love for us was unmeasurable. The fraud. The hateful, fucking bastard.

I let the anger surge and roar and then subside, washing over me. The experience was profound. It gave me a sense of release and then I slumped exhausted in my seat, luxuriating in a sense of deep peace like nothing I'd ever experienced before. "Oh Dad," I whispered to myself, "now that you are gone, you can't hurt me anymore. I'm free to be me." I wanted to scream it from the rooftops – I'm free, I'm free! "And you know in spite of my anger, I don't hate you; I pity you. I've realised the truth and I know that what you purported to be love was worthless, it was simply your own unmet needs which drove you to possess me and demand that I adored and worshipped you. But you were the loser; you ended up with nothing."

Subconsciously, I reached for my chicken salad wrap and bit hungrily into it, savouring the mix of flavours and the soft roll. Until today, I'd have picked out the filling and nibbled a bit of the wrap discarding most of it. I smiled as I wiped the crumbs from my mouth and then surprised myself because as the refreshment trolley was wheeled past, I confidently heard myself asking for a coffee and a Kit Kat. Tears spilled down my cheeks, I realised that the delights of food could once again play a part in my life. I knew that food and not eating no longer needed to control me. I was free of that or certainly on my way to freedom. The chocolate made my mouth water with delight. I settled back in my seat confident that I really did have a positive future ahead of me – no doubt, there would be challenges and disappointments as well as moments of delight, but I knew and I could be oh so sure that Mum's love for me and for Jonty would last forever.